Also by Samantha Chase

DISCARD

A Dash of
Christmas

SAMANTHA CHASE

sourcebooks
casablanca

Published by Sourcebooks Casablanca, an imprint of Sourcebooks
P.O. Box 4410, Naperville, Illinois 60567-4410
(630) 961-3900
sourcebooks.com

Printed and bound in Canada.
MBP 10 9 8 7 6 5 4 3 2 1

Prologue

"ELIZA, QUICK! TURN ON YOUR TELEVISION! DO YOU SEE this?"

Eliza Montgomery was used to her sister-in-law's theatrics, but right then she sensed something more urgent in her tone. And considering they were on the phone, Eliza could only imagine the look on her face. "Give me a minute, Monica," she said, reaching for the TV remote. "What am I looking for?"

"It's all over the morning news shows," Monica said. "I saw the promos and couldn't believe it! I mean, I met them at your house, at Joseph's funeral! I guess you just never know about some people, right?"

"Wait…what? Who are we talking about?" Scanning quickly through the channels until she landed on *Good Morning America*, Eliza wracked her brain for who on earth she was going to see.

"That poor, sweet girl," Monica went on. "I knew, you know. I just *knew* when I met them that she was too good for him. And that was before you dropped the bombshell on how she was the one you had hoped to set Carter up with!"

A migraine was starting to form behind Eliza's right eye. "Are you talking about Emery? What's happened? Why is she on the news?"

Monica made a *tsk*ing sound and explained. "Her weasel of a fiancé, that's why! Turns out he was messing around with everyone and a lot of it wasn't consensual." She paused. "I'm telling you, it's a disgrace the way these men in powerful positions take advantage of women. It's disgusting."

Before Eliza could comment, her sister-in-law was on another roll.

"William talked to him—the fiancé—quite a bit that day at your house, and later on he told me he didn't get a good feeling about him. He told me the bad things Joseph had said about him in the past."

That was a bit of a shock. "Really? My Joseph? I didn't think he even knew this Whitman boy."

"I'm sure with all of you living in the same town and Joseph having business with so many corporations, they would have crossed paths at some point."

"Hmm…maybe."

"Either way, William was more than a little turned off by Whitman's attitude. Apparently with good reason. You know what an excellent judge of character he is."

Just then, the segment came on and Eliza was transfixed.

"According to sources, Congressman Whitman is accused of multiple counts of inappropriate sexual behavior," the news anchor reported. "While this story is just breaking, it appears Whitman's behavior has been an issue for several years, dating back to his law school days. No official statement has been issued, but we did catch Whitman's fiancée, Emery Monaghan, leaving her home this morning."

Eliza gasped at the look of utter devastation on Emery's face as she fought her way to her car while the media shoved their cameras and microphones in her face. Eliza's heart broke for her. The news anchor was still talking, but all Eliza could focus on was how she wished they would leave Emery alone. Wasn't the situation hard enough without adding a circus to it?

"I can't imagine what she's feeling," Monica said, interrupting Eliza's thoughts. "I hope she has her family around her to support her."

"If I remember correctly, her family is the reason she's in this position."

"What do you mean?"

"Oh, come on, Monica. Isn't it obvious? A young politician on the rise? What parents wouldn't want their daughter to date him? He comes from a wealthy family and a long line of politicians."

"Poor girl. What do you think will happen now?"

"I have no idea. But I hope her parents will back her up no matter what she decides." Eliza paused. "I don't know them very well, but from what I remember of all the years Carter and Emery were in school together, they weren't the warm and fuzzy types."

"That's a shame. I hope someone's in her corner. She's got to be humiliated."

They both went silent as the news story about Whitman's career continued, showing photographs of him with Emery.

"Is it just me or does she not look happy in any of those photos?" Monica asked.

Eliza remembered Emery as the girl with the beautiful smile who always had a kind word for everyone and was very encouraging to her classmates. The woman in this footage bore little resemblance to the girl she remembered.

"Although, she didn't look too happy at Joseph's funeral either," Monica went on. "But I just attributed that to the circumstances. Have you seen her since?"

"I have. It's funny—I hadn't seen her in years before the funeral, but since then, I've run into her in town several times. Just last week I saw her at the nail salon," Eliza said, thinking back to the conversation. "She was as pleasant as always, but..."

"But what?"

"I don't know. I think maybe this wasn't breaking news to her. She was talking about wanting to change careers and making a move. I just figured she was referring to her fiancé needing to move for his job. You don't think—"

"She was already looking for an escape? A way out of a bad relationship? Um, yes!" Monica said giddily. "Eliza, you have to find a way to get in touch with her. We can help her—maybe find her a job so she can start fresh. We can—wait, what is it she does for a living?"

"Something with marketing, I believe. A content manager, maybe?" Eliza sighed loudly.

"So how did you leave things? Did you mention any openings with Montgomerys?"

"Honestly, Monica, it wasn't even on my mind at the time." She paused. "Although..."

"Yes?"

"I did mention the cookbook project I've been hounding Carter about."

"And?" Monica asked hopefully.

"Well, this is all speculation, you understand, right?"

"I do."

"She seemed genuinely interested in the project. She even had some suggestions about marketing it."

"But...I thought this was all just a charity project—something local. You're even printing it locally, not through a publishing house, right?"

"We are," Eliza explained, "but that doesn't mean we can't do some creative PR to get attention and raise more money for a good cause, right?"

"Mm-hmm."

"Maybe I can reach out to her and see if she'll help me brainstorm a bit?"

"Oh, Eliza, the timing is awful. You know she's not going to be answering her phone or returning emails," Monica said, and Eliza could almost see her pouting. "It's a shame you don't have her private contact information."

A slow smile spread across Eliza's face. "Perhaps I do."

Monica was quiet for a moment, then cleared her throat. "And it's really a shame your condo in Manhattan sits empty so much of the time."

"That's true."

"And you know what else?"

"Is there more shame?" Eliza teased.

"Very funny," Monica replied. "I'll just throw this out there. More than anything, it's a shame how Carter has been so difficult with this project. It's not like you ask a lot of him. The least he could do is finish this cookbook and give you a little peace."

"Well, it's not like he isn't busy, Monica."

"It's a *shame*," Monica said with emphasis, "how he doesn't have an assistant or some sort of project manager keeping him on task. Say...someone who brings out Carter's competitive side."

"Ooohhh ..." Eliza drawled as it all began to make sense. "That's an interesting idea."

"Trust me, Eliza, I know all about doing whatever it takes to coax even the most reluctant Montgomery into action! If we play our cards right, Emery will be making a move to the Big Apple very soon and enjoying the real estate on Park Avenue."

Eliza's smile grew. "And you want to know a weird coincidence?"

"I do!"

"I think Carter's going to be enjoying that same real estate at the end of the month. Wouldn't it be awfully convenient if they were both there at the same time and working toward the same cause?"

"I do believe this is a proud moment," Monica gushed. "I feel a little like the student has become the teacher!"

Laughing, Eliza commented, "Well, it took me long enough, and besides, we're out of children."

"Bite your tongue. The grandkids are getting older and eventually will benefit from all our wisdom."

"What we've just worked out for Carter could be the most rewarding match yet!"

"If we play our cards right, there could be an engagement for Christmas!"

Eliza smiled. Truth be told, that was her dream.

Chapter 1

EXHAUSTION—MENTAL AND PHYSICAL—WAS GOING TO be the death of him.

And his mother was fully to blame.

Carter Montgomery climbed into the back of the sleek town car and confirmed the address with the driver before returning his attention to the phone conversation with his mother. To most, Eliza Montgomery didn't appear capable of it, but right now she was most certainly going to kill him.

"Mom," he began wearily as he leaned his head back against the cushions, "I did what you asked of me. I did what I could afford to do. In case you've forgotten, I'm a bit busy right now."

"Yes, yes, yes, I know. We *all* know, Carter," Eliza said with a hint of annoyance. "But a promise is a promise, and I didn't expect you to renege on this! You know how important this project is to me. With everything I've gone through in the last year, you would think—"

"Okay, okay," he quickly interrupted before she reminded him of all the ways she had been struggling since his father died. It wasn't something he liked to think about, but it was a subject she had used with increasing frequency since she'd approached him with this project some time ago.

A cookbook.

A holiday cookbook.

Rolling his eyes at the thought of it, Carter wondered what he could possibly do to appease her at this point. He'd chosen the recipes, had some photos taken, and written the foreword. What else was there? It wasn't like this book was going to press with a major publisher, for crying out loud. It was a little self-published cookbook for a local charity. Why was she making such a big deal out of it?

"Look," he said, starting again with a little more patience. "I am struggling with this Montauk place—the permits aren't all in and I'm having trouble finding the right staff. And I gave you everything you asked for in regards to the book, Mom. You wanted recipes? I gave you recipes! You wanted a little personal touch? I wrote one!"

She sighed.

It was long enough that he knew he'd only prolonged the inevitable.

Here came the guilt trip.

"This is the first project I'm heading up in a long time, Carter. My original plan was to do it last holiday season, but…well, with losing your father, I just couldn't. Our group put out a cookbook with contributions from our members and it wasn't a very big hit and we didn't raise a lot of money. But one with your name and reputation behind it *will*."

"Mom…"

"Besides selling it as part of our annual fundraiser, I'm sure we could attract a bigger crowd by placing the book in your restaurants, with a percentage of the proceeds coming back to the charity."

"Wait, wait, wait." He rubbed his temple. "Now you want to branch out and place this book in my restaurants? When did we talk about this?"

"I don't see why you're getting so huffy," Eliza snapped back. "It's good PR for you too."

While she did have a point, it also meant he would have to put a little more effort into the project since it was going to be in *his* restaurants. When it was just something they were going to sell as a charity fundraiser, Carter hadn't put much thought into making the book look polished. Using a smaller press and doing a print-on-demand sort of thing was just fine with him. His mother had organized a team to handle the formatting and cover design, and by that point he'd be well and truly out of the process—but now?

Rubbing his temple wasn't doing a damn thing for him right now except reminding him that his head was pounding. It was late—he'd been traveling all day and he was looking forward to two full days of sleep before heading out to Montauk to look at the progress on the restaurant. Currently, he was in Manhattan and staying at the family condo because it was easier for him to get the flight out of LaGuardia to the island.

Okay, that wasn't entirely true. He wanted to be lazy and spend some time eating at a few of his favorite restaurants in the city before dealing with all the stress and aggravation the next several weeks were going to bring.

But even with all the stress sure to come his way on this project, it was nice to know he'd have something to look forward to at the end of each day to help him unwind. He had opted to rent a small house in Montauk since the summer season was over—it meant a little more privacy while enjoying spectacular views. He hadn't appreciated that sort of thing until he'd visited his brother Christian and his new bride, Sophie, at their place in San Diego and realized how relaxing the sound of the waves could be.

"Carter? Are you still there?"

And it was farther away from his mother and, if luck was on his side, would have lousy cell service.

"Yeah, Mom. I'm still here," he said and then yawned. "Can we pick this up again next week? I just landed—I'm in the car going to the condo and I just can't focus on this right now."

"The condo? You mean your apartment?"

"No, the family condo in the city."

"You mean you're in New York already? I thought you said you were flying in on Monday!"

He groaned. He *had* mentioned that earlier in the week to get out of being guilted into going upstate first. All he wanted was a little time to himself before tackling the mess out on the east end.

"I wish you had let me know," she said quickly. "I—I would have had food brought in or maybe driven in myself so I could see you."

"It was a last-minute decision," he said and immediately felt guilty.

"A likely excuse."

"It's not an excuse. And honestly, Mom, I'm legitimately tired. I worked all week down in New Orleans and grabbed a late flight and—"

"Yes, I get it. You're tired. Your restaurants don't open until lunch time, Carter, and I've visited you often enough to know what a typical day is like for you."

He wasn't sure if that was working for or against him at the moment.

"So…"

"So I found someone to help with the cookbook project," she said. "Someone who has looked at everything you've sent in and knows exactly what we're looking for and will be able to work with you one on one to make this the kind of cookbook we can all be proud of."

He was blind in one eye from the pain in his temple.

"Mom, I don't think I have time to sit down with whoever this is. They'll have to make an appointment with me—you have my assistant's number—and *if* I have the time, I'll make it work. I've already told you the next few weeks are going to be crazy for me!"

"You won't have to worry," his mother said sweetly. "It won't be intrusive, and really, you'll hardly know she's there."

He didn't like the sound of that.

Carter was just about to comment when his phone beeped with an incoming call. Looking at the screen, he saw it was the general contractor for the new restaurant. With a sigh, he said, "Mom, I need to go. The contractor is beeping in. I'll talk to you during the week, okay?"

"But Carter, I didn't get to explain—"

"No time right now. For this guy to be calling at ten on a Friday night, it can't be good. I love you!" He quickly disconnected before she could say anything else, and for the next fifteen minutes got caught up confirming meeting schedules for Tuesday. When he finally hung up and placed his phone on the seat beside him, Carter was surprised to see they were still at least twenty minutes from his destination.

"Gotta love New York traffic on a Friday night," he murmured. With his mind racing from the two conversations, he had no idea how his brain was ever going to shut off.

Picking his phone up, he tapped out a text to his assistant not to put any calls through or accept any appointments for anyone having to do with the cookbook project. He knew it was childish and that he couldn't put it off forever, but he also knew there was enough on his plate to get through before dealing with this.

Phone still in hand, Carter passed the time catching up on the news. As odd as it seemed, reading national and world news worked to clear his mind in ways little else did. If he were at home or at one of his restaurants, cooking would be the way to go. Hell, he'd created some of his most famous dishes while stressed out and using cooking as a distraction. But since that wasn't an option right now, digital news it was.

Politics. Pass.

Sports. None of his teams were playing.

Finance. Not in the mood.

And that was when he saw it—the story that had been popping up in his news feed regularly for weeks now.

Emery Monaghan.

Well, the story was more about her fiancé than Emery herself, but...

Carter shook his head as yet another picture of the less-than-happy-looking couple appeared. He'd known Emery since elementary school, and with their last names being so close in spelling, all through middle and high school they'd sat next to each other in homeroom. She was smart and outgoing and—

A complete pain in his ass.

Of course, that didn't mean she deserved what she was going through.

Her douchebag fiancé? Yeah. That guy deserved it all, and more.

Unable to help himself, Carter scanned the story, which reported how more women had come forward and accused the guy of inappropriate and unwanted sexual advances. It filled him with disgust. Where did guys get off doing this sort of thing? When had this become the norm? And what did it say for society that this was being brought to light with more and more frequency?

Carter's curiosity about Emery, however, was piqued. Where was she, and how was she handling all of this? There weren't any new pictures of the two of them—any photos used were from months ago. Even when he'd run into the two at his father's funeral last year, neither had looked particularly happy.

And not just because it was a funeral.

Either way, the article said little about her except that no one had seen her since the story broke. No doubt she'd had no choice but to go into hiding to avoid the media. Carter snorted with disgust. That wasn't going to be easy. It wasn't often that someone could completely slip off the radar and go undetected in this day and age. No doubt she was holed up in her own home or with a friend or family member.

"That's got to suck," he said and focused on the picture again. With a small smile, he realized Emery still looked exactly the same. Her dark hair was long and straight, she wore little makeup—not that she needed it—and her classic sense of style hadn't changed. Emery Monaghan reminded him of Audrey Hepburn. There was just something about her that drew you in. She had always been kind to everyone in school.

Except to Carter.

Yeah, all these years later and it still rankled.

The girl had seemed to go out of her way for everyone in their school except him. Why? Maybe it was because he was just as smart as her but didn't have to put in as much effort. And that wasn't him bragging, it was just a fact. Academics came naturally to him but they weren't nearly as important to him as they were to Emery. They had butted heads their entire school lives, right down to graduation day when she took the podium as valedictorian and he as class president.

Tossing the phone aside, Carter closed his eyes. "This is definitely not helping me relax."

Sex, he thought, sex right now would be a great distraction. He eyed his phone and wondered if there was anyone he would consider calling. His last relationship had ended three months ago. Not that it mattered. Ivy lived in New Orleans and he was in New York, and hooking up with an ex is never a good idea. So that left—

"Frustration," he murmured. "Add frustration to the list."

"Sir?" the driver asked, meeting his gaze in the rearview mirror.

"Sorry," Carter said. "Just talking to myself." He was saved from saying or thinking anything more as they pulled up to his building. He could almost feel his head hitting the pillow. Maybe a solid eight hours of sleep and nothing pressing to do tomorrow would help him unwind a bit.

And then his stomach growled.

There was no possibility of cooking, because there wasn't anything stocked in the condo. When he came to the city, Carter always preferred to go shopping for fresh ingredients if he was going to make something himself. More times than not, however, he simply walked around until he found a restaurant to try. But just because he was in the city that never slept didn't mean he didn't need sleep.

Climbing from the car, he tipped the driver, grabbed his luggage, and walked up to the doorman.

"Good evening, Mr. Montgomery," the man said with a tip of his hat. "It's good to see you again."

Smiling, Carter responded, "Thanks, Seth. It's good to be here." He paused. "Hey, any recommendations for someplace that delivers?"

The doorman studied him for a moment. "There is an amazing sushi place that just opened a couple of weeks ago that everyone is raving about. I know they deliver, but on a Friday night you may be waiting for a while."

Carter laughed softly. "Even at this hour?"

Seth nodded. "I'm sure the place is still packed. Earlier tonight one of the residents mentioned the line being out the door." He considered that. "The wait might be worth it. You know, if you're into sushi."

It wasn't one of his favorites, but right now, it did sound pretty good. Considering his options, he said, "Where's it at?" Seth gave him the address. "Thanks. Keep an eye on my luggage and I'll be back."

"I thought you wanted delivery?"

Five minutes ago, he had. But once he stepped outside and breathed in the semifresh air, the idea of a little walk and some food had suddenly revived him. "After being in town cars in traffic and flying, it might be good to stretch my legs for a bit." With a smile and a wave, Carter made his way up Park Avenue and hopefully towards a new favorite place to eat.

She might not have been a prisoner, but that didn't mean Emery Monaghan wasn't acting like one.

Here it was, a Friday night, she was staying in one of the most exclusive neighborhoods in Manhattan—a place where she could easily blend into any crowd—and yet she was still afraid to go outside for any length of time.

"Ugh… I have got to get over this," she muttered as she looked out the window at the city below. Her view from the tenth floor showed busy sidewalks, and no doubt every single one of those people walking them was heading out for a night of food and fun, and what was she doing? Standing there in a pair of boy-shorts and a T-shirt, eating a microwaved frozen pizza.

"Living the dream, Emery Grace," she said to herself, stepping away from the window to grab another slice of pizza. Somewhere down in the city was some of the best pizza in the world, but here she was eating its lousy frozen cousin. "I loathe myself."

Yet she continued to eat three more slices.

With a full belly, Emery considered what to do next—curl up on the couch and binge-watch something on Netflix or curl up in bed and binge-watch something on Netflix. Either way there would be crumbs, because by the second hour, she was going to want something to snack on. Never in her life had she been more thankful for her speedy metabolism than in this last month. The sheer amount of junk food she had consumed would have made any normal person easily gain twenty pounds. But Emery? If anything, she'd lost seven.

It was the only thing she had to brag about, except… there was no one to brag to.

Huffing out a breath, she collapsed on the couch and picked up the television remote. As soon as she clicked on the TV, she remembered why she was sticking strictly to Netflix.

"More troubles for Congressman Derek Whitman," the newscaster said. "It seems his alleged sexual advances to his staff may not be his only crimes."

Emery groaned and almost changed the channel.

Clearly, she was a glutton for punishment because she had to hear what else was going on. Her mother had been calling for days begging her to come back and keep up appearances, and each time Emery had strongly declined.

Then she stopped answering the phone.

Part of her wondered if some of those ignored calls this morning had been to warn her of these new allegations.

"Footage of the disgraced politician appeared online earlier today showing him out and about with a woman who has been identified as an Instagram lingerie model. The two are seen checking into a hotel in Atlantic City last month and not leaving for two days…"

After that, Emery shut the television off and tossed the remote aside. A few weeks ago, she would have thrown the remote and anything else she could get her hands on. But now, she was numb to it all. It stung—that didn't go away—but not in a way she could explain. Her relationship with Derek had died a slow, painful death over the last six months—when she thought there was only one affair. Once the story broke in the news about all of his disgusting ways? She couldn't get away fast enough.

Much to her parents' chagrin.

And Derek's legal team's.

The exact moment they had shown up at her home

and suggested she stand by her man was the exact moment Emery knew she needed to get the hell out of Dodge.

And fast.

As if dealing with her parents wasn't bad enough, she had the smarmy lawyer trying to convince her to "do the right thing." The way he'd looked at her had made her skin crawl, and once she had gotten all of them out of her house, she'd felt the need to run even more.

And in a twist of fate, that evening she had gotten a call from a most unexpected acquaintance—Eliza Montgomery.

The Montgomery family had been a part of her life since she was nine years old, and although they weren't close friends, they were still a constant for her. Having moved back home last year to be closer to Derek and his office, she had found herself running into Eliza quite a bit. She'd gone to her husband's funeral and Emery's heart broke for the family.

Even for Carter.

But although they were cordial to one another that day, Emery had to admit to herself just how much it bugged her how good-looking Carter had gotten with age. And how much she resented how successful and confident he had grown while her own life was less than idyllic.

Okay, it was pettiness, pure and simple, but there it was.

Her entire life, Carter Montgomery had been a thorn in her side—he was arrogant to the point of obnoxious, yet people flocked to him. She'd had to work twice as hard for the same amount of attention and grades in school. It was maddening, the minimal effort he'd put into everything.

But here she was, ready to work with him as a favor to his mother. She wanted to compare it to making a deal with the devil, but that wasn't quite accurate. Basically, she'd made a less-than-desirable deal for the sake of her own peace of mind.

Peace that would, no doubt, be hard to come by once Carter showed up here next week.

"Not gonna think about it," she said primly as she stood and stretched. In the kitchen, Emery cleaned up her dinner mess and half-heartedly wiped everything down. Cleaning was not something she enjoyed, and since it was only her here at the moment, she knew she could let it slide. On Sunday she'd put the effort into cleaning the place up before Carter arrived. "And if he has anything to say about it, I'll tell him he can kiss my butt."

Feeling somewhat better, she roamed around the place as if some form of entertainment would magically appear.

This is ridiculous. I should be able to go outside and walk around! With her decision made, Emery quickly changed into jeans and a hoodie before putting her hair up in a messy bun and sliding on the non-prescription glasses she used to disguise herself. Grabbing her phone, keys, and purse, she locked up and was in the elevator before she could change her mind.

Down in the lobby, she was relieved to see the doorman talking to an older couple. The guy was nice enough but could be extremely chatty, and the last thing she wanted right now was to engage in conversation with him. No, right now she wanted to get out for some fresh air—as fresh as you could get in Manhattan—and maybe some ice cream for dessert.

It wasn't like she was going to skip out on dessert just because she went out for a walk.

She was feeling depressed, not crazy.

Slipping out the front entryway without detection, Emery turned to the right and began walking. The temperature was cool and she was glad she'd chosen a hoodie. It was mid-September and during the day it was unseasonably warm, but the temperatures definitely dipped once the sun went down. Either way, she was loving it.

It didn't take long for her to realize that waiting until this hour wasn't the best way to kill time—all the good shops and boutiques were closed. Sure, she could find a random place to window shop, but to what end?

She wished the Christmas displays were up. Every year people complained about how the holiday season started earlier and earlier—but right now she wished there were festive displays to look at to kill the time. Not only would it be a fantastic distraction, but she loved Christmas so much that it would have put her in a better frame of mind.

Ugh. Think of something else.

Food!

Yeah, lately that had seemed to be her only form of distraction.

There was no shortage of places to eat and it had her cursing her choice of frozen pizza for dinner. Right now she could be enjoying something infinitely better *and* killing time.

And this is why I'm in the predicament I'm currently in—I make the worst decisions.

Hindsight and all that.

Deciding to enjoy window shopping, Emery walked around for well over an hour before finally stopping to get herself a medium hot fudge sundae with cookies-and-cream ice cream. She took her dessert and joyfully dug in while heading back to the condo. The walk was spent with her focus primarily on the ice cream and only marginally on where she was going. Not that it mattered; she hadn't gone particularly far—or even off the beaten path—she'd simply walked on the same side of the street for multiple blocks until she was ready to turn around.

Yeah, you're a rebel, Emery.

As she approached the condo, she groaned when she spotted Seth standing by himself. There wasn't a doubt in her mind he'd try to start a conversation with her, so she did the only thing she could—pulled out her phone and pretended to be on a call.

When she got closer, she began talking.

"Oh, I know, Mom, it's crazy!" Emery said with a brief smile and wave at Seth as he opened the door for her. "I wish I knew. I honestly wish I knew."

The elevator was in sight and she felt mildly victorious when—

"Oh, Miss Monaghan? I forgot to tell you—"

But she didn't let him finish.

Actually, she pretended she hadn't heard at all and practically dove into the elevator as soon as the doors opened.

"Crisis averted," she said, sliding her phone back into her purse and pulling out her keys.

On the tenth floor, the elevator doors opened and she happily made her way to her door. Her ice cream had been yummy, the walk had felt good, and the fresh air would definitely be helpful in falling asleep.

"Emery for the win," she said, unlocking the door. Inside, she locked it back up then she kicked off her shoes and made her way to the bedroom. The fresh air really had done wonders for her, and as she stripped off her jeans and hoodie, she knew that if she slid between the sheets without doing anything else, she'd be asleep in no time.

Still…some water wouldn't hurt.

With a shrug, she walked out to the kitchen, grabbing a bottle of water from the refrigerator and taking a long drink before putting the cap back on and stretching. As she did every night, Emery double-checked the locks on the front door before shutting off the lights on her way to her room. Closing the bedroom door, she pulled back the duvet on the bed and slid between the sheets.

Remember to ask Eliza where she got these, because they're fabulous. The sheets were glorious, the pillows were perfect, and if she were honest with herself, this whole experience was like staying at a five-star resort rather than someone's home. And considering this wasn't the Montgomerys' primary residence, it was even more impressive. *Maybe I should send her a gift basket to thank her.*

Thoughts of whether to send flowers or chocolates or both swirled in her mind as she got comfortable and turned out the light. As predicted, it didn't take long to fall asleep. One minute she was thinking of baskets, and the next—

A sound in the distance woke her up.

Emery wasn't a particularly light sleeper, but after the whole situation with Derek, there had been many nights when the media were outside her home making all kinds of racket in hopes of getting her to come out and talk to them. It had put her on edge then, and apparently, she hadn't gotten over it yet. Holding her breath, she waited until she heard it again.

And she did.

Cursing quietly, she climbed from the bed and tried to think of something she could use as a weapon. The last thing she wanted to do was turn on the light and alert whoever was here to her presence, but in the dark she wasn't quite sure of what she could get her hands on.

And where the hell was her phone?

With her ear pressed against the bedroom door, she thought she heard the sound of someone in the kitchen. She could hear the refrigerator door opening and closing and then the same with a cabinet or two. *Seriously? Someone breaks in and makes themselves at home? What in the world?*

With no other choice, Emery reached into the closet and pulled out a shoe—more specifically, a stiletto—and silently opened the bedroom door.

Sure enough, the light was on in the kitchen and she could see the shadow of whoever was in there making themselves something to eat. On tiptoes, she made her way down the short hallway in stealth mode, stopping with her back against the wall. Her heart was racing as she considered her options.

Jump out and scream?

Sneak up behind him and scream?

Use one of the moves from her self-defense class and scream?

It didn't take long for her to notice a pattern, and she had to rack her brain for the best way to handle the situation. Glancing back down the hall, Emery remembered tossing her purse on the upholstered chair in the corner of her room. Maybe she should just go back and—

She screamed.

A large figure had loomed in front of her—his arm against her throat and his entire body pinning her to the wall. It took all of three seconds before he released her.

"Just what the hell do you think you're—*Emery*? What are you doing here?"

Simple enough question—but breathless and wound tight from fright, Emery passed out cold.

Holy crap… He'd killed her.

Carter dropped to his knees and gently shook her the second Emery collapsed. "Emery? Emery, come on now… wake up!" Fear had him by the throat when he realized how rough he'd been with her a moment ago. He had no idea anyone was staying here and thought she was a burglar— how was he supposed to know it was Emery? And for that matter, he was still confused as all get-out why she was here.

Giving her another small shake before checking her pulse, he continued to coax her to wakefulness.

His hand getting smacked away was kind of a shock.

"You still know how to make an entrance, Montgomery," she murmured, slowly sitting up. Looking around as if still a little dazed, she took her time before letting her eyes land on him. And when they did, they were shooting daggers.

"Are you okay?" Hesitantly, he reached out to help her to her feet and once again she moved his hand away. It wasn't until she was up and steady on her feet that he realized how little she was wearing. "Um…Emery?"

"What is your deal, Carter? Why would you attack me like that?" she demanded.

"Yeah, so... I had no idea you were here and—could you please go put some damn clothes on?" If he wasn't so freaked out over what had just happened, he would have laughed at her shocked expression when she looked down and realized she was in nothing more than boy shorts and a clingy shirt.

With a muttered curse, Emery spun around and practically sprinted to her room, slamming the door behind her.

It took a minute for Carter to breathe normally. Resting a hand on the wall, he tried to gather his wits. When had everything gotten out of control? Why didn't his mother mention any of this to him? How could she not come out and tell him that the one person who'd aggravated the crap out of him for most of his school years was staying in their condo? If it wasn't so damn late he'd call his mother and find out, but now he had no choice but to talk to Emery and find out from her instead.

Walking back into the kitchen, he finished his drink and waited for Emery to come back out.

And waited.

And waited.

It was already after midnight and all Carter wanted was to get undressed and go to bed. His dinner had gone longer than planned because he'd got to talking to the owner, who'd then introduced him to the chef and it became a very lengthy thing. The food had been spectacular, and before he knew it he'd lost track of time. The entire time as he walked home, all he could think of was how satisfied he was and how ready he was for sleep.

That plan was shot to hell now that he had to deal with Emery.

He finally realized she wasn't coming back out, and that just got him all riled up again. Stomping down the hall, he knocked on the door. "Emery?"

No answer.

Great, maybe he really had hurt her and she was passed out again. He threw the door open, and she let out a small scream when she spotted him.

From under the blankets in the bed.

Son of a…

His first thought was how he was going to strangle her, but then realized he knew exactly how to get back at her.

Leaning lazily in the doorway, he crossed his arms and simply stared at her. The small bedside lamp was on, so he had no problem seeing every emotion play on her face—and he remembered each and every expression from all those years in school together.

First she was shocked.

Then she looked at him expectantly.

When he did nothing but quirk a brow at her, she got mildly annoyed.

Followed by majorly annoyed.

The huff of frustration was next, along with narrowing her eyes at him, and Carter had to fight a smile because he had forgotten how much fun this could be.

"Dammit, Carter! What do you want?"

His eyes went wide. "What do I want? Seriously? I come home to my family's place and find you here! And I believe I asked you exactly what you were doing here and you chose not to answer!"

"I fainted, you idiot!" she cried, clutching the duvet to her chest.

Then he moved from the doorway and sauntered across the room, looking at all of her things scattered about before sitting on the edge of the bed. "Whatever," he said casually. "I figured you'd grab a robe and come back out and talk to me like an adult. Clearly only one of us has matured." He gave a careless shrug and looked at her with an easy grin.

Yeah, she looked ready to spit nails.

And it was awesome.

"Only one?" Emery sputtered, sitting up straighter. "Look, what is your deal, Carter? You knew I was going to be here! We're working on the cookbook this week!"

For a moment he was too stunned to speak.

Or blink.

Or breathe.

"Um…what?"

She nodded vigorously. "The cookbook? The one you gave a half-assed effort to? Any of this ringing a bell?"

Now he was annoyed. "Yes, I'm familiar with the project," he deadpanned. "What I'm not familiar with is what any of it has to do with you."

Emery's mouth opened and then quickly closed as she looked at him with disbelief.

They were at a stalemate, continuing to stare at one another. It was making Carter crazy. All he'd wanted was to come back to the condo after enjoying a good meal and get some sleep. Now his mind was racing, he was more than a little ticked off at his mother, and—and what? Studying Emery, he couldn't quite say what he was feeling.

Annoyance. Always stick to annoyance where Emery Monaghan is concerned.

Good advice.

Unfortunately, now that they were both a little calmer he could see the effects of her fiancé's scandal on her. She looked tired—and not just because it was late. He could see the circles under her eyes. Normally, whenever they used to spar, those same eyes would twinkle.

They were fairly dim and wary now, and that—for some reason—had him wanting to hunt down the bastard and punch him in the face on principle. No doubt Emery could be a pain in the ass, but she didn't deserve to be treated the way Whitman had treated her.

No one did.

With a loud sigh, Carter raked a hand through his hair and stood, his eyes never leaving hers. "It's late. Let's just talk about this in the morning, okay?"

Emery nodded.

"You gonna be okay?" he asked, figuring maybe she wasn't saying much because he'd hurt her earlier in the hallway. "I mean, I know I got a little rough out there and…are you hurt?"

She shook her head.

While it had been fun giving her the silent treatment only minutes ago, Carter found it less than entertaining to be on the receiving end. Moving in close, he braced his hands on the bed on either side of her hips and leaned in until they were nose to nose. "I'm not leaving until you say something."

And that's when he saw it.

A hint of a twinkle.

"Something," she said quietly, her lips twitching.

He surprised himself by placing a soft kiss on her forehead. "Good girl." Stepping away, he made his way across the room and stopped in the doorway, his hand on the door knob. "Get some sleep. We'll figure this all out in the morning." Carter had the door almost completely shut when he turned and looked at her one last time. "Good night, Em."

"'Night, Carter."

This time he shut the door and walked across the hall to the other guest room. It had been on the tip of his tongue to tell her she was sleeping in his room, but what would have been the point? They were both more than a little stressed out, and while he couldn't speak for Emery, Carter knew he'd feel more in control the morning after a good night's sleep.

And an early morning call to his mother.

Remembering his suitcase was still in the living room, he hung his head and went to retrieve it. Trudging to the guest bedroom, his limbs suddenly felt like lead and the thought of doing anything more than climbing into bed seemed too much.

Closing the bedroom door behind him, Carter placed his luggage in the closet, stripped down to his boxer briefs, and tossed the duvet and sheets back. The cool cotton felt amazing against his skin and as soon as his head hit the pillow, all of his muscles began to relax. For several minutes he tried to make himself think of all the things he was going to have to address tomorrow with Emery—mainly, how he didn't need or want her help. But...

He yawned instead and thought of how vulnerable she had looked as he walked out of her room, and dammit, he didn't want to focus on that. Yeah, she'd had a rough time of it recently, and yeah, she probably needed something to keep her mind off of the cheating scumbag she was engaged to, but that didn't mean he had to be involved in any way, shape, or form. Uh-uh. No way. Not his problem.

Rolling onto his side, Carter punched his pillow and let out a long breath. And as he lost the fight to keep his eyes open, his last thought was how he wished he'd gone directly to Montauk, because the sound of the waves would be awesome right about now.

"What the hell are you eating?"

Emery choked and coughed for several moments before she could respond. "It's a Pop-Tart, Carter." She waved the chocolate pastry in the air for emphasis.

His hair was a mess and he was wearing a pair of flannel pajama pants and a T-shirt. He looked fairly exhausted. Emery glanced at the clock and saw it was a little after eight o'clock, but she had a feeling Carter could have used another eight hours of sleep.

"Why would you eat something like that?" he grumbled as he walked over and made himself a cup of coffee.

"Because it's delicious," she said, feeling happy with her choice of a chocolate-filled, chocolate-covered breakfast. "It's even better with a tall glass of milk!" Which she then held up for him to see.

He groaned. "Is it because there isn't a lot of food here? I planned on shopping at some point today. I'll make sure to get you some real breakfast foods so you don't have to eat...that."

Rolling her eyes, Emery popped another piece into her mouth. When she was done chewing, she asked, "What do you mean by real breakfast foods?"

Shrugging, Carter added milk and sugar to his mug before facing her. "Eggs, cheese, fruit...you know, *real* foods."

"I'm not a fan of any of those things," she said casually. "Especially the fruit." She shuddered for emphasis.

"What do you mean you're not a fan of fruit? Everyone likes fruit!"

"Not me." She took another bite of her breakfast and had to fight the urge to laugh. There was a vein bulging at his temple and if he gripped his mug any tighter, it would shatter. "Although…does jelly count? Like grape jelly? Because I love a good peanut butter and jelly sandwich."

No doubt his molars were being ground into dust.

"Sometimes I eat strawberry Pop-Tarts. That probably counts as fruit, right?"

Slamming his mug down on the kitchen island, he muttered a colorful array of words as he paced back and forth. It was highly entertaining, and it felt good to feel… happy. Yes, that's exactly what Emery was feeling right now. Happy. There was a lightness in her chest that hadn't been there in years.

Damn.

It really had been years since she'd felt silly and carefree and…

"Do you think there's fruit in jelly beans?" she asked, knowing full well there wasn't. "Do you think that's why I don't like them?"

"Emery…"

She took the last bite of her toaster pastry and smiled sweetly at him. When she stood up, she walked over to the refrigerator and opened it. "I know there's not much here, but I did buy a box of Lucky Charms and there's milk." She paused and scanned the contents. "There's some white bread for toast." Peeking her head out from behind the door, she looked at him. "And I do have some jelly, so you could put that on it if you'd like. You know, get some fruit in for breakfast."

"That isn't quite what I had in mind, and I think you know it," he said.

With a shrug, Emery closed the refrigerator, threw away her napkin, and rinsed out her glass. Taking her seat again at the island, she figured now was as good a time as any to start talking about the project.

"I looked at the recipe files you sent over and I think I know how we can improve on them," she said.

Carter's bark of laughter stopped her from going any further.

"Excuse me," she said stiffly. "What's so funny?"

Leaning on the granite, Carter took a moment to compose himself. "Emery, you just sat here explaining your eating habits, which could rival any five-year-old's, and you think you're going to give me advice—me, a trained chef—on how to improve my recipes? I mean, do you not see how ridiculous that sounds?"

Well… She hadn't until he worded it like *that*.

Unfortunately, now it felt like a challenge and she never backed down from a challenge where Carter Montgomery was concerned.

Studying him for a moment, she cleared her throat and prepared to make her case. "Actually, I wasn't implying that I could *improve* your recipes. After all, I'm not a trained chef—as you so nicely pointed out," she said in a no-nonsense tone. "However, the recipes you chose are completely uninspired and typically something that can be found in just about any cookbook anywhere. I think my sister-in-law has a similar one that all the moms from her daughter's preschool put together."

He straightened as his expression went fierce. "Now, wait a minute."

Because she had been studying the files for the last several days—including this morning over her Pop-Tart—Emery reached across the island for her folder and opened it before speaking again.

"Stuffed Holiday Turkey?" she asked and then looked at him. "Uninspired." She flipped to the next recipe. "Glazed Christmas Ham? Aren't there companies who do that for you so all you need to do is heat it up?"

"Not if you want to—"

She held up a hand to stop him. "You went from boring to ridiculous," she stated, glancing at most of the remaining recipes. "Everything else contains ingredients most people wouldn't eat or would be too intimidated to try to make." Closing the folder, she eyed him. "And what is your obsession with gouda?"

"Excuse me?"

"You heard me—so many of those recipes involve gouda. There are other cheeses, you know."

"Are you sure? Because judging by your earlier comments, I'd bet good money you couldn't name more than three."

Slowly coming to her feet, Emery took a few steps toward him. "Just because I don't like to eat your pretentious food doesn't mean I'm ignorant, Carter. And don't think for one minute that you're better than I am because you cook fancy food for a living. I know where you came from and I happen to know you grew up eating the same things I did, so don't try to act superior to me."

She waited for some sort of snarky comeback, but none came. Instead, Carter let out a breath and reached for his coffee, taking a long drink. When he was finished, he carefully put the mug back down and said, "I'm going to grab a shower and then walk around and do a little shopping for lunch. Want to join me?"

Seriously? That's all he had to say? Emery was about to say just that when Carter reached out and put a finger over her lips.

"Uh-uh-uh," he said with a grin. "I never said I was ready to talk about the cookbook project or that I was going to work on it at all. It's early, I've barely had my coffee, and I already had my weekend all planned out." He took his finger away before leaning in a bit closer. "And none of those plans involved you."

"How is that even—"

His finger was back over her lips.

"Be ready in thirty minutes," he said and then walked away before she could say anything else.

Once Emery heard his bedroom door close, she felt conflicted.

Go out shopping with Carter? Ugh. Food shopping had never been her thing. But if she went with him, she'd get a glimpse into his process and maybe it would help her help *him* with the cookbook.

The idea had merit.

Honestly, it wasn't that the recipes and files he sent for the book were bad. Most people wouldn't give them a second thought except to be a little in awe of or intimidated by them. But after speaking to Eliza, Emery knew what she had envisioned and nothing Carter had sent was it.

Eliza wanted a cookbook that was specifically for the holidays and would fit every family—not just the super wealthy. She wanted something that said home and family and Christmas. It was important that the book give a sense of love and be filled with stories and recipes to remind readers of traditions and the emotions they evoked.

It was a tall order for a cookbook.

And clearly a tall order for a man who was doing the project under protest.

But she was up for the challenge. And while her first thought this morning was to call Eliza and find out why it was that Carter genuinely seemed confused about her presence here at the condo, Emery decided there was no need to involve her. This was something they could work out on their own as two mature adults.

Carter opened up his door and called out, "I suggest you get moving if you're going shopping with me! And just so you're prepared, we'll be hitting numerous fresh markets and will be doing a lot of walking. Wear comfortable shoes!"

She heard the door shut again and sighed.

Fresh markets? Walking? Couldn't he just order his food online like a normal person? Why did they have to walk all over the city and go to multiple stores? Couldn't they find everything in one place?

This was Carter Montgomery she was dealing with.

Of course he was going to make a production out of a simple shopping trip.

Stretching, Emery contemplated being lazy for a little while longer and making Carter wait for her. Unfortunately, she knew he wouldn't and she needed to get him onboard with the things she had planned for the cookbook revisions.

If she went into this looking to tick him off, they'd spend the bulk of their time arguing and nothing would get accomplished. And really, it wasn't any way to thank Eliza for being the only person in her life who actually took her predicament seriously and offered her a solution.

And refuge.

Even if said refuge came with Carter attached to it.

Beggars couldn't be choosers, right?

Resigning herself to the fact that she was going to have to play nice, she made her way back to her room, picked out an outfit, and went to take a shower. Her mind was spinning with how she was going to pull off being interested in watching Carter choose produce and whatever else he had in mind for this little excursion. But if she'd learned anything in the last two years with Derek, she'd learned how to fake it.

Smiles, interest, and orgasms.

Ugh… Why even go there? Smiles and interest she had mastered a long time ago and it would definitely help her while working on this project. But the orgasms? Um, yeah, that had nothing to do with Carter. And while she knew it wasn't fair to judge, there was a part of her that sort of categorized both men in the same way. They were both very attractive, very charismatic, and knew how to schmooze to get their own way. Well, she'd let herself get fooled by one; it wasn't going to happen again. And besides, she knew Carter pretty well. At least on the surface. She knew all his lines and all the ways he tried to get the best of her and she was ready for them. There was no way she would let him win with this project.

They were going to argue. He was going to make excuses. And Emery was certain there would be many,

many times when they would want to strangle one another. It wasn't anything new. She'd lost count of how many times he'd infuriated her back in school. Even the thought of some of those incidents brought a sense of rage. Yes, that was the emotion she had come to relate to Carter and it seemed like time apart had done little to dim it.

Either way, she would deal with it. Why? Because she was an adult. She'd dealt with a cheating, disgusting man she had almost married. Compared to Derek, Carter would feel like a walk in the park.

At least, that was what she was going to keep telling herself. Why? Because his mother deserved to get what she wanted and Emery would do whatever it took to make that happen.

Even if it meant faking smiles and interest at a farmers' market.

Chapter 2

THEY WERE ON THEIR THIRD FARMERS' MARKET AND had easily walked about five miles. Carter hid his grin behind a melon as he watched Emery huff with annoyance for the tenth time in so many minutes.

It wasn't as if he was doing this to torture her—although it was certainly a perk—this was just how he shopped and what he had planned to do all along. Granted, he could have just gone out by himself, but...

"You know, by the time you finish shopping for lunch, it's going to be dinner time," Emery murmured as she walked over and examined the display of fruit.

Carter looked at her. Her hair was up under a baseball cap, she had on a huge pair of sunglasses, and if he had to guess, he'd say she'd picked out one of the least flattering outfits she owned—long baggy shorts and a T-shirt that was about three sizes too big for her. They hadn't had regular contact for many, many years, but with all the pictures of her in the news lately, he knew she tended to dress way more stylishly than this. For the last two hours he'd been fighting the urge to say something about it, but he wasn't sure what.

His stomach growled, and while it would have been great to shop a little longer, he had all the ingredients he wanted for lunch. Glancing around, he spotted a booth selling baked goods and realized dessert would be a definite treat.

"I'm going to head over and grab some pastries for dessert. Any requests?"

But Emery wasn't looking at him. Her eyes were trained on something several rows over and she'd gone pale.

"Emery?"

Turning her head toward him, she was about to say something but then seemed to change her mind before returning her attention in the same direction. If Carter wasn't mistaken, she looked ready to bolt. He took a step toward her and spoke her name again.

"Um...no requests," she said quickly, moving away from him. "As a matter of fact, I'm... I mean, I've got a bit of a headache. I'll grab a cab back to the condo. Don't rush on my account."

"Emery, wait," he said, reaching for her. "I'll go with you. We don't need dessert. We can just—"

"Brownies!" she said, but she was already several feet away. "I'd love some brownies. I'll see you later!"

Setting the melon back down, he tried to go after her when the entire display rolled off the table, landing at his feet. Cursing wildly in between apologizing to the owners, Carter looked up and realized Emery had vanished into the crowd. It took several minutes to get the melon mess cleared up and by the time everything was back in place, he knew it would be pointless to run after her. No doubt she was already in a cab and well on her way back to the condo.

He looked around and wondered what could have spooked her. Knowing Emery like he did, it was doubtful a headache would have caused that kind of reaction. And besides, she would have mentioned having one several times in hopes of moving him along. No, this wasn't about her not feeling well as much as it was something or someone that had made her want to flee. Not that he could begin to imagine what, because there were so many people milling about and he had no real idea about her life and…

"I'm losing my mind," he grumbled, apologizing again to the fruit owners. He handed them a fifty to cover any lost produce and made his way over to the bakery booth. Maybe if he plied Emery with brownies, she'd tell him what the hell had just happened. The sheer amount of sweet confections was overwhelming, so not only did he purchase two brownies, but he got a variety of Italian cookies, a couple of croissants, and two fruit danishes.

Mainly because he thought she'd enjoy him being a bit of a smartass.

With a sense of purpose, Carter strode out of the market area and hailed a cab. No way was he going to walk with all the food he had purchased and knowing that answers awaited him at home. Of course, it still took him longer than he wanted to get there, but once he paid the driver, he all but sprinted into the building and prayed the elevator wouldn't take too long.

He burst through the front door, then slammed it shut, and almost felt bad when he saw Emery jump. Placing the shopping bags down on the kitchen island, he stepped across the room to her. "Want to explain to me what happened back there?"

Her eyes went wide. "I—I told you. I had a headache. I just took something for it and…and I'm starting to feel better." She looked toward the kitchen. "So, what are we making for lunch?"

"Peanut butter and jelly," he said, his voice low and calm.

"Peanut butter and—" She looked at him like he was crazy. "But you bought the shrimp and crabmeat, the artisan bread, and all kinds of other stuff. Why aren't you making something with that?"

"Answer my question first."

"I already told you."

Taking a step toward her, he growled, "The truth, Emery."

In all the years they'd known each other—and all the years they'd gone head to head with one another—never before had he seen Emery Monaghan deflate before his eyes like she did right then.

And it made him feel like he'd kicked a puppy.

Before she spoke, she sat down on one of the massive sofas and let her head fall back against the cushions.

"First, I want you to admit that you could have gotten everything you wanted to use for lunch at the first market," she said with her eyes shut.

Unable to help himself, he smirked. "I disagree."

Emery lifted her head and glared at him.

"Okay, fine. I *probably* could have gotten everything there, but I'm glad we went to the others because I found even better stuff at each of them."

Resting her head back again, she took a moment before saying anything. "I've been staying inside since the story about Derek first broke. Back home..." She shuddered. "It was awful. The press was relentless and I had zero privacy."

There was nothing Carter could say. He'd never experienced anything remotely like it, so he nodded and sat on the edge of the sofa across from her.

"I had to climb over the fence in my backyard and go to a neighbor's house to have my mother pick me up so I could get away undetected." She let out a snort of derision.

"Everyone wanted a comment from me, but there was no way I was going to speak publicly. I couldn't. I was angry and embarrassed and just...ugh. I was mortified by the whole thing."

Another nod. Not that it mattered. She wasn't even looking at him.

"It didn't take long for the press to start sniffing around my parents' place, my office—they were everywhere. I couldn't go anywhere or do anything. It was like being trapped." She paused and finally turned her head to look at him. "Then your mother called."

Ah, now we're getting somewhere.

"I had run into her at the nail salon about a month prior to...well, you know. Anyway, she reached out and asked if I needed anything." Emery gave him a small smile. "Don't get me wrong, I had friends who all made the same call and offered to help out, but I knew your mother was being genuine."

"And your friends weren't?"

She shrugged. "I can't really explain it. Most of my friends are Derek's friends too. It all just felt...awkward. I was already getting pressure from my parents and from Derek's lawyers to make an appearance with him and show my support." Sitting up, she cried, "Can you believe them? I was supposed to show my support of the man who did disgusting things to all those women on top of cheating on me! What was there to support?"

"Emery..."

But she wasn't listening. Standing, she began to pace. "Your mother calling was like a lifeline for me. She could hear in my voice how stressed I was and offered me the opportunity to come and stay here. On one hand, I felt guilty for considering it, but on the other, I was desperate and thankful to have the option."

As much as he hated to ask, he had to. "And how did the whole cookbook project play into this?"

"I kept saying how guilty I felt and how I didn't want to take advantage of her. We talked about how I had to take a leave of absence from my job because all the media attention was causing too many issues at the office. I was at a loss for something to do and couldn't really afford not to work." She looked at him helplessly. "That's how I ended up here."

Crap. So he was basically stuck with her or would end up being the world's biggest jerk.

Not going to focus on that right now.

"I'm guessing you saw someone you didn't want to see at the farmers' market," he said after she had been quiet for a minute.

Nodding, she replied, "One of Derek's attorneys, with his wife." She sighed. "I don't think he recognized me—probably didn't even see me—but I'm not ready for anyone to know where I am."

That was a little shocking. "So...no one knows you're here other than my mother?"

"I told my parents I was going to Martha's Vineyard." She shrugged. "We vacationed there when I was growing up, so it seemed like a plausible place I'd escape to."

Sliding down the arm of the sofa until he was on a cushion, Carter raked a hand through his hair. "Wow. Emery, I—I had no idea." He paused. "They've got to be worried about you."

"I don't think so. Derek's like some sort of god in their eyes. They loved the idea of having a politician in the family."

"And after all these allegations?"

Another shrug. "Boys will be boys."

"What? How is that possible? How could they not care? Especially when it involves their own daughter!"

"Like I said, they love the idea of a politician in the family and believe Derek is the innocent victim of some sort of witch hunt."

"And you don't?"

She laughed. Like a near-hysterical sort of laugh. When she looked at him, she wiped a tear of mirth from her eye. "Carter, this isn't the first time Derek's been accused of this sort of behavior. Hell, it's not the first time he's been caught cheating!"

Now he was angry. Like seriously pissed off. "Then why would you stay with him?" he yelled. "Were you so in love with the guy you were willing to put up with his bad behavior? Hell, my sister Megan dated a guy who was a real class act— not quite as bad as your ex, but there's enough similarities that I can see. And she walked away. It was hard and it messed with her self-esteem for a while, but she was strong enough to do it."

All of a sudden, he realized what he was saying and the whole kicking the puppy thing immediately came back to him.

"Emery, what I mean is—"

She held up a hand to stop him. "I know what you mean, Carter, and believe me, I wish I had been stronger and didn't let so many people influence my decision. But I did and now here I am, in the middle of this nightmare—and all I'm trying to do is stay sane."

And he wasn't helping one bit.

"Can I ask you something and then we'll let this topic go for now?"

She nodded.

"Did he ever... I mean, other than the cheating, did Derek ever...?"

Emery shook her head. "Derek never abused me in any way, shape, or form. If anything, he was just cool and detached. He almost always treated me with respect, and other than making demands on my time to help him with his career, well—that was it. It's weird, because everyone asks if he exhibited the kind of behavior he's accused of while we were at home." She looked up at him sadly. "And he never did. He cheated on me, yet he always managed to convince me that he was sorry and it wouldn't happen again. But the rest? I guess I should consider myself lucky."

Somehow, that wasn't quite what he'd call her, but it filled him with relief to know she hadn't been abused the way so many others had been.

Without a word, he stood and walked into the kitchen and pulled out one of the bakery boxes. Cutting the twine, he opened it, took out one of the brownies, and brought it to her like a peace offering.

"I'm going to get started on lunch," he said gruffly and moved away before Emery could say anything.

In the kitchen, he washed his hands and began pulling ingredients from the bag. He rinsed, he chopped, he seasoned. Though it was mindless work for him—he could prepare a simple seafood salad with warmed bread in his sleep—even cutting up the fresh fruit didn't bring him any joy, and Carter normally enjoyed tasting the sweet pieces as he worked.

All he could do was think about what Emery had just shared with him. Hearing the anguish in her voice had affected him deeply and angered him more and more.

And the thing was, there was a part of him that wasn't sure why.

Was he upset because—for all intents and purposes—they were friends? And that he hated how something like this could happen to her and that it seemed like no one was around to support her?

Or...

And this was the one that really stung...

Was he upset because it all fell on him not to rock the boat? He couldn't throw her out, he couldn't ask her to leave. There was no way he could refuse to work with her, which meant she might have to come with him to Montauk.

To his retreat.

There weren't enough ocean sounds to calm the tension that would undoubtedly course through him at being forced to spend so much time with her.

She would make him crazy.

She would annoy the hell out of him.

She would challenge every single thing he did.

In short, it was going to be everything he didn't need right now.

Just then, Emery walked into the room. She had a smudge of chocolate on her cheek. Carter couldn't help but laugh softly.

Or maybe it was just what he needed.

At this rate, she was going to get spoiled.

And it was only one meal.

One incredibly delicious meal served by one incredibly delicious man.

Where the hell did that *thought come from?*

Rather than think about it too deeply, Emery chalked it up to acknowledging something she'd always known— Carter Montgomery was too handsome for his own good.

With a quiet sigh of relief, she leaned back in her chair and said, "My compliments to the chef." And she meant it. "That was wonderful, Carter. I certainly don't expect you to cook for me, but I'm very thankful you did." She let out a small laugh. "I had half a frozen pizza for dinner last night and had planned on eating the other half for lunch."

He looked at her as if she was insane.

Come to think of it, that's the way he'd been looking at her almost since he arrived at the condo less than twenty-four hours ago.

"You're in one of the food capitals of the world and you ate frozen pizza?" he asked incredulously. "How…? I mean, why?" He shook his head. "Even if you didn't want to go out, Emery, you could have found some place that delivered."

She shrugged. "It's really not a big deal."

The look he gave her said he didn't believe her.

"Really. I stocked up on the basics and…I'm good."

Carter reached for his glass of water and stared at her for so long that she definitely started to squirm. "And what do you plan on doing for dinner?"

Dang. She was really hoping he was going to offer to cook again.

With a careless shrug, Emery reached for her own drink. "I don't normally plan that far in advance. I guess since I didn't finish the pizza for lunch, I'll have it for dinner."

He gave her a curt nod before he stood up and walked over to the refrigerator. Without a word he opened it, reached inside, and pulled out her foil-wrapped pizza.

And threw it in the trash.

"Hey!" Jumping to her feet, she stormed over to him. "What did you do that for? I wasn't asking you to eat it!"

"It's offensive."

"Offensive? Seriously?"

"Yeah. Seriously. If you want pizza for dinner, we'll go out and—"

"Oh no," she said, quickly cutting him off. "Been there, done that today. I'm good."

His shoulders sagged. "Emery, you can't stay inside forever. This is a city of eight million people. It would be almost impossible for you to run into the same person twice in one day at two different locations."

"You don't know that."

He sighed loudly. "Yes, I do. Come on, you need to get out. We'll go and—"

"Look, Carter," she began and hated how bitchy her tone was, "I get that you're concerned or you feel sorry for me or...whatever. But the fact is I'm not your responsibility, okay? Just because I choose to stay in doesn't mean you have to. If you want to go out to eat, you should. I'm not stopping you!"

And there it was again.

The look.

The glare.

Only this time, Emery wasn't going to squirm or apologize or back down. Whether he wanted to believe her or not, she wasn't up to going out and looking over her shoulder the entire time. In a word, she was spooked. This was the first time this week she'd seen anyone she knew, and while Carter was probably right—it would be almost impossible for her to run into the same guy again—she just wasn't willing to chance it. It wasn't worth it.

Not even for pizza.

"Good to know," he said finally, walking back over to the table and clearing away the dishes.

Good manners prevailed and Emery stopped him, trying to take the plates from his hands. "Let me. You cooked, I clean. That's the rule, right?" But Carter wouldn't release the plates in his hand. She tugged a little harder, huffing with agitation. "Dammit, Carter!"

"There are no rules here, Em. There was no agreement for the meal. I don't mind cleaning up. It's not a big deal."

"Well, it is to me, okay? So…just let me do this," she said wearily. This time he released the plates and she simply said "Thanks" and cleared the table—and cleaned up the kitchen too. Although she had to hand it to him, he did a pretty good job of cleaning up after himself while he cooked. If she hadn't been so distracted earlier, she would have loved to watch his process so she could start thinking about the book and how they could incorporate his habits into it.

Though they had yet to talk about it, she believed it would be best for them to do it sooner rather than later. Emery overheard him talking and figured he was on the phone. It gave her time to come up with a plan on how she could make a presentation to him and get him to hear her out without any snarky comments or push-backs.

A girl could dream, right?

Looking around, she was pleased with how neat and

clean the kitchen and dining room looked, so she went in search of Carter. But he was in his room, the door was closed, and he was still talking.

"No biggie," she murmured, going into her own room and getting out the files that she had been studying earlier, along with the notebook she had been using to jot down her ideas. Considering she hadn't expected him to arrive so early—Eliza had mentioned him flying in on Monday—she had enough notes to make a basic presentation. If she'd had more time, she could have made a great PowerPoint presentation that would have blown him away.

Maybe she wouldn't bring up the subject until tomorrow and spend the rest of the day working on putting something a little more impressive together. Maybe she could—

Carter's door opened and he was still talking.

"No, it's fine. I'm heading there now. Don't worry about it," he was saying. "It's okay, I didn't have anything else planned for today. This weekend was all about relaxing before heading out to Montauk."

Montauk? Why was he going to Montauk? And for that matter, how long was he going to be there? How could Eliza expect her to work with Carter if he wasn't going to be here?

Not wanting to disturb him, Emery hung back in her room until she heard him say goodbye, then she casually made her way to the living room. "Everything okay?" she asked.

"What?" he asked distractedly, turning toward her. "Oh, uh…yeah. I'm going to head out for a while. I need to meet up with one of my lawyers and sign some papers."

"On a Saturday?"

For a moment he looked at her as if he didn't understand

her question. Then he relaxed. "Well, I don't get to New York as often as I used to, so he sees me whenever I'm here."

"That's very nice of him."

He nodded and they stood in awkward silence.

"Anyway," he said, "I should go. I guess I'll see you later."

"Sounds good." She was about to ask when he'd be back but remembered telling him to go out and do whatever he wanted without worrying about her. So…he was going out and it wasn't any of her business when he'd be back.

When she finally got out of her own head, she saw him standing by the front door, keys in hand. Looking at her over his shoulder, Carter said, "There are a couple of fruit danishes in the box on the counter and there's another brownie if you want it for dessert. Help yourself."

And then he was gone.

The idea of any kind of baked good with fruit was beyond unappealing, but the brownie was a possibility.

Just not right now.

Then again, after her chocolate Pop-Tart for breakfast and her prelunch brownie, maybe she should save the darn thing for tomorrow.

Or at least wait until after dinner.

Or maybe she should utilize the gym here in the building to work off the first two treats, and then come back for the third. The treadmill was a great place to focus on her work and clear her mind of everything else.

With the perfect afternoon plans, Emery made quick work of changing into yoga pants, a tank top, and sneakers before grabbing her iPod, a bottle of water, and her keys. Feeling invigorated, she quickly made her way to the elevator and down to the gym.

The gym room was deserted, which was fine by her. The fewer people she came in contact with, the better. With her favorite playlist on and the speed of the treadmill just right, she settled in for a workout for both body and mind.

She immediately got warm and cursed herself for not being more faithful to a workout routine. Emery focused her mind instead on envisioning how she wanted Carter's book to look. Going by the examples Eliza had given her and adding them to her own ideas, she envisioned something that looked more like a family gathering than a chef alone in a pretend studio. Perhaps she could convince the Montgomerys to set up for Christmas early this year and do a photo shoot at their family home upstate or at the condo.

Loving that idea, she made a mental note of her vision and kicked up her speed on the treadmill by another half mile per hour.

A little breathless, she imagined Eliza's home decorated for the holidays, the whole family around the table enjoying a meal Carter had created—food that was special but not… ridiculous.

Seriously, she needed to get him to back off the gouda.

Eliza had said she wanted emotion—to engage readers with their senses, remind them of family traditions and how food plays into that. This seemed like a foreign concept to Emery—she and her family were never the type of people who had food traditions.

Ever.

Her mother never enjoyed cooking, and every holiday was a catered meal where someone else created the menu—even if no one enjoyed any of the selections.

Which was how she had developed her junk food habit.

She hid snacks in her room because so many of the meals they had weren't enjoyable.

While her parents loved the idea of being rich and fancy and having events catered by some of the best restaurants in the city, Emery would choose going to a diner for a big fat burger any day of the week. Or something as simple as meatloaf and mashed potatoes.

Yeah, she was a comfort food kind of girl.

Looking straight ahead, Emery caught her reflection in the mirrored wall and studied herself. She was taller than a lot of women she knew and felt like she had zero curves. She'd kill for a few more curves and a few less inches in height. It was unrealistic, but somehow she'd always wished she was someone other than who she was.

There was a depressing thought.

All through school she'd had issues with her appearance. Chalk it up to the pressures of being a girl and how the female population was generally made to feel bad about the way they looked, but Emery felt it more than most. She didn't get asked out like most of her friends, didn't date a lot in high school or college. She had blamed it on being focused on her studies, but inside, she knew it was because of her looks.

And the depressing thoughts continued.

Thinking about school and the awkward teen years brought her thoughts right back to Carter. He never seemed to have one of those phases. He'd always been good-looking and confident, and if memory served, he'd been dating the cute girls since around the age of thirteen. She'd never admitted this to a single person but…she'd been jealous. Yeah, there'd been a time when she'd had a crush on him and knew it was pointless. Boys who looked like him never dated girls who looked like her. It was part of the reason they had the relationship they currently did. Emery had built a wall between them—being adversaries with him was easier than facing his indifference.

Some therapist would have a field day with her if she ever tried to explain that logic out loud.

But even if she did have to explain it, one look at Carter would be all it took. Tall with a lean, muscular build, dark hair that needed a good cut, gray eyes that seemed to see right through you, and the perpetual five o'clock shadow? Um, yeah. If the therapist was a female, all Emery would have to do was show a picture of Carter Montgomery and it would all make sense.

And it didn't make Emery feel any better.

She picked up the speed until she was in a good jog— breathless and getting sweatier by the minute.

She was going to deserve that damn brownie by the time she was done.

And now that she thought about it, it would make the perfect dinner.

"What's this?"

Carter looked up from the dough he was rolling out and grinned. Emery had clearly just emerged from the shower because her hair was wrapped up in a towel, turban-style, she didn't have on an ounce of makeup, and was wearing a flannel robe.

A man's flannel robe.

Seriously, did she not have a better wardrobe than this? After the shorts and T-shirt disaster earlier, he was really beginning to doubt it.

Putting his attention back on the task at hand, he said, "Pizza dough."

"Pizza dough? Why?" she asked, stepping closer. He noted her curious expression.

"I was in the mood for homemade pizza," he replied. He immediately knew she didn't believe him.

"Really?" she asked sarcastically.

"Uh-huh. Really."

"This from the man who earlier today told me about the wonders of being in one of the food capitals of the world, and you're telling me you'd rather stay in and make your own pizza than go out for one. Do I have that right?"

He gave her one of his most dazzling smiles. "Nailed it in one."

She huffed and moved closer, watching what he was doing. "Why would you want to make this much of a mess?" Then she looked around the kitchen. "And don't you need some sort of stone oven or something for this to be good?"

He laughed softly. "Preferable, but not completely necessary. When my parents purchased this place when I was a kid, we never cooked. If we were in the city, we were eating out. About a half-dozen years ago, they did this major renovation on the place and I begged them to go big on the kitchen. My father said it was a frivolous waste of money since no one stayed here long enough to use it and—more specifically—I was selfish to ask such a thing."

"Wow."

He nodded in agreement. "Yup. That was my reaction

too." Then he shrugged. "Although to be fair, he had a point. No one stayed here for extended periods of time, and I'm the only one in the family who enjoys cooking, so…"

"Still," she began, resting her hip against the granite, "they all could have benefitted from it when you were here together. Plus I'm sure if you ever sold the place it would have only added value."

"I thought that as well but kept it to myself. There wasn't anything you could argue with where my father was concerned. Especially when it came to my career choice."

Emery sat on one of the stools and watched him. "He didn't approve of you being a chef?"

With a mirthless laugh, Carter said, "Hardly. It was either be in the finance business or nothing to him. We argued for years, and finally I put my foot down and told him it didn't matter what he said or what he threatened with, it wasn't going to happen. I'm not a suit-and-tie guy and I don't want to sit in an office all day."

"And what did he do?"

Carter reached for a rolling pin and began working on stretching the dough. "He disowned me for about a year—wouldn't talk to me, wouldn't allow my mother to have me home for the holidays… It was crazy."

"So what changed? Did he ever come to appreciate your success and all you accomplished?"

"Eventually. But it wasn't until my second restaurant opening. That's when I started getting a bit of a following." Another laugh. "I had been featured in several magazines and my restaurants were getting rave reviews. He figured if I was getting that much attention, I must be making money."

Her brows furrowed. "Wow."

He ducked his head. "I know."

"Still, it must be nice to know he was proud of you."

Instantly, he stopped rolling and gave her a hard look. "I never said proud, Em. He acknowledged my success, but it was always followed by a snarky comment like 'Still, it's not as secure as being in a real job.'" He shuddered as if hearing his father's voice in his head. "The pressure to work harder and always be on top of my game has been exhausting. I can never relax and enjoy what I've accomplished because I have this fear it's never going to be enough."

He stopped and cursed himself.

Dammit, why had he just shared any of that? The only other person in the world he'd shared that with was his brother Christian.

Without looking at her, Carter turned and started pulling ingredients out of the refrigerator. Fresh basil and mozzarella, fresh and canned tomatoes, artichokes, mushrooms, onions, garlic, and pepperoni. He had no idea what kind of toppings Emery liked on her pizza, but everyone he knew liked pepperoni.

Placing everything on the counter, he walked over and pulled a deep pan out of the cabinet and set it on the stove. Normally, he enjoyed letting his sauce cook all day, but for tonight they'd have to make do with a quick one. Using canned tomatoes wasn't his choice but he'd doctor them up, and with all the other toppings, it would taste fantastic.

And yes, he was definitely tooting his own horn, but he knew it to be true.

His back was to Emery as he began chopping, dicing, and mincing ingredients. He opened the cans and then the bottle of red wine he had purchased on the way home. No

Italian meal—even just pizza—should be eaten without a good bottle of wine. That would be sacrilege.

Olive oil, garlic, onion…it all began to heat in the pan and the aroma filled the air. Carter inhaled deeply and smiled.

Behind him, Emery cleared her throat. "I guess I'll dry my hair and get dressed so I can…you know…go grab something for myself."

Carter immediately took the pan off the flame and turned the burner off. He turned toward her in complete confusion. "Why?"

"Why what?"

"Why are you going to grab something of your own? I'm making us pizza!" And yeah, okay, he was sounding a bit like a crazy person with the snap in his voice, but did she honestly believe he was going to stand here and make himself a fabulous dinner right in front of her and not offer her any? Did she think he was that big of a jerk?

Stupid question.

Her hazel eyes went wide and there was a hint of panic in her expression. "Um… I just thought, you know…" She cleared her throat again. "I told you earlier I don't expect you to cook for me."

Yes, she had told him that and at the time he hadn't commented. So if blame had to be placed on this misunderstanding, it was on him.

Not that he was going to admit it.

"Look, we're both here, and obviously I enjoy cooking and you…don't." He paused to see if she'd take offense to that, but she didn't. "So if I'm cooking and you're here, it's safe to assume I'm cooking for both of us. Okay?"

And then the strangest thing happened.

Emery blushed.

Like, seriously, her cheeks turned pink and she averted her eyes, and it was absolutely adorable.

"Em?"

With a quick nod, she said, "Okay." When she looked up at him again, she fidgeted with the towel on her head. "I still need to go dry my hair and get changed." She paused. "I'd ask if there was something I could do to help, but I think we both know the answer to that."

His quick laugh escaped before he could stop it. "Go. And you don't have to rush. It'll easily be an hour before we eat and I've got everything under control. So…go."

"Thanks."

He stood back and watched her walk down the hall toward her bedroom, and once the door was closed, he went back to the stove and put the pan back on the burner and continued to cook. Once things were seasoned and simmering to his liking, he pulled his phone out and did the one thing he had hoped to put off for a few more days.

He called his mother.

"Carter! What a surprise! I thought after the way you threw me off the phone last night I wouldn't hear from you for a while," his mother said as soon as she answered the phone.

"I think we both know why I'm calling sooner rather than later," he said.

"I did try telling you last night, but you weren't listening to me."

"Mom…"

"And on top of that, you lied to me about your travel

plans!" she cried. "Am I so horrible to be around that you find it necessary to lie to me rather than allowing me to see you when you're in town?"

Twenty-three seconds! That had to be a new guilt-trip record.

"You're not horrible, Mom, and you know it. I need a couple of days to decompress before dealing with all the new restaurant issues, and yet somehow that didn't happen. Do you want to guess why?"

"Let's not play this game, Carter," she said stiffly. "I get it. You're at the condo and so is Emery, but in my defense, she needed a place to go and when you mentioned going to New York to me several weeks ago, I couldn't be sure if you meant the city or out to Long Island. See, if you were a little more *honest* with me—"

"Okay, let's not play that game either," he interrupted. "I think it's very nice how you helped Emery out. But if you had told me, I would have gone straight to Montauk and avoided all of this."

"Carter..."

"Do you have any idea how awkward this is?" he asked softly, not wanting Emery to overhear him. Quietly, he stepped into the hall, heard her blow-dryer running, and breathed a sigh of relief. He made his way back to the living room. "I come home to find a stranger in the house—"

"Emery's hardly a stranger."

"I thought someone had broken in. Emery was asleep and also thought someone had broken in, and we both scared the crap out of one another and I attacked first and asked questions later!"

"Oh, Carter! You didn't hurt her, did you?"

He decided to omit some details. "No, Mom, I didn't hurt her, but it certainly freaked us both out!"

They were getting nowhere. He walked back into the kitchen and stirred the sauce. "Mom, this wasn't a good time for you to do this. I gave you recipes, photos, and you have my name to put on the book. If there's anything else you want to add, you can—photos, anecdotes, whatever. You know what you want and you can totally do it. I can't put any more time into this. I'm leaving for Montauk on Monday and—"

"So take Emery to Montauk with you," she stated simply.

Damn. I walked right into that one, didn't I?

He sighed wearily and raked a hand through his hair.

"It won't matter. I still don't have time to put into working with her. This trip is for me to focus on the problems with the restaurant."

"But Carter—"

"Look, clearly you have faith in Emery or you wouldn't have offered her the position, right?"

No response.

"All I'm saying is if she knows what you want and she has all the materials, then she'll be able to make it work. And honestly, why would you even *think* choosing Emery to help me was a good idea?" he asked. "She's been a thorn in my side since we were kids!"

"Carter," she said a little more firmly, but he cut her off.

"I'm sorry, Mom. This is the best I can do."

Not knowing what else to do or say, Carter glanced toward the stove and saw steam coming from under the lid of his saucepan. Walking over, he lifted it and gently stirred the sauce, relieved nothing had stuck. It smelled good, but suddenly his appetite was gone.

Lowering the flame, he replaced the lid and sighed.

"I really am sorry. The timing is just…"

"It's fine, Carter. It was selfish of me to ask so much of you when you're already overwhelmed with work." She paused. "Now, if you'll excuse me, I'm meeting the girls for book club tonight. I'll talk to you soon." And before he could respond, she was gone.

Much like he'd done to her the night before.

Tossing his phone down on the kitchen island, he braced his hands on the granite and hung his head.

He cursed himself, not that it did any good.

It was like he was being punished, though for what he had no idea. For years he'd run a very successful business. His restaurants were world-famous and he had been interviewed and done segments on both daytime and nighttime talk shows, so why was everything going to shit now?

He poured himself a glass of wine and took a sip, but that wasn't going to be enough to mellow him out.

Putting the glass down, Carter stepped back over to the stove and stirred the sauce, looking at the dough sitting on the counter. He had rolled and stretched it, then formed it back into a ball again earlier, for no other reason except he was trying to keep himself busy. Now he had to roll it out again and get it onto the large pizza stone. It was the last thing he felt like doing. He turned off the burner beneath the sauce.

The walls were closing in on him and there was only one thing to do—leave. He'd take a long, brisk walk, and he could deal with the dough and the rest of it later. Keys in hand, he was halfway to the door when he heard Emery ask, "Going someplace?"

It wasn't as if she had intentionally eavesdropped on his conversation with Eliza; it just happened to turn out that way.

After she had finished drying her hair and getting dressed, Emery had heard Carter speaking on the phone. She could hear the frustration in his voice and knew she was a contributing factor to it. And while that had been enough to get her hackles up, it wasn't until she listened closer that she realized there was more to the story. She didn't know what, but it wasn't just her presence that was freaking him out. In the end, she'd heard how tortured he sounded at letting his mother down, and she could only imagine how Eliza must have reacted.

Dammit, she hated this. Hated how this was a problem and she was in the middle of it.

This was supposed to be a reprieve for her—a sanctuary with a bit of busy work to keep her mind occupied. What it was now was an awkward situation for the three of them with no means of escape.

Okay, maybe escape wasn't the right word, but… she hated how this was Carter's family home and she was encroaching on his space and his need for solitude. The fact that he was leaving told her so.

"You shouldn't be the one to go, Carter," she said cautiously, not wanting to upset him any further. "I'll leave."

When he turned to face her, she could tell he was wound tightly. His fists were clenched at his side, his expression hard. "What are you talking about?" he said gruffly.

"I—I heard your conversation with your mom." She sighed and took a tentative step toward him. "I had no idea my being here or helping with the book was going to cause so many problems."

"The book is the problem, Emery, not you," he corrected, but it didn't make her feel much better.

"Still, it seems like I'm just adding to an already difficult time for you, so... I'll find someplace else to stay until you leave for wherever it is you're going next."

Carter continued to stare at her and Emery wished he'd say something—anything! When it appeared he wouldn't, she turned to head back to her room to pack up a few things. A couple of nights in a hotel wouldn't be the worst thing in the world, right? There was room service and well, she was sure there would be other perks but they escaped her right now.

She'd gone all of two feet when Carter called her name. Slowly, she looked over her shoulder at him.

"Don't go."

His voice was raw and it wasn't hard to tell there was a battle raging within him. Normally, Emery enjoyed watching Carter squirm and struggle, but for some reason seeing him this emotional after a call with his mother affected her in a way she didn't expect.

She felt compassion for him—a need to comfort him and tell him it was going to be all right.

She made her way toward him. "I think it would be best for everyone if I did. You didn't deserve to be blindsided like this, and I'm sorry it happened this way. I truly believed you were aware of what was going on and you were coming here specifically to work on the book. I had no idea your trip here had nothing to do with it or that you were so against giving it more attention."

Carter's shoulders sagged a little. "At any other time…"

"I know," she said softly, moving a little closer. "I get it. Hey, there isn't anything I can do about whatever else you're dealing with, but on this particular subject, I can. I'll work with the files you sent your mother and I'll make it into something closer to what she's looking for, okay? And in the meantime, I'll stay out of your way so you can have at least one night's peace."

They stood in silence for a long time, and as much as Emery wanted to pack and get out of his way, she couldn't seem to make herself move. In all the years they had known one another, they had bickered and poked fun at each other and essentially gone out of their way to make the other miserable. It was what they did. It was comfortable. But right now, she couldn't think of a single snarky or antagonistic comment.

And that freaked her out.

Swallowing hard, she took a step back. And then another. Next thing she knew, she had spun and was walking back to her bedroom, mildly trembling. She went straight to her closet and pulled out her weekender bag. Knowing she wouldn't be going out or doing anything other than vegging in her hotel room, she walked over to her dresser and pulled out a couple of pairs of yoga pants, a few T-shirts, a pair of pajamas, and a pair of shorts and tossed them in the bag. Next, she opened her lingerie drawer and was pulling out a handful of panties when a large male hand closed over hers. Gasping with surprise, she turned and found herself face-to-face with Carter.

While they both held her panties.

Awesome.

Emery wanted to be outraged—or at the very least annoyed that he had invaded her space when she was clearly trying to be the bigger person here—but for some reason she couldn't seem to make herself speak or react.

What was happening to her?

"This is crazy," he said, his voice deep and low and borderline hypnotic.

So he felt it, too? This sudden crazy pull toward one another? The change in the air around them?

"I already said I didn't want you to go, Em," he went on, and that's when she realized what he was talking about.

Forcing her gaze away, she carefully pulled her hand and underwear from his. "I think it's for the best." Then she moved away, tossing her garments in the weekender bag along with the rest of her clothes. For a few minutes, she busied herself collecting odds and ends—her laptop, her e-reader, her iPod—before going into the bathroom and grabbing her toothbrush, makeup, and brushes. Anything else she needed she'd get from housekeeping. When she walked back out into the bedroom, she found Carter sitting quietly on her bed.

And her weekender bag emptied.

Okay, *now* she was outraged.

"Seriously, Carter?" she cried. "Why can't you just let me do this?"

He shrugged. "I already told you. It's not necessary."

"To me it is! There's no reason for me to stay here. And might I remind you, I've been a thorn in your side since we were kids!"

It pleased her that he paled a little at having his words thrown back at him.

"I would think you'd be thankful that I was leaving," she said, hating the tremor in her voice. "One less thing for you to worry about."

The curse that flew out of his mouth followed by a huff of annoyance didn't really surprise her. This was them. This was the relationship they had. And honestly, she preferred this to the strained silence and whatever it was that she was feeling just minutes ago.

Carter stood and walked over until they were toe to toe. "What I said to my mother," he began and then stopped. "What I mean is, that was said in the heat of the moment and really, it couldn't have been news to you. I've been telling you that to your face since we were twelve."

"Eleven, but…whatever," she corrected and smirked when he growled with frustration.

"That! That right there is why I said it! Can't you just let some things go?"

"*Me?*" she cried. "How about you? I was being the bigger person here! I was putting your feelings first, and where did that get me, huh? I should be in a cab on my way to a hotel with room service, but instead I'm here arguing with you again! Why couldn't you just let me leave?"

They both instantly fell silent and Emery felt herself holding her breath while she waited for his answer.

"What's the matter?" she finally asked. "Is it possible the arrogant Carter Montgomery has nothing to say for himself for the first time in his life?"

Yeah, she was taunting him, but…she needed to. Needed things to be like they always were. If she didn't get them back on solid ground—back on the familiar turf of a lifelong rivalry—she wouldn't know what to do. For years she'd been aware of Carter as a person. She couldn't deal with suddenly being aware of him as a man.

When his only response was a slight tick in his jaw, she figured she'd poke the bear a little more. "Did you burn the sauce? Is that why we're not eating yet? Or maybe you realized all that pretentious crap you bought was no better than grabbing a couple of slices from the pizzeria on the corner." She noted he seemed to be almost inflating before her eyes—his posture straightened, his shoulders seemed to grow broader…

Go big or go home, right?

Leaning in, she said, "I bet you really don't know *how* to make homemade pizza. At least not *good* homemade pizza." She let out a devious little laugh. "Probably thought I would be too naive to know the difference. You probably could have served up one of my frozen pizzas and I wouldn't know the difference."

He was breaking molars now, no doubt.

"Not that it matters. I've got some microwave popcorn I can have for dinner, along with the last brownie. That's the kind of stuff I can count on—and will probably be a lot more enjoyable."

This time when Emery tried to move away, Carter's large hand on her arm stopped her.

She had to hide her smile of satisfaction. "Problem?" she asked innocently.

"You've got a real smart mouth, Emery, but you don't know what the hell you're talking about."

"Oh, really? Care to explain?"

But he shook his head. "As a matter of fact, no. I don't."

She shrugged. "Fine, whatever. Now, if you'll excuse me, my dinner awaits."

"If you so much as think of making popcorn for dinner, I'll strangle you," he said, tugging her closer.

When she leaned in until they were nose to nose, she said, "I dare you."

"Such a smart mouth," he said right before he claimed it.

Chapter 3

FOR TWENTY-PLUS YEARS, CARTER HAD IMAGINED SOME pretty creative ways to shut Emery Monaghan up.

Snarky comebacks.

Throwing stuff at her.

Making references to their younger days guaranteed to embarrass her.

Kissing her?

Never.

And yet now that he was doing it? Holy hell, it was amazing.

She was taller than most women he'd been with and he found it nice not to have to bend down quite so much. And while she didn't look to be soft or curvy, he'd never been more wrong. As Emery's body seemed to melt against his, he felt every soft curve and his hands itched to touch them. But first…first he reached up and fisted his hand into her dark hair out of curiosity and was amazed by how soft it was.

Like silk.

Emery let out a soft little moan as his fist tightened in her hair. The sound was the sexiest thing he'd ever heard from her lips.

And yeah…those lips. Soft and wet and so damn good that kissing her could possibly be his new favorite pastime.

Emery broke the kiss and pulled away from him breathlessly. "What the hell, Carter?"

Uh-oh. Was it possible he'd misread the whole situation? She had kissed him back and then there was the moan and...

"Seriously, why would you do that?"

Okay, yeah. She was pissed.

Not turned on.

Dammit.

"Well?" she demanded.

What could he possibly say? He couldn't explain what had possessed him to kiss her even if he wanted to. One minute she was insulting him and the next—

No idea.

In order to save face, he was going to have to make it sound as if it wasn't a big deal.

Even though it was.

A major one.

With a shrug, he said, "It seemed like the only way to shut you up." Then he held up his hands and added, "And it worked." Without looking at her again, he walked out of the room and straight to the kitchen. Why? He had no idea. He was still a little irked about his conversation with his mother, and on top of that, he was turned on. Spotting his keys on the kitchen island where he'd tossed them before going after Emery, Carter considered going out like he originally planned. But if he did, no doubt he'd come back to find Emery gone. And he couldn't let that happen. If anyone was going to leave, it was him.

Just...not yet.

The kitchen was a bit of a mess and the last thing he wanted to do was cook—which was an oddity for him—but he was starving. Glancing over his shoulder at Emery's bedroom, he wondered if she was packing again or just avoiding him.

Only one way to find out.

He walked with a sense of purpose and collided with her in her bedroom doorway. Carter reached out to steady her, but Emery moved away too fast.

Crap. Was this how it was going to be now?

Unable to resist, he looked over her shoulder and saw that her bag was exactly where he'd left it. Hopefully, that meant she hadn't repacked anything yet.

"Look," he began slowly, "can we just forget the last hour? I'm sorry for what I said to my mother, okay? Can we please just grab some dinner, since the meal I was prepping is running too late now?"

Her eyes narrowed at him suspiciously. Without a word, Emery stepped around him and walked to the kitchen. He found her with the lid to the pan in her hand, sniffing the sauce. Turning her head toward him, she said, "What's wrong with this? It smells perfectly fine to me."

This would probably be the wrong time to remind her how she also enjoyed frozen pizzas and eating popcorn for dinner and how her overall knowledge of good food was questionable.

"The dough's not ready. It's going to take too long."

She looked around and saw the ball of dough. "I know I'm no chef, but I didn't think pizza dough was particularly difficult."

Normally he'd agree, but...

And then she smiled.

Like a genuine smile—not evil, no snark, just... beautiful.

"Aww, did someone have a temper tantrum and now you don't feel like cooking anymore?"

Okay, so much for the lack of snark.

Why argue it? With a nod, he said, "Pretty much. How about we go down to the place on the corner and get a couple of slices?"

Rather than respond, Emery walked to the pantry, scanned the contents, and pulled out a box of spaghetti and waved it at him. "You've already got the sauce made, why not just have this with it?"

"Because I really wanted pizza."

She rolled her eyes and placed the pasta back on the shelf.

"We'll make the pizza tomorrow," he said with a bit of a huff, hoping she'd give up and agree to go eat with him. He needed to get them back on level ground and just...not be here right now. "I'll put the dough in the refrigerator and we'll make it for lunch tomorrow, if you'd like."

Emery peeked her head out from behind the pantry door. "We should make it now."

"Now?" he asked.

"Yes." She stepped out of the pantry, shut the door, and walked over to lean against the island. "I didn't want to admit this, but I was kind of looking forward to watching you make it."

He quirked a dark brow at her. "Seriously?"

She nodded.

Now he was a little suspicious. "Why?"

Instead of answering, she rolled her eyes and groaned. When she finally looked at him again, she replied, "Honestly? I always thought it was cool the way they toss the dough in pizzerias and I was curious if you were going to do that here, and maybe...I don't know, maybe you could show me how they do it."

For a moment, he couldn't speak. "Wait—you want me to teach you how to...toss pizza dough?" he asked incredulously. "Did I get that right?"

She nodded.

Almost enthusiastically.

And damn, now he really wanted to do that for her.

"Okay," he said and smiled when Emery bounced on her toes excitedly and clapped. "But there are a few things I'm going to need you to do."

The look of panic on her face was almost comical.

"You're going to wipe down the countertop for me and then chop some vegetables. Think you can handle it?" He wasn't being condescending—simply asking the question.

"That I can do," she answered with a smile.

A smile he was beginning to like seeing far more than he'd ever imagined.

Carter made quick work of instructing her on what he needed prepped and busied himself rolling out the dough.

Standing in the middle of the kitchen, Carter knew he had to get a grip on his thoughts and feelings.

There was more than one pizza stone in the kitchen, so he might let Emery make her own. She could top it with whatever she wanted and maybe feel a bit accomplished at having done it herself. Especially after he taught her how to toss and stretch the dough on her own.

He smiled.

There was nothing for him to feel awkward or weird about.

There was nothing sexy about making pizza.

Everything was going to be just fine.

He'd never been more wrong in his entire life.

Carter had to admit it to himself—the art of cooking and eating was sensuous. He just had no idea it could be quite like this over something as ridiculous as pizza.

Emery had flour on her face, her shirt, her jeans... pretty much everywhere. Her laughter at the process was infectious.

Carter stood close behind her and guided her hands in the motions of working the dough properly.

"I think this is a lost cause," she said, and he was almost ready to agree. They had made multiple dough balls and had thrown several out already when she had lost control and either sent them to the floor or mangled them beyond repair. Carter knew she was frustrated, but he had to hand it to her, she had a good attitude.

"Come on," he said, still amused. "This one's gonna be the one. I can feel it."

Her head came back and almost landed on his shoulder as she continued to laugh. "I'd wave the white flag, but I've already strewn enough flour around this kitchen to make it look like a snowstorm blew through."

Gently grasping her shoulders, he made her straighten. "You got this. Remember, pick up the dough and let it drape over your hands," he instructed. "Your right palm should be up and that's the hand you're going to use to spin, okay?"

She nodded.

"Ready?"

"Not even a little."

Carter reached around and carefully wrapped his hands

around hers. He had a feeling she still wasn't going to be able to do this unless he guided her. So far, she had tried watching and mimicking his moves without success. This was the only thing he could think of to help her get the gist of what she needed to do.

Together they began working the dough—first stretching it using their knuckles, tossing it from left to right and back again before slowly spinning it. It was awkward working like this and he knew it wouldn't be perfect, but once they got in sync and had the motion going, he could step back.

Emery gasped with delight as the dough began to spin the way it was supposed to. He was careful not to spook her and make her lose the rhythm. "Focus," he murmured close to her ear. "You've got this."

Was it his imagination or did her breath catch? Swallowing hard, Carter tried to convince himself to take a step back—to lower his arms and let her take over—but he couldn't. He inhaled deeply, enjoying the sweet scent of her skin, and moved in just a little bit closer until his chest was against her back.

"Are you ready to toss it?" he asked thickly, amazed at how aroused he was.

"I…I don't think I can."

His mouth was practically against the shell of her ear. "C'mon, Em. Do it."

She groaned. And it was sexy as hell. He encouraged her one more time and smiled when he watched the disc go up a few inches from her hand and then she instantly caught it, keeping the motion going.

"Ohmygosh!" she said excitedly. "I did it! I really did it!"

Beaming with pride, Carter forced himself to take a step back. "Keep going. You got this."

And for another minute she did. On her last catch, she quickly dumped the rounded disc onto her pizza stone before turning to him with pure joy on her face.

And then she launched herself into his arms.

Carter readily caught her and hugged her close. Her long legs wrapped around him and it was all he could do not to spin and press her against the wall so he could kiss her and relish the feel of her in his arms.

"I did it!" she said again. "I can't believe I really did it! And I was good, right?" Her hazel eyes were big and bright and her cheeks were flushed and she was killing him.

So good, he thought. She was so very…very good.

Moving quickly, he did his best to unwrap her from around his waist and placed her on her feet. He was enjoying himself a little too much and soon Emery would know *exactly* what he was thinking.

And feeling.

And wanting.

Dammit.

Emery looked at him with confusion and Carter had to think fast so he didn't do or say anything to embarrass either one of them. Clapping his hands together, he said, "We don't want to let the dough rest too long. We need to get the sauce and toppings on it as soon as possible."

She glanced at him and then over at his own dough, which had been sitting on the stone for the last fifteen minutes.

"I'm starving," he said, his voice higher than he'd ever heard come out of his own mouth.

Without looking at her, he moved to the stove and

brought the pan of sauce over to the island, ladling some first onto his dough and then hers. Once he was done, he put the pan back before trying to remember what came next.

When it seemed to take longer than it should, Emery prompted, "Um… Carter?"

"Toppings!" he said enthusiastically. "Now you can go wild with whatever toppings you want. We've got the sautéed vegetables, pepperoni, three different cheeses—"

"None of them are gouda, right?"

It would have been easy to let that comment slide them into snarky territory, but he didn't take the bait. "Nope." He began covering his pie with an assortment of cheese. "So, what's your favorite topping? Did we miss anything?"

"I'm a total pepperoni girl," she said, taking the cheese from him. "Although there's a place back home that makes a fantastic eggplant pizza."

"Grilled or fried?"

"Fried. Sometimes I get that with pepperoni. But only when it's just me. Derek hates it."

Right then and there, Carter wished he'd had some eggplant to fry up for her, and had to bite his tongue to keep from making a nasty comment about her ex. Not that she would blame him, but the last thing she needed was a reminder of what an ass she'd almost married.

"I happen to love eggplant," he said. "I make a really good eggplant rollatini. It's one of my mom's favorites."

"Do you ever make it for the holidays?" she asked casually.

"Years ago we used to make it on Christmas Eve. It was one of the many dishes we made." He added some of the sautéed vegetables to his pizza. "Back when we were kids, there were so many family members around on Christmas

Eve that it was a buffet. It wasn't until we got older that it all became a little more formal and turned into a complete sit-down, five-course meal."

"And which do you prefer?"

He laughed softly, arranging the slices of pepperoni strategically around the pizza. "Buffet," he said without hesitation. "I love the variety and some of those dishes we only have once a year so."

And that's when it hit him.

That was the sort of thing he had skipped in the cookbook. It had been years since he thought about the Christmas meals from his childhood. All this time he'd been focusing on his later years—like when he started cooking professionally and opened his first restaurant—but he could probably add meals like the one he had just mentioned to Emery. Hopefully, that might fulfill his mother's wishes for the book.

When he looked over at Emery, he saw her smiling broadly as she added toppings to her pizza. "Having fun?" he asked.

Without looking at him, she nodded. "You'll probably make fun of what I'm thinking."

"This time I won't. I promise."

She paused and looked at him—her skepticism clear—then went back to placing pepperoni carefully around her pie. "I was thinking how whenever I buy a frozen pizza, it never has exactly what I want."

"That's because it's frozen pizza."

Huffing, she shook her head. "I knew you'd make fun."

"I wasn't!" he argued. "I'm just saying it's one of the reasons you don't get what you want. Frozen pizzas only come in so many varieties."

"Oh." Relaxing, she went on to explain. "Anyway, I love a supreme pizza, but I don't like sausage. So everything you bought fits me perfectly." Turning her head, she smiled at him again and Carter felt it all the way to his toes. "Thank you."

"You're welcome," he said, his voice gruff as he processed this new feeling. He studied his pizza. It was ready for the oven, but he waited for Emery.

"All set!" she chimed.

He looked at her pizza—it was much more chaotic than his, but what she lacked in talent she more than made up for in enthusiasm. First he placed his stone in the oven, and then carefully took hers and placed it alongside his.

They worked together to clean up the incredible mess they had made while Carter shared his ideas about the recipes from his childhood. Emery didn't gush or tell him he was brilliant or anything, but he knew she was pleased with his brainstorming.

"So if I type up the recipes and maybe add a passage or two about why they mean something to me, would that be helpful?" he asked, almost afraid to broach any topic that might cause tension in what was becoming a rather enjoyable night.

"Sure," she said. "Any idea how many you might be adding?"

"I'm not sure. Maybe a dozen?"

Emery finished wiping down the granite and rinsed out the sponge. "I think that would be great. If you can get them to me before you leave for Montauk, I'd appreciate it."

After putting the kitchen back in pristine condition, Carter poured them each a glass of wine before checking on their pizzas. Emery was immediately at his side, peeking into the oven with him.

"Oh wow!" she said with awe. "Those look fantastic!"

She's right, he thought. Reaching for the oven mitts, he removed each stone from the oven and placed them on top of the stove. Emery was still at his side, practically bouncing on her toes. Her excitement over something as simple as homemade pizza was really adorable and he had to remember to keep that thought to himself.

"Could you get us a couple of plates and I'll slice these up?" he asked. Emery nodded enthusiastically.

Within minutes, they were sitting at the dining room table and Carter found himself holding his breath, waiting for Emery to take her first bite. And yet she was staring at the two slices on her plate as if she wasn't sure what to make of them.

"Problem?"

"It's not as crispy as I thought it would be and I'm afraid if I pick it up, it's just going to fall apart and make a big mess and you'll make fun of me. But if I eat it with a knife and fork, you'll also make fun of me." She looked at the pizza once more, then laughed. "I think I'm willing to be messy and say to hell with what you think!" Then she picked up a slice, took a massive bite out of it—half the toppings fell off and onto her plate—but she looked like she didn't have a care in the world.

Rather than make her feel self-conscious, he put his attention on his own pizza, made his own mess, and together they shared what was quite possibly the most perfect meal.

She missed him.

A week later and still all Emery could think about was how much she missed Carter.

It was like she was living in an alternate universe or something.

Their pizza dinner last Saturday night had been a turning point. At least, that's what it felt like to her. They had cautiously morphed into a couple of friends who were comfortable around one another. By the time Carter left Monday morning, they had laughed together more than they had in all the years they'd known each other.

That wasn't to say it had been a completely blissful thirty-six hours. That would have been way too bizarre. Her eating habits seemed to annoy him more than anything else—if she wasn't eating what he was, then she was in the wrong. What Carter didn't understand was how most of what he ate held little appeal to her, while he—surprise, surprise—refused even to try to see her side of things or taste anything she was eating.

Her breakfast Pop-Tarts were a definite problem for him.

So was the chocolate-covered popcorn she snacked on while checking her emails.

Then there was the time she turned down surf and turf for a couple of hot dogs.

And though she got it—sort of—it still annoyed her. Carter was a chef. Food was his life. But the fact that he cringed at the thought of hot dogs from a street vendor made him a snob, in her opinion. When they walked into a gourmet deli to get some items for lunch and he grilled the poor girl behind the counter for a solid twenty minutes over how fresh everything was, that only confirmed it. And all those fancy salads he bought? Most of them she didn't like. One of them she actually spit out into her napkin. She hadn't done that since she was five.

Of course he had reprimanded her, because that salad—which still made her shudder to think about—contained beet pasta, goat cheese, and walnuts and was one of the trendiest salads he'd ever seen.

The only salad Emery enjoyed was a caesar and when she told him so, he groaned with disapproval.

She'd called him a food snob, he'd called her uncultured, and they'd each eaten their meal of choice in silence.

Ironically, once food was *off* the table, things were fine between them. Carter had written up those recipes for her and then she had offered to work with him on the commentary. He had dictated and she'd typed. Together they edited it all, ending up with a very sweet passage that Emery felt defined everything Eliza was hoping for with the cookbook.

All week long, Emery had gone through the recipes Carter had given her and created a document with each one in the order she felt they should be. While it was starting to come together, she'd texted Carter twice with questions and he'd been more than willing to help her out, sending her a couple more anecdotes and commentaries. It was all nice and sweet and what she was asking for, yet it still felt lacking. What was she missing? What were they *both* missing?

Eliza herself seemed pleased with the progress, but Emery could tell something wasn't there for her, as well. And yet none of them could put their finger on it. It was maddening! Unable to stand looking at the computer screen any longer, she stood and stretched, contemplating finding something else to do. It was a beautiful Sunday morning, and what she wanted right now was to go out for a long walk and enjoy it.

So that's what she did.

In a pair of faded skinny jeans, a navy blue hoodie, and sneakers, Emery slipped on her sunglasses, grabbed her phone, keys, and cross-body purse, and headed out. The temperature was perfect, the sun was shining, and as she predicted, being outside lightened her mood in an instant.

She walked with no real purpose. She window shopped, ate when she was hungry, and simply enjoyed people-watching. For hours Emery walked at her own pace, realizing just how much time she'd been spending locked up in the condo as a way to avoid the possibility of anything negative.

Had it worked? Yes.

Was she tired of it? Yes.

Maybe her self-imposed exile could be coming to a close. It had been a month, and Derek's name was in the news less and less each day. Maybe she could consider going home. Making a mental note to call her mother later in the evening to get a read on the situation, Emery continued with her stroll.

By four o'clock, she was beat, her belly was full, and she had a bag full of goodies for later. She had discovered that New York bakeries were her weakness. As she turned the corner by her building, Emery reached into her purse and pulled out her keys, not really looking where she was going, and walked right into someone.

"Oh! I'm so sorry, I—" When she looked up, she paled.

It was the same gentleman she'd seen last weekend in the farmer's market when she was with Carter. Martin Ashley, one of Derek's attorneys.

He gave a tight smile and said, "Good afternoon, Miss Monaghan. You're not an easy woman to find."

Swallowing hard, Emery tried to think of a way out of this situation. She did not want to talk to this man or talk about Derek.

Ever.

Doing her best to look bored, Emery waited him out, figuring he'd say what he had to say and then leave.

"Our firm has been trying to get in contact with you with no success. It's very important for Derek's defense for you to be there at his side."

Although she knew he couldn't see behind her dark glasses, Emery's eyes went wide. "You're joking, right?"

Martin's expression never changed. "Not at all. We have several court appearances coming up this week, and your appearance and show of support would go a long way in helping Derek's case."

This time she couldn't help it—she laughed.

Actually, she snorted.

"I hate to break it to you, but I'm not looking to help Derek's case. At all. You see, I believe he's guilty and if the prosecution asked, I'd testify to that. So really, you're wasting your time here."

Now he looked irritated.

"It's perfectly understandable that you'd feel a little… let's say *distressed* by what Derek's been accused of. However, the two of you have been together for so long and the public is used to seeing you with him, and they no doubt expect you to follow the words of the law. A man is innocent until proven guilty, after all."

Is this guy for real? she thought with disgust.

"Save your breath. It's not going to happen. I'm not showing up to any court, I'm certainly not going to support Derek, and I'd really like you to leave now."

Taking a step back, Martin held up his hands in mock surrender. "It's a public sidewalk, Miss Monaghan." Then he paused and looked up at the building. "Nice place you're staying. I'm not sure the residents would appreciate the press setting up camp out here in hopes of getting a statement from you."

Emery felt like she was going to be sick. This bastard was threatening her.

"Come to court on Tuesday and no one knows of your whereabouts. Refuse and I'll make a couple of well-placed calls to alert the press as to where you can be found and how you're just itching to talk to them. Think about it," he said smugly before walking away.

Everything in Emery revolted. If she didn't get inside soon, she most certainly was going to be sick right here on the street.

With her head down, she quickly made her way inside the building and into the elevator. Luckily, she was alone and she paced and silently prayed she could hold it together for a few more minutes. By the time the doors slid open, tears were streaming down her face and her heart was racing. With a cry of despair, she sped down the hall and let herself into the apartment, slamming the door behind her. The bag of food, her keys, phone, and purse all dropped to the floor as she sprinted to the bathroom and lost her hold on everything she had eaten today.

By the time she felt well enough to move, her entire body felt beaten and bruised. Her head was pounding, and more than anything, she wanted to yell and scream and cry at the unfairness of it all.

Off in the distance, Emery could hear her phone ringing. The last thing she wanted was to talk to anyone, so she ignored it. Slowly, she came to her feet and got her bearings. Next, she brushed her teeth. Her arms felt like lead and her body was shaking as she moved herself to the kitchen, opening a can of Coke. She sat and sipped it while trying to relax.

And still her phone continued to ring.

"Oh, just shut up," she murmured, too weak to yell. It finally stopped. "Thank God."

But then the house phone rang and the sound made her jump. Uncertainty waged within her—was it her place to answer it? Was it just a coincidence that it rang right after her own phone stopped?

Then it too stopped.

She said another prayer of thanks and took a sip of her soda.

And the damn phone rang again.

"Okay, that is way too much of a coincidence," she said, slowly coming to her feet. Grabbing the phone, she said, "Hello?"

"Emery? Are you all right?" It was Eliza, her voice laced with concern.

"Um…yes," she said hesitantly.

"Are you sure? I just received a call from someone asking if it was our condo you were staying in! I don't know who he was and he wouldn't tell me, but when I tried to deny it, he claimed he'd talked to you today."

Emery began to cry.

The entire time she cried, Eliza did her best to calm her

down and promise that everything was going to be all right, but Emery was doubtful. She was alone and scared and had no idea what was going to happen next. Just when she had thought things were getting better, they had crashed and burned around her.

"Tell me what you need me to do. We have other homes you can go to. We have family down in North Carolina who would be more than willing to give you a place to stay. My sister-in-law, Monica, and her husband, William, have a lovely guest house you could stay in and—"

"No. No, I couldn't impose like that," she quickly interrupted. "I've already somehow managed to drag you into this mess and you don't deserve that."

"What are you going to do?"

As much as it pained her, she replied, "I'm going to go home and make my appearance in court."

Eliza gasped. "You can't! Oh, Emery, please don't. Don't put yourself in that position!"

"I don't really have a choice. I'll make a deal that if I show up, it's the one and only time, and hopefully they'll agree. And maybe—just maybe—the press will eventually grow tired of not getting any response from me and leave me alone."

"Please don't do anything rash. I'm sure you just need a couple of days to think this through."

"That's just it, I don't have a couple of days. If I don't show up with Derek to his court appearance on Tuesday, his attorney will tell everyone where I am. That's going to cause a problem with the residents here in the building and it will make problems for you as well. I can't do that to you, Eliza. You've done more for me than anyone else I know and it wouldn't be right for me to be so selfish."

"Emery, you're the least selfish woman I know and I hate this." She paused. "Just…just give me until the morning, okay?"

"For what?"

"We have quite an extensive legal team at Montgomerys. Let me make some calls and—"

"Eliza, no," Emery said firmly. "This isn't your battle to fight. I appreciate it—more than you know—but I have to figure this out on my own."

"Let me at least get you some advice," Eliza said. "I'm not saying you have to take it, but if we can put off this sleazy lawyer and prevent him from going to the press, then you'll have some time to figure things out."

"I don't know…"

"Do you trust me, Emery?" Eliza asked softly, almost lovingly. Like a mother should sound.

"You know I do."

"Then at least give me a couple of hours. Please."

It was pointless to argue. "Okay. Thank you."

Emery hung up. Her instinct was to flee—not to her home, but anywhere else.

Groaning, she collapsed on the sofa. It wasn't running away, she reasoned—and not for the first time. It was a matter of self-preservation. Emery had dealt with the problem when it hit—she'd broken up with Derek and told him she wanted no part of this scandal. And where had that gotten her? Forced to move out of her own home just so she could have a little peace, quiet, and a place to breathe without being watched and hounded. That wasn't too much to ask, was it?

Apparently.

Glancing over at her phone, Emery thought about

calling her mother and trying to talk to her but…to what end?

Rising, she grabbed her can of soda and walked around aimlessly from room to room as if one of them was going to suddenly have answers for her. There were four bedrooms and four bathrooms, the living room, dining room, and kitchen. Each was beautifully decorated and held many framed photos of the Montgomerys. It wasn't until she was walking around the master bedroom that she stopped and picked a photo up. It was of Eliza's three children—Christian, Megan, and Carter—and it made her smile.

On the left was Christian. He looked serious—his smile was sweet but didn't quite meet his eyes. On the right was Carter, eyes full of mischief, his smile wide like someone had just told him a good joke. His hair was a bit askew and darker than his brother's, but what stood out more than anything was how much they looked alike. It was their temperament that was so different—she knew this from the few times she'd met Christian.

Standing between them was their sister, Megan. Her smile was as big as Carter's and she was hugging both of her brothers close. It was such a sweet photo and looked like it hadn't been taken that long ago. For a moment, Emery stared at it and wished she had siblings she was close to. Her two older sisters were married and living on the West Coast now, and—not surprisingly—neither had offered any advice or support when the news about Derek broke.

Yeah. Not surprising. They'd never been close. Emery had been the smart one, the one her parents bragged about because of her accomplishments. Growing up, her parents always made the comparisons and when Eva and Ella—yes, their parents really went there with the names—each got married, they moved as far away as possible and rarely kept in touch. Not that it mattered. They hadn't been close growing up, so nothing had really changed.

"God, there's way too many depressing things swirling in my brain right now," she muttered, placing the picture of Carter and his siblings down. It felt a little awkward and voyeuristic to be in Eliza and Joseph's bedroom, and she was about to walk out when she spotted a picture of Carter alone on the small desk in the corner.

Walking over, she picked it up and her heart skipped a beat. It was a photo of Carter at one of his restaurants. He was standing in his chef's jacket, holding a glass of wine in one hand and a whole lobster in the other. The look on his face was pure joy. His eyes were looking directly at the camera—so right now they felt like they were looking directly at her.

Carefully, she put the picture back down but continued to stare at it. They hadn't talked any more about the kiss Saturday afternoon, and Emery thought she'd done a good job of acting as if it wasn't a big deal. The reality was that she was a big fat liar. That kiss had been a *very* big deal. A huge deal, in fact. Everything about it had awakened things in her that she hadn't known existed.

For starters, she'd had no idea a kiss could consume her. From the moment Carter's lips had claimed hers, she had felt like everything changed.

And since then? It had played on a constant loop in her head. Even if she closed her eyes right now, she'd still be able to feel his lips on hers, smell his cologne, and remember how it felt to have his hands up in her hair. She groaned. It was the sexiest thing ever—and that in and of itself was a depressing thought. She was almost thirty and had been dating since she was sixteen and engaged for two years. Yet one brief kiss from Carter Montgomery trumped every other kiss she'd ever experienced.

And he could never know.

Ever.

Still, she couldn't quite get over the fact that he'd done it. His response seemed reasonable at the time, but the more she thought about it, the more it didn't.

Why are you looking for trouble?

Unfortunately, this was how her brain worked. Ever since she'd first caught Derek cheating on her last year, Emery second-guessed just about everything in her life. What signs had she missed? How could she not have known? And that spilled over to other aspects of her life, like questioning why Carter would kiss her when he'd never done anything like that before. And that question led to things like "And why didn't he do it again?" and "Does he want to kiss me again?" which eventually led her to "Oh no—am I a bad kisser? Is that why Derek cheated?"

Then her self-esteem plummeted and she wanted to cry.

"Now I need a snack," she said with annoyance and stormed back to the kitchen to find something to eat. Technically, it was dinnertime, but the need for something quick and easy was too strong to ignore. Maybe it was nerves, maybe it was just her own stupid quirk, but right now she needed to keep her hands and her mouth busy.

Popcorn!

Pulling out a packet of microwave kettle corn, she tossed it in the microwave and got out a cold can of soda.

That's when she spotted the string cheese. It was protein

and that was nutritious, right? Snagging a stick, she placed it on the counter before reaching for a bowl for the popcorn.

"Should probably eat the cheese first," she reasoned, opening it up and taking a bite. Within minutes, her freshly popped kettle corn was in a bowl, the cheese was gone, and she had an icy cold can of soda in her hand. Living the dream.

In the living room, Emery sat, reaching for the remote and immediately turning to Netflix without glancing at the regular cable channels. She wasn't in the mood for a movie, but binge-watching something could be fun. As she scrolled, a slow smile crossed her lips.

The Office.

Yes. That's what she needed. A comedy to take her mind off this miserable day—miserable life!—and make her laugh and relax. A little wackiness should do the trick. Settling in more comfortably, the bowl of popcorn in her lap, Emery decided to start at season one, episode one and enjoy the ride.

Four episodes later, the popcorn was gone, the soda was gone, and the urge for something chocolate was strong.

One of the bakeries she had stopped in earlier was famous for their black-and-white cookies, and as she opened the box and pulled one out, she could see why. It was perfect—it smelled amazing and she knew it was going to taste even better.

Because no cookie should ever be eaten without milk, Emery poured herself a tall glass and settled back in to enjoy the last two episodes of the first season. It was like sitting with a bunch of old friends who were trying to cheer her up. It was dark outside and with only one small lamp lit, it made for a very cozy atmosphere. When her snack was finished, she reached for the afghan on the back of the sofa and wrapped it around her as she reclined.

When Netflix asked if she wanted to start on season two, she figured why not?

By the third episode, her eyes were heavy and she was losing the battle to stay awake. *Why fight it? I've got nothing else to do.* By then, time had lost all meaning and it would take too much effort to see what the actual time was. It was dark, she was tired, and that was really all she needed to know.

Normally, silence was her preference for falling asleep, but tonight there was something comforting in hearing other voices around her.

Did that make her crazy or pathetic? *Hmm...*

It made her sleepy. Very, very sleepy. With a low hum, Emery felt herself beginning to drift. A door opened and closed in the distance and as her mind was begging her to go to sleep, she had to wonder what was happening in the scene because the sound of the door seemed so completely out of place. Her eyes refused to open, forcing her to listen to the scene a little more closely.

Only...she couldn't focus. Exhaustion was pulling her under and she couldn't fight it any longer. A yawn escaped and with her next breath she smelled something wonderful. Something delicious—and she hoped it was going to be a dream about food. Not that she was hungry, but food dreams were almost as good as sex dreams.

Mmm...sex dreams.

She'd had a few of them over the last week, and all of them had starred Carter.

Mmm...Carter, food, and sex. Now *that* was practically the best dream she could imagine.

Was there a way to encourage the dream to start? In her mind, she envisioned a shirtless Carter cooking dinner for her. Yeah, definitely shirtless. He'd smell fantastic and he'd feed her with his hands…those magnificent hands. She moaned as she could practically feel his finger on her tongue.

"Mmm…Carter," she purred.

"Emery?"

Hmm—he didn't sound as turned on as she did, though he looked it, she thought. Somewhere in her subconscious she knew something wasn't quite right, but she couldn't put her finger on it. He said her name again and Emery felt herself coming more awake, losing hold on the images she desperately wanted to hang on to.

"No," she moaned. "Not yet…"

Then she felt a hand on her shoulder and it was enough to jolt her to full wakefulness. Her eyes shot open, and there before her sat the man who just moments ago was seducing her with his bare chest and talented fingers.

And he didn't look the least bit amused.

Chapter 4

FIVE HOURS AGO, CARTER HAD BEEN SITTING ON THE beach enjoying the view and feeling completely at peace.

Then his mother had called and shot all that peace to hell.

It wasn't her fault, he knew that, but once she had told him about the call she had gotten, he was beyond tense. Then she told him about her conversation with Emery and he was back in his house getting everything he needed to make the long drive back to the city. Even though he'd flown there on Monday, it would have taken too long to find a flight back. Driving his rental car made the most sense and gave him control over his schedule.

During the entire lengthy drive, Carter's mind was going. His mother was calling a lawyer to see what she could do to help protect Emery's privacy, and he was proud of her for doing that.

That led him to consider calling his own attorney to get a second opinion. Might as well let the man do something, since everything else had fallen into place in the last week and there were no more fires to put out. All of the permit issues had been resolved, the construction was finally starting, and Carter's presence in Montauk wasn't all that necessary.

And while he was thankful how everything had worked out, it left him at odds with what to do with his time. There was no reason for him to take the extended break he had originally planned, but the idea of going back to work wasn't nearly as appealing as he thought it would be. He was enjoying the peace and quiet and the slow pace of life. He had extended his lease on the house.

Carter had taken to sitting on the beach with his tablet and reading in the mornings before going for a swim in the private pool the house boasted. Going into town each afternoon to shop for food had allowed him to experiment with some recipes, and he was feeling great. Creative. Happy. Relaxed. And just when he'd decided to embrace this sudden vacation, all hell had broken loose in Manhattan.

Not going to Emery wasn't an option. As soon as his mother described the way she had sounded on the phone, Carter had sprung into action.

He'd analyzed his sudden protectiveness of her for the last hour of the drive and hadn't come up with any answers.

Now he was here, sitting on the sofa, trying to wake her up. Not very hard, mind you, but still…

Then she'd said his name in her sleep. A throaty purr that had him envisioning other ways to wake her up. Sexier ways. Unfortunately, he realized almost immediately how wrong that would be and how this certainly wasn't the time for something like that. He remembered the horrified look on her face last week after he'd kissed her and wasn't particularly anxious to see if that was a one-time reaction or not.

Better to keep his distance and not find out.

Still, the sound of her saying his name in her sleep was—

"Carter?"

Beside him, Emery was slowly coming awake. Her voice was sleepy and slightly confused—as if she wasn't sure she was really seeing him.

"Hey," he said softly. "Sorry to wake you."

Lazily, she sat up. The afghan that had been covering her dropped to her waist as she stretched and yawned before looking at him. "What are you doing here?"

Okay, so her sleepy voice was an obvious turn-on. Carter scooted a little farther away from her and cleared his throat. "Um... I heard about what happened earlier."

"You did?" Her brow furrowed with her question and she looked completely adorable. "How?"

"My mother called."

"Oh." He knew immediately that she was embarrassed. Her head dropped forward and he could see the flush to her cheeks.

Without thinking, he reached out and tucked a finger under her chin and gently lifted her face so she was looking at him. "You okay?"

For a moment he thought she'd put on a brave face and tell him everything was fine. It was how things always seemed to be. Even when she was struggling with something, Emery never budged an inch—as if she thought showing that side of herself made her weak. He was prepared for it and was ready to tell her it was okay to be upset.

Then she surprised him.

Wordlessly, she shook her head and tears formed in her eyes. He cursed the bastard responsible for making one of the strongest women he'd ever known look this sad and defeated. So yeah, he reached out and pulled her into his arms and held her as she cried. For now, she needed this. Maybe she had cried earlier, maybe she hadn't—but right now she was and he was going to let her do it.

They sat like that for several long minutes, and when

Carter felt her moving away, he pulled back and held his breath.

"Thank you," she said quietly, wiping her face. Letting out a long breath, she studied him. "I held it together as best I could and swore I wasn't going to cry again, but—"

"Hey," he cut her off, "it's okay to vent. I think you're more than entitled to."

Shaking her head, she stood and walked to the kitchen.

He followed.

And wished he hadn't.

Besides the half-finished cans of soda on the coffee table, popcorn bowl, and crumbs on the living room sofa, he saw the remnants of multiple snacks along with bakery boxes—one of which was still open. Good Lord, did the woman ever eat a sensible meal?

Not the time to focus on that.

She pulled a bottle of water from the refrigerator and handed it to him before grabbing one for herself. Without a word, Emery took a long drink before looking at him again and when she did, she let out a weary sigh. "Okay, I think I'm better now. Sorry about that."

"We already covered it. You don't have to apologize."

"Agree to disagree," she murmured, walking back to the living room. "What time is it?"

"Almost ten."

With a gasp, she faced him. "Seriously?" She shook her head as if to clear it. "Wow. I thought it was later."

There wasn't anything he could say, so Carter waited.

Once she was seated and seemed a little more awake, she reached for the TV remote and shut it off. "So…why are you here? I didn't think you were coming back to the city."

Crap. Out of all the possible dialogues that ran through his head on the drive here, none of them dealt with how he'd answer that question.

"Um, well…" He shifted in his seat and studied the bottle of water in his hands. "Okay, here it is."

She looked at him with wide eyes and a serious expression, and Carter's mind went blank.

"Carter?"

Right. An answer. "I talked to my mother about what happened earlier," he began, "and I don't think you should go to the courthouse on Tuesday."

"You don't?"

He shook his head. "No. I don't."

Her shoulders sagged. "Oh."

"Here's the thing—you don't need to do it. It's not going to benefit you in any way, Emery. It's not like you're going to voice your support of Derek, right?"

"Right."

"So then, why do it? Why go?"

"Because it's not fair to put your mother or the residents of this building in the kind of position I'm being threatened with. I don't want a media circus out front. That's why I came *here*, because there was a media circus on my front lawn!" She threw her head back against the sofa. "If I go, then maybe I can get my point across that I'm done."

"Or…"

She lifted her head and looked at him, curiosity written all over her face. "Or?"

"Or you get your own lawyer who will block anything they try to drag you into and…and come with me to Montauk."

All of a sudden, he felt like he couldn't breathe. He

waited for her to tell him he was crazy or that his idea was stupid or…argue for the sake of arguing.

But she didn't.

She didn't say anything.

And her silence was almost as irritating.

"Why—" She stopped and cleared her throat. "Why would I go to Montauk with you? I mean, I appreciate the offer, but—"

"Clearly, we still have work to do on the cookbook, right?" he asked, effectively cutting her off.

"But you said you were too busy. That you had problems with the construction on the new restaurant and didn't have time to work on this."

"Yeah, well… Things sort of righted themselves faster than I thought they would and now I've got some free time, and I know you need to work on this project and now you need a place to stay and—"

"Carter?"

"Hmm?"

"You're rambling," she said with amusement.

With a huff, he said, "I know."

"Why?"

"Why what?"

"Look, we've known each other way too long and you've never once been anything other than an overconfident jerk most of the time. You never hold back on what you have to say to me, so why are you starting now?"

Good question.

"Can't I just be nice?" he snapped and then instantly regretted it.

Until she smiled.

The evil, condescending smile she usually gave him.

"I wouldn't know," she said sweetly. "Based on our history, that is."

"I was never mean, Emery."

"No, but you also weren't particularly nice. You were smug and sometimes out-and-out rude. So you'll have to excuse me for not knowing what to make of all this."

He stood and paced a bit. "You need a place to stay and I need to finish this damn cookbook and get my mom off my back. There! Satisfied?" he yelled.

Judging by the look on her face, she was.

Very.

"If I go to Montauk," she began carefully, "you'll seriously put in the effort to work on this book?"

"Yes."

"You realize we're running out of time—the book has to be ready for the first of December so it can be sold through the holiday season."

"I'm aware."

"And you'll need to do everything I say so we can get this done. With no arguing." She batted her eyelashes at him in a look of pure innocence, but he knew her better than that.

"Within reason," he countered.

"Define reason," she said with a smirk.

"Considering the fact that the kitchen looks like a frat house did the food shopping, you have to accept that any of your suggestions on recipes will not be taken seriously. You know that, right?"

"Hey!" She jumped to her feet. "There is nothing wrong with my taste in food. Just because I don't eat a snooty meal every night doesn't mean my suggestions are going to be bad!"

He stepped in close—toe to toe—and asked, "Did you have any normal meals this week since I've been gone?"

"I've had pizza—"

"No, no, no—a real meal, Emery. Something you cooked yourself. Something with a meat, a vegetable, and a starch—you know, a balanced meal."

She eyed him defiantly. "That's just *your* definition of a balanced meal. Technically, it describes my pizza. It had pepperoni and green peppers. Meat and vegetable, all served on a starchy crust."

She had him there. But...

"Was it a frozen one? Because they don't count."

"Stop making up food rules!" she cried, stomping her foot. "Your way isn't the only way!"

"All the people who eat at my restaurants would disagree," he replied smoothly, taking a step back.

"You are so damn smug," she muttered. "You couldn't pay me to eat at one of your restaurants!"

Okay, that one was hitting a little below the belt. "Challenge accepted."

"What?" She looked at him like he was crazy, and clearly, he was.

"I bet that by the time we're done with this book, you'll be so enamored of my cooking you'll be begging for a table at one of my places."

Emery laughed long and loud. When she calmed down a bit, she looked at him with amusement. "Carter, you don't have any restaurants here in the city, and there is nothing you could possibly make that will have me getting on a plane to New Orleans or Florida or wherever else you have a place to eat a meal."

He shrugged. "We'll see."

"Uh-huh. Sure."

"Why don't you go and pack and we'll get going," he suggested.

"Carter, I was asleep just a few minutes ago. Can't we leave early tomorrow morning? You just drove three and a half hours to get here. We're not in a rush to get out of town, are we?"

A couple of hours of sleep sounded pretty good right now, he thought. "No. We're not in a big rush, but I'd like to get on the road as early as possible."

"Why? Do you have a meeting or something tomorrow?"

"No, but I'm a bit of a morning person and I'd just like to get back to the beach as soon as possible. It's what kept me sane all last week, and after this conversation tonight, I'm desperate to get back."

"No one asked you to come here," she said defensively, crossing her arms over her middle. "I was handling everything."

He opted not to argue.

"I know you were," he said evenly. "Can we just agree to get on the road before eight? This way we can get a good night's sleep. Okay?"

"Can I ask you something?"

He nodded.

"Why the beach? I mean, isn't it a little too cold to be anxious to get back to it?"

Shrugging, he replied, "I like it. And you know that after growing up in upstate New York, the cold really isn't an issue. Trust me, you're going to love it too. Throw on a sweatshirt and go out and listen to the waves. It's very tranquil."

She still eyed him suspiciously, but she agreed. Wishing

him a good night, Emery went to her room to pack, leaving Carter alone with his thoughts.

"Might as well clean up first," he said, walking around to pick up the popcorn bowl, bottles of water, and cans of soda. In the kitchen he tossed the trash, washed the dishes, and wiped down the countertops. His mother had a cleaning service that came in once the place was empty, so they'd be here when Carter confirmed they were gone.

Speaking of which…

Pulling his phone out of his pocket, he typed out a quick text to his mother letting her know Emery would be heading to Montauk with him in the morning. No doubt she was already in bed, but at least she'd get the message when she woke up.

Putting his phone down, he looked around the kitchen, pleased to see everything in order. Tomorrow he'd throw any leftover food in the trash and take it out on their way to the car. Walking out of the room, he shut off the light, checked the front door lock, and headed to his bedroom. When he'd left the beach earlier, he wasn't sure how all of this was going to go and had packed an overnight bag just in case, and now he was glad he had.

Closing the bedroom door behind him, he realized just how tired he was. It reminded him of his first night here a week ago. Too tired to do much of anything, he simply stripped down to his boxers, pulled back the duvet, and slid beneath the sheets. Reaching over, he turned out the light.

Now he was well and truly stuck with Emery, he thought. He was taking her with him to his retreat. She was going to invade his space, more than likely make a mess, and aggravate the crap out of him.

No doubt he'd be willing to sleep in a tent on the beach before long.

Still…he was doing a good thing. The right thing.

And maybe, just maybe, they wouldn't kill each other.

The sunrise was magnificent.

The scent of the ocean was invigorating.

The thought of standing in the kitchen with Carter made her want to say bad words.

Lots and lots of bad words.

For almost five days they'd been coexisting together in his magnificent house. Emery knew it was a rental, but that didn't diminish how spectacular it was. When they first arrived on Monday, she hadn't been impressed with the front. It looked like a basic—and small—two-story shingled home. But once they stepped inside? Wow.

It was the kind of place she envisioned when she pictured a summer house on the beach. It was perched on a hilltop overlooking the ocean. The entire setup was perfect and the beach décor throughout the home completed the coastal vibe. There were ocean views from every room, and they'd had perfect weather to make that view spectacular every day.

Then she'd stepped outside, unable to believe the outdoor space could be just as amazing, and yet…it was. There was the heated pool—which she loved—and it included an infinity hot tub. And yes, she'd spent a lot of time sitting there. Often, she used the excuse of needing time away from Carter, but the truth was it relaxed her and she hadn't felt that for a long while.

Maybe never.

There were seating areas around the pool, as well as a bar, an outdoor kitchen, a fire pit, and a private outdoor shower. It was going to be a real chore to go back to her everyday life after spending a week or two here.

Did Carter live like this all the time, she wondered? Was this place as exciting to him as it was to her? The only room that seemed to excite him was the kitchen, and she could see why. Top of the line appliances and a large marble-topped island to work with were perfect for him. He'd complained that it wasn't larger, but he was cooking only for the two of them, so he didn't really need more.

Until today.

Today they were going to work on preparing a full Christmas dinner. It was still only the two of them, but he was going to cook as if it were for at least ten more. Apparently, he'd had some inspiration in the previous week and wanted to try making it for the masses, so to speak. Personally, she didn't think any of the recipes he was preparing sounded very festive—definitely not like a Christmas meal—but she'd let him try it his way first.

A slow smile spread across her face when she thought about what she was going to do to help.

Not with the food—that wasn't allowed—but with the overall atmosphere.

Carter was going shopping around ten this morning. Once he was gone, a holiday décor consultant was coming in to help her decorate the house for Christmas. And while Emery would love to take all the credit for the idea, Eliza had helped come up with it. Emery's job had been to find the right person to come in on such short notice and to make it happen.

And the best part? Carter had no idea. With any luck, he'd be gone for a couple of hours and by the time he got home, everything would be in place. It would look like a Christmas wonderland if all went as planned.

Growing up, her family had always hired professionals to come in and do all of their holiday decorating. Emery could remember wanting to do some of it on her own, but her mother was a stickler about wanting everything perfect. Once she had moved out on her own, however, Emery had gone wild when the holidays came around. Derek had mocked her more than once for her…enthusiasm. She waved the thought away. Thinking about the holiday décor made her smile: a huge Christmas tree, tons of lights, ornaments that actually held some sentimental meaning to her…

"Damn," she said, wishing she had some of her things here with her. Oh well. It wouldn't matter if she had her own stuff or not. It wasn't Christmas yet and this was all just for show. Still, in her mind she could clearly envision how she wanted the house to look.

Festive.

Welcoming.

She'd promised Eliza she would take tons of pictures to use in the book. And how cool would that be?

Deciding to take a few more minutes to relax before the day got crazy, Emery stretched, reaching for her cup of coffee. It wasn't her favorite drink to start the day, but Carter hadn't let her pick any of the groceries. Frowning, she remembered how he had gone shopping while she was out walking on the beach. Now all she had to choose from were fruits, vegetables, and other assorted fresh foods he had yammered on and on about.

No toaster pastries.

No popcorn.

No chips or dip.

The bastard.

If she hadn't made plans for the decorator to come in today, she would have gone into town herself and gone shopping. For comfort food.

Now she was twitchy. The coffee tasted flat in her mouth and all she wanted was a piece of cake or some cereal with milk. This was like a detox from junk food, and it was probably a huge contributing factor to why she was so on edge and wanting to say bad words.

"Ah, there you are."

Emery's spine stiffened at the sound of Carter's voice. It was on the tip of her tongue…all the rage, all the bad words, but she kept them in and focused on the waves crashing on the shore. If she was lucky, he'd think she was meditating or something and leave her alone.

He sat down beside her.

"I'm making a list of all the things we're going to need before I leave to go shopping. Any requests?" he asked.

Don't seem too anxious, don't seem too anxious…

Forcing down another sip of coffee, she kept her eyes forward. "I could go for some cereal," she said mildly and out of the corner of her eye she could see him nod. "And maybe some…you know, snacks. Chips, salsa—nothing major."

He was silent for a moment. "Anything else?"

She pretended to think about it. "I really could go for some kettle corn popcorn." Again, she tried to sound blasé, like she wasn't dying to have all of those things right here, right now, instead of his stupid, pretentious gourmet coffee. *Gah!* She hated it! Hated it!

"You're looking pretty fierce there, Em. Something on your mind?"

Dammit. Now she could actually feel herself frowning— her entire face scrunched up with rage. Shoving her cup down in the sand, she turned to him.

"I'm not a prisoner here, Carter!" she snapped. "I am an adult, and I can pick the food I want to eat and you can't stop me from eating it! You think you're so smart—shopping when I'm not with you and then stocking the house with things only you like. Well, let me tell you something, buddy, that's just wrong!" She paused only long enough to take a breath. "I get that you're a control freak and all, but this is insane! You don't want me here? Fine! I didn't ask to come here with you. If memory serves, you. Asked. Me. So why am I being punished, huh? Why am I being treated like some... some addict who you're forcing to detox, huh? Huh?"

Okay, now she was sounding like a crazy person, and rather than go on, she jumped to her feet and walked closer to the water to calm herself down.

His hand on her shoulder had her practically jumping out of her skin.

"Hey," he said calmly, and that grated on her last nerve. "You sure you're okay?"

She saw red. Turning, she faced him and knew she was about to unleash on him again and didn't want to do a damn thing to stop it.

"Has it ever occurred to you that your way isn't the only way?" she yelled. "That you're not the only one whose feelings matter?" Her voice caught and she hated it—along with the sting of tears she felt. Thankfully, she had on sunglasses so he wouldn't see them, but the look on his face showed that he realized how upset she was.

"Emery—"

"No!" she quickly interrupted. "I don't have any control over anything in my life right now and all I'm asking for are some simple creature comforts, but you won't allow it! Like you're the boss here, but you're not! You're *not*, Carter," she repeated for emphasis, poking him in the chest with her finger.

This time, before she could do or say anything else, he reached out and grabbed her wrist in his hand and held it tight. And then she waited. Waited for him to make some snarky or superior comment about how he was doing it for her own good or how she just didn't appreciate good food.

But he didn't.

"I'm sorry," he said gruffly. "At the time I thought—I thought it was funny, but now…" He didn't have on any sunglasses and the emotion she saw in his eyes was enough for her to know how sincere he was.

"I hate this," she said quietly. "I hate how this is my life right now."

In a move she was only mildly surprised by, Carter pulled her into his arms and hugged her. Like he knew how much she needed comfort—even if it was from him.

She burrowed close and remembered just how much she was coming to love the feel of him, the smell of him… It was a little crazy to be thinking that way, because for most of her life all she could focus on were the things she hated about him. Why was that all suddenly feeling petty and childish and pointless? Why did he have to be so tall and so strong? Why did she have to love the fresh, citrusy smell of his cologne? Or how great his large hands felt as they smoothed up and down her spine?

Thinking about it was just as overwhelming as the way her body was reacting to his. Carter's arms tightened around her and he placed a soft kiss on her forehead. "I wasn't thinking," he said. "It was inconsiderate of me and I...I guess it just seemed like harmless fun. I had no idea you were this upset over it."

"Yeah, well, I am," she said against his chest.

Although—who knew bananas tasted good even without peanut butter? Or that a crisp, cool apple could be so sweet?

Not that she was going to share *any* of that with him. Especially right now. But...there it was. When life returned to normal and she was back at home in her own place, there was a definite possibility of adding some fresh fruit to her shopping list.

Pulling back, Carter looked down at her and gave her a lopsided grin. It was boyish and adorable and she had to fight the urge to caress his jaw.

"C'mon. Let's go back up to the house and we'll work on the list together. You can put exactly what you want on it and I promise to buy it, okay?"

Emery felt herself relax a bit more and smiled up at him. "Thank you."

Together they walked hand in hand back to the house. Carter stopped briefly to pick up her forgotten coffee mug and then they continued on. Once inside, he let her go and walked over to the kitchen island, where he had a notepad and pen waiting. They talked for several minutes about what he was purchasing for the meals he was going to prepare for the cookbook, and when he was done, he slid the pad across the granite toward her and encouraged her to write down everything she wanted.

Because they were in a good place right now, she thanked him and then added about a half-dozen items to the list. When she slid it back over to him, he looked at it with surprise.

"That's it? You're sure you don't want to add anything else?"

She frowned and glanced down at the paper again. "I think that's everything. Why?"

He shrugged. "I just figured you'd want to punish me or make me crazy by adding at least twenty things that aren't good for you."

As much as she wanted to take offense to that statement, it was exactly where her mind had gone first, so she had to laugh. "I thought about it, but then decided to be the bigger person here. Plus I have a feeling we're going to be eating all the food you make tonight for days. I won't have any room for junk food."

Laughing with her, he nodded. "That's probably true. But if you'd like, I'll add a couple of desserts to the menu that aren't for the book. How does that sound?"

"Cookies!" she blurted out. "We should bake Christmas cookies!"

Carter's eyes went a little wide. "Seriously? You want to bake—"

"I do! I really do! And before you say anything, I'm not talking about the refrigerated cookie dough kind of cookies, I'm talking real cookies we bake from scratch and use cookie cutters and make icing and—"

"Okay, okay, okay," he said, still chuckling. "I get it." Then he paused. "I hadn't planned on adding that to everything else we have going on today."

"We don't have to bake them today," she quickly amended. "Let's save them for tomorrow! Oh, it's going to be awesome. I'm sure you have some great recipes, right? Although if I could make a request—I know they're not Christmassy, but could we just make a small batch of chocolate chip cookies? I love them when they're hot out of the oven and the chocolate is all melty. They're perfect with a tall glass of milk."

She realized how ridiculous she was sounding, and by the serious look on his face, she knew he was thinking the exact same thing.

"So…?"

With a curt nod, Carter said, "Sure," before reaching for the list and writing a bunch of things down. Ten minutes later he was heading for the door. "I'll be gone for at least three hours. You sure you don't want to come with me?"

She waved him off. "I'm sure. I'd just slow you down. Plus I downloaded a new book today that I think I'll read out by the pool, so…you go. But call me when you're on your way back!"

He looked at her suspiciously. "Why?"

"Just in case I want you to pick up something specific for lunch," she said sweetly. He nodded, but didn't look completely convinced. Luckily, he didn't question her any further before walking out the door. Looking over at the clock, she let out a long breath. The decorator was due in fifteen minutes.

Running over to the front window, Emery watched as Carter pulled out of the driveway. Once his brake lights were out of sight, she sprang into action. There were shelves and a mantel to clear, furniture to move, and once that was done, she grabbed her trusty notebook full of directions for what she wanted and where. This was all stuff she had discussed with the decorator already, but she held on to it like a lifeline for reference.

Five minutes later she opened the door with a big smile on her face. "Let's do this!"

It was as if the truce they had silently called never happened.

Emery had called him no less than three times in the last hour with requests for things to add to the shopping list and what she wanted for lunch.

She was trying to kill him.

It was the only explanation.

Now, as he loaded the final bag of groceries into the trunk of his car, Carter was thankful he had brought a large cooler and filled it with ice to keep the perishables cold. Although if he stayed out much longer, it would all be pointless.

The last addition to her list had been rather specific ingredients for ice cream sundaes. How the woman could possibly think about desserts or sweets after all the food they were going to make plus the baking they had planned for tomorrow, he'd never know. Either way, there was no way he would comment on it or deny her since she had her meltdown this morning.

And yeah, he still felt like major crap for that one.

It really had been done in the name of fun. He hadn't thought about how Emery might not see it the same way. It just seemed natural for them to have something to argue about since it was their thing, but he really felt bad about doing it.

Lesson learned.

Not that he was going to refrain from picking fights with her. There was no way that was ever going to happen. It would be like someone asking him not to cook. It was just part of who he was. Who *they* were.

Though unfortunately, lately...Carter was having a hard time with what exactly they were.

Maybe it was all the close proximity. Maybe it was that they were both mellowing with age.

Or maybe it was because he was so damn attracted to her that he could barely stand himself anymore.

Probably a combination of all three—but primarily that third one.

Holding Emery in his arms this morning on the beach had been both pain and pleasure. It was his natural instinct to want to offer comfort, but it didn't take long before his mind started to wander. That was why he'd led them back into the house, because within minutes there would have been no way for him to hide the effect she had on him.

He was seriously losing his mind—so today's plan to cook was the perfect solution. It was a ridiculous amount of food. He knew that. But it would guarantee he'd be busy for hours. As much as Emery would ask if she could help—and that still made him laugh—he wouldn't allow it, because the kitchen was his domain and things would go smoother if he worked alone.

And it would be better for his peace of mind as well.

Just thinking back to the night they'd made pizza together was enough to make him break out in a cold sweat.

Emery's body pressed up against his, the smell of her perfume, the feel of her hands working under his...

He cranked up the AC in the car and let out a long, frustrated breath. Putting the car in gear, he drove through town, cringing when he pulled into the parking lot of the local fast-food burger place. That had been her last request for lunch. Some sort of double cheeseburger she absolutely had to have, she claimed. Whatever. All Carter knew was there was no way he was going to eat any of it. He'd purchased some fantastic options of his own to make a sandwich, and on top of that, with all the cooking he was going to be doing, he'd be tasting as he went.

The chef never went hungry.

As his car inched along in the drive-thru line, however, the aromas coming at him weren't nearly as offensive as he thought they would be. If anything, it brought him back to being a teen, when he and his friends would hit all the fast-food places after school. He hadn't eaten anything like that in years. His car moved closer to the menu board and he seriously considered forgetting all about his own plans for lunch and giving in to his curiosity. After all, if he ate the way Emery did and still didn't like it, he'd at least have some credibility in her eyes, right?

The picture of the french fries had his mouth watering. He loved french fries—crispy, lightly salted... He almost groaned at the thought. No doubt the burger would be subpar, but for one meal, could it really hurt?

By the time he was at the menu board, his mind was made up. He ordered enough food for four people, mainly because he was curious about a number of things on the menu and he'd think about how ridiculous he was being later on.

And because he had promised, he called Emery as soon as he had the food and before he left the parking lot. "I'm on my way," he said casually, waiting to pull out onto the main road.

"So you're, like…what, five, ten minutes away?" she asked.

"Um, yeah. About ten. Why?"

"Just curious," she quickly replied. "I'll make sure the table's clear and ready."

"The table was clear when I left. What have you been doing?"

"Sheesh, relax! It was just a figure of speech." She let out a low snort. "Anyway, I'll see you in a few minutes."

He was about to ask if there was anything else she needed but decided against it. There was no more room in the trunk and the bag of food he just picked up reminded him of how hungry he was. "Okay. See you in a bit."

The temptation to grab a handful of fries was great, but he resisted—reminding himself he only had a few more minutes of driving and he'd be back at the house.

Turning onto the block, he noticed a strange car pulling out of his driveway and instantly tensed up. Who was it? Was it just someone turning around? Had someone found out where Emery was?

With his foot on the accelerator, he sped down the block and into the driveway, barely missing the garage door in his haste to stop and get out of the car. The food was forgotten as he jogged to the door, only to be stopped short by Emery opening it and stepping out onto the front steps. Her eyes wide, she greeted him with a smile.

"Hey! Where's the fire?"

He was breathless and grasped her shoulders more to steady himself than anything else. "What—I saw... Are you okay?"

She looked at him quizzically. "Yes," she said cautiously. "Are you?"

His eyes scanned her face and it took him a few long moments before he realized he was overreacting. She looked fine—concerned, but fine. He instantly released her and took a step back. "Uh...yeah. Sorry. I—I saw a strange car pulling out of the driveway and I thought..." He stopped and raked a hand through his hair, unsure if he should tell her what he was thinking, because he didn't want to freak her out. Not right now.

"You thought someone found me," she said, her expression going a little soft.

Rather than speak, he nodded.

Emery reached for him and Carter realized it was one of the few times she'd been the one to do it first. Her soft hand cupped his cheek and her smile was sweet. "Thank you for being so concerned. I'm fine. No one was here."

Shaking his head to clear it, he took another step back and then turned toward the car. "If you grab the lunch bags from the front seat, I'll grab the cooler from the trunk and we'll deal with the rest after we eat, okay?"

She all but skipped to the car in her excitement to get her junk-food fix on, and all Carter could do was laugh.

"There's an awful lot of food here, Carter," she called back to him. "It almost looks like there's enough food here for more than one person."

Yeah. He knew he was going to catch some grief from her over this, but he'd deal with it.

"Or maybe I just figured you had some catching up to do," he replied, hefting the cooler out. Placing it on the ground, he slammed the trunk closed and caught Emery standing only two feet away with a knowing smirk on her face. "What?"

"It got to you, didn't it?" she asked. "The smell. The delicious smell. You could practically taste the salt on the french fries. Admit it."

Leaning in close, he said, "I admit nothing. Now come on before it all gets cold."

They walked to the door and Emery went ahead of him, holding it open for him. It took all of three seconds before he realized something was off. Different. Something was—

He dropped the cooler at his feet and stared in shock. *What the…?*

Emery came to stand beside him and he could feel her vibrating with excitement. "Surprise!"

Turning his head, he looked at her like she was crazy. "What is all this? Why… I mean, how…it's…it's…"

"It's inspiration!" she replied giddily, walking ahead of him into the kitchen where she promptly began setting up their lunch. "Your mother and I talked about it and I thought today would be the perfect day to do this. You'll cook, we'll take some pictures, and I think it will go a long way to helping you get in the spirit of this project."

Slowly, Carter walked around. The entire living room had been transformed into a winter wonderland. Where everything had had a beachy, coastal feel this morning, it was all replaced now with elegant Christmas décor. He had no idea how she had pulled it off in such a short amount of time, but it was amazing. Looking toward the dining area, he found the table elegantly set for a large family holiday dinner.

It was perfect for what they were doing.

Carter finally found his voice. "How did you manage all this?"

Looking pretty pleased with herself, Emery continued to put their lunch out on the table as she explained. "It took longer than I thought it would. That's why I kept calling and giving you extra stops to make." Grabbing a couple of french fries, she grinned at him. "But I found a decorator who specializes in this sort of thing, and it's all rented and they come in, set it all up. They'll be back in a few days to take everything back." She motioned to the table. "Let's eat!"

He joined her and found it hard to focus on the food in front of him—he was still in awe of the transformation of the house. "I can't believe you pulled this off."

She smiled and picked up her burger. "I'm extremely organized and efficient. In other words, I had a plan."

Picking up his own burger, he looked at her and saw how pleased she was, unsure if it was because of a job well done or the greasy treat she was eating. His stomach growled, and he needed to ignore how unhealthy the meal was and just… go for it. "Well, color me impressed," he said, referring to her, but realized it could also have meant the meal.

It was surprisingly good.

And satisfying.

When neither had spoken for several minutes because they were too busy eating, Emery leaned over and said, "Welcome to the dark side. We have empty calories."

Carter almost choked on his food but managed to

swallow it down before reaching for his drink. Her sense of humor was something he was finding to be utterly charming.

Add that to the list.

There was no time to dwell on it, however, because he was almost done with his burger and was seriously enjoying it.

Now *that* deserved some dwelling.

"Admit it," Emery said from beside him, leaning back in her chair. "You enjoyed it."

"Never."

She laughed, husky and sexy, and...he seriously needed a distraction.

Reaching over, she looked in the second bag and then gave him a knowing glance. "Who are these chicken nuggets for?"

"Oh, um... I thought you might like them," he said, not wanting to look at her. Carter busied himself with finishing his fries—which were salted to perfection.

"Hmm. I don't know if I could eat them right now." He heard her rummaging around in the bag again. "And what about this? Is this some sort of apple pie?"

Busted!

"Maybe."

She laughed again—loud and hearty. "Carter Montgomery, you better admit right now that you bought all of this for you because you remember what it's like to eat like a normal person!"

He lost the battle with his own laughter. "I will do no such thing."

Standing, Emery took the bag with the extra food and made her way across the kitchen. "Well then, as much as I appreciate the thought, I'm way too full to eat another bite, so...I'll just throw this out."

"Wait...what?" he cried, coming to his feet. "Why would you do that?"

With a careless shrug, she replied, "These things never reheat well, so it's pointless to save it. Besides, what do you care? I can give you the five bucks they cost you, if you'd like." The bag was dangling over the trash pail, and the look on her face was full of challenge.

And amusement.

"Emery," he began as he took a step toward her. "Just... put the bag down."

"And nobody gets hurt?" she teased before letting out a very feminine giggle.

Deciding to stall, Carter studied her. "I just hate to see food go to waste."

"All you have to do is admit you got it for you. Just say the words and I'll put the food back on the table." She shook the bag for good measure. "Come on. I dare you."

Those were fighting words.

Before he could question it, he lunged for her and Emery let out a high-pitched squeal before taking off around the kitchen island. By their third time around, Carter caught her around the waist and spun her while she cried out, "Uncle! Uncle!" They were both laughing hysterically by the time he collapsed back in his chair with her in his lap. It took several minutes for them to calm down.

"Man, you just cannot *stand* to be proven wrong," she said, but made no attempt to move from the circle of his arms.

This was dangerous territory. He knew that. It felt far too good to hold her. Turning his head, he inhaled the smell of her shampoo, daring to lean in farther until his lips were touching her ear.

Softly, he murmured, "Just give me the apple pie, and nobody gets hurt."

It was meant to be funny—a small joke to go along with all the teasing they'd been doing—but it didn't feel so funny when Emery let out a low moan at his words.

"Make me," she whispered, and—holy crap. It was all Carter could do not to haul her over his shoulder and take her inside to his bedroom.

Her name came out as a plea as Carter ran his tongue along the shell of her ear. Emery trembled in his arms as they tightened around her. The bag fell to the floor and she shifted ever so slightly so they were nose to nose. Then it was her turn to sigh his name. Her hand came up and cupped his cheek, and for a moment, he was afraid to move. Afraid to breathe. He didn't want to risk doing anything to break the spell or ruin the moment.

It would kill him.

Reaching up, he mimicked her pose by cupping her cheek. He owed it to her to be honest.

"This isn't about making either of us stop talking," he said gruffly. "This is about me kissing you because I have to."

Slowly, Emery licked her lips. "Good."

It was as if everything happened in slow motion from there as if they were being drawn together by forces beyond their control, and when their lips touched, they both sighed and eased into it.

All Carter could think was how this was possibly his sweetest victory ever with Emery—knowing she wanted his kiss just as much as he needed to kiss her.

Chapter 5

DON'T THINK, JUST FEEL...

That's what Emery told herself as she sank into the kiss with Carter. It was pointless to pretend she didn't want it and she was tired of fighting it. For almost two weeks she'd done nothing but think about it—especially when she was alone in bed at night—but she never thought she'd get the chance to experience it again.

She'd never been happier to be wrong.

The way Carter kissed was like nothing she'd ever experienced before in her life. She'd gladly give up chips and dip and popcorn if they could be replaced with his lips.

Whoa.

There was no urgency. There was no desperation. What there was right now was a slow simmer that was building up to something more. Kissing Carter was like watching him cook—he was meticulous in his preparations, and then his actions became a little more intent before things came to a sizzle.

Yeah, she was totally okay with the cooking metaphor, because it fit them so perfectly.

His jaw was rough and scratchy against her fingers, but his lips were so incredibly soft yet firm. She hummed softly as his tongue touched hers, and felt herself melt against him. The moment was so perfect, so arousing, so completely and utterly unexpected, and Emery wouldn't change a thing.

Well—maybe she wouldn't have gotten onion on her burger had she known this was coming.

Carter ran his hands up and down her spine before one came up and anchored in her hair. It gave her a bit of a thrill how he was holding her to him as if he was afraid she'd move away.

Like the last time.

Not gonna happen.

So many times since that kiss she'd kicked herself for freaking out the way she had. It wasn't that she hadn't wanted him to kiss her, she just wasn't confident enough in herself—or him—to trust why he was doing it. The fact that he clarified why he was kissing her this time was probably the sexiest thing he could have done.

His mouth moved from hers as they both gasped for breath, but he simply moved on to her throat and began nipping, licking, and kissing his way around.

"You smell so damn good," he murmured hotly against her skin. "And you taste even better."

Part of her wanted to joke and say she smelled like the french fries she had just eaten, but now definitely wasn't the time. Playtime was over. She wanted serious. She wanted heat. She wanted him to…

Rather than think, she firmly cupped his jaw and brought his lips back to hers.

That's when everything changed.

Where before it was a slow simmer, now it was a full-on sizzle, threatening to boil over.

Yeah. She was cooking.

They moved together to get more comfortable, and Emery ended up straddling his lap and oh Lord, did *that* kick things up to a whole other level. Standing and kissing Carter? Sitting cradled in his lap while kissing Carter? That was nothing compared to the full-bodied experience of kissing him while feeling him intimately pressed up against her most sensitive spots.

Which were now burning for more of him.

Maybe it was because it had been so long since she'd felt desirable.

Or maybe it was because it had been so long since a man had touched her like this.

Or maybe it was just because every minute of every argument she had shared with this man was meant to lead to this.

If anything, Emery began to kiss him with more urgency and Carter matched her. Now their moves were frantic—clinging and touching and grinding to get closer. She wanted to pull off her shirt and watch him take his off and feel them skin to skin. She wanted to see and touch and feel every inch of him.

At that moment, as if reading her mind, Carter reached down and gripped her ass hard.

They were done being polite. They were done with the gentle exploration. Whatever they had started now took on a life of its own.

He stood with her wrapped around him. Emery locked her ankles behind his back, her hands raked up into his hair and gripped it hard, willing him not to stop. She had no idea where they would go or if she was ready for what was to come; all she knew was she wasn't ready for this moment to end.

Opening one eye, she saw they were moving out of the kitchen, across the living room. Would they go to the couch? The floor?

Carter broke the kiss again as he stopped in his tracks and looked at her. They were three feet away from his bedroom door. His bedroom was here on the main floor; hers was upstairs. And right now, she was thankful for the proximity of his.

His eyes were so dark with desire that she couldn't look away. She swallowed hard and prayed he wasn't going to change his mind. That sanity hadn't returned, because she wasn't sure how she'd be able to respond—or stay here and look at him for another day or even another minute—knowing he didn't want her as much as she wanted him.

"Be sure," he said, his voice low and rumbly, a warning. "Because once we go through that door, I don't think we can turn back."

She nearly sobbed with relief. "Keep walking, Carter."

With a curt nod, he captured her lips again and kissed her right there without moving, until she thought she'd go mad. When he finally lifted his head, he gave her a sexy grin. "You're still not the boss of me, Em," he teased.

But then he walked into his bedroom and gently placed her on the center of the bed. She was glad to let him call the shots. The look he was giving her made her feel like she was the feast and he was starving.

Carter's hand rested on her ankle and began skimming up her leg.

"Do you remember the first night I showed up at the condo?" he asked, his voice still low and gruff.

Emery nodded.

"You were wearing a clingy little T-shirt and a pair of panties and I just about swallowed my tongue." He shook his head and let out a long breath as his hand continued to touch her. "I didn't want to think of you like that," he said, lowering his voice, "as an incredibly sexy woman—but now I can't seem to think of anything else. You realize you've turned me upside down since then, right?"

Seriously? Emery shook her head, unable to believe what he was telling her. It wasn't possible. She'd never believed she could be the kind of woman capable of making a man—any man—feel like that. Especially not someone like Carter.

He smiled down at her. "You can shake your head all you want, but it's the truth." Leaning forward, he braced both of his arms on the bed on either side of her head until she could feel his breath on her face. "And the night I kissed you? It had nothing to do with shutting you up and everything to do with me wanting you."

Gasping, her eyes went wide. But before she could shake her head again with disbelief, Carter was kissing her. Devouring her. And it was glorious. She wrapped herself around him, reveling in how good he felt—welcoming his weight as she pulled him down on top of her—and gave as good as she got.

On and on it went until she lost all concept of time. She was on sensory overload and the only thing she knew was that she wanted—*needed*—more. Her clothes felt too restrictive. Every inch of her body was humming and straining and desperate for the feel of Carter's skin brushing against hers.

It was madness.

It was heaven.

It was...

Carter sat up and rolled away from her and off the bed. Emery blinked up at him in confusion. Was this it? Were they done? Did she do something wrong?

Oh God, she thought, was she bad at this?

Then, much to her delight, Carter peeled his shirt up and over his head, and Emery forgot to breathe.

He was magnificent to look at.

Reading the naked desire on her face, he grinned down at her. "Watch out, Em. Because I'm going to look at you just like that when it's your turn."

Somehow she doubted it, but it was nice that he would put it out there.

He kicked off his shoes, peeled off his socks, and then his jeans were gone and he stood beside the bed in nothing but navy-blue boxers that barely contained him.

She was pretty sure she was gaping.

Reaching for her hand, Carter gently tugged her up to a sitting position and then to her feet. His smile was feral as his hands snaked under her T-shirt. "My turn," he murmured. His hands slowly slid up her ribcage, taking the shirt with it, and in the blink of an eye, it was off.

She said a silent prayer of thanks that she had on a sexy push-up bra, because once he saw her without it, no doubt he'd be a little disappointed.

Body-image issues sucked.

Holding her breath, Emery watched as Carter's gaze roamed over her. It was as exciting as it was nerve-racking. His hands cupped her breasts and it felt so good that soon her head slowly fell back, she closed her eyes, and let herself feel. The last thing she wanted was to watch him for any signs of disappointment.

"You're perfect," he murmured, and then his lips were kissing her through her bra and she trembled in his arms. "So perfect."

Before she knew it, she was down to nothing but her panties, and they were moving back onto the bed. And just as she had predicted, the skin to skin contact was amazing. Carter was all smooth muscle and she couldn't seem to stop touching him—his chest, his arms, his back... It was like she couldn't get enough. The good thing was, he did the same to her. Their lips and hands were never idle, and it was the most foreplay she'd ever experienced.

Rolling them over, Carter looked up at her, his hands instantly cupping her breasts again. The raw heat she saw on his face was almost enough to make her orgasm right then and there.

"This is how I pictured you," he said after a long minute.

Unable to help herself, Emery was moving against him, showing what she wanted them to be doing rather than talking.

"Just like this," he went on. "I wanted to watch you take control, to take what you want, because that's when you're most spectacular."

His words were another form of foreplay she had never experienced before. There wasn't anything particularly dirty about them, yet they had the same effect.

And just when she thought this was it—they were finally going to do this—Carter flipped them over again until she was flat on her back. He grinned down at her.

"Then I realized this was the way I wanted you the first time." His voice was a near-growl as he took her lips in a kiss that was rough and wild and untamed and so exactly what she wanted. "Let me have you like this," he said breathlessly between kisses. "Just like this."

And she did.

If anyone had told him fast-food burgers would work as an
aphrodisiac, he would have told them they were insane.

But now?

Um…yeah. He was totally blaming it on the fast food.

Well, that and the fact that he had pretty much been on
sensory overload where Emery was concerned for weeks
and it didn't matter what it was that they were doing, he had
wanted her.

Still wanted her.

And they had barely caught their breath from the first
time.

She was sprawled out beside him—half of her gloriously
naked body on his—and his hand was tracing lazy circles on
her spine.

She destroyed him.

Even now, lying here thinking about the events of the
last hour, he couldn't wrap his brain around it. In his entire
life, he'd never met a woman who made him feel the way
Emery did. She challenged him, angered him, amused him,
and aroused him—and clearly not just in the ordinary and
mundane aspects of life, but here in the bedroom as well.
They were so compatible here that it—

It scared the hell out of him.

Yeah, no woman had ever made him feel like he'd found
his other half before.

But this woman did.

Beside him, some of the tension was coming back into
her body and he knew she was probably having the same
inner dialogue as he was.

What had they done?

This was something people did every day. Sex was amazing and fulfilling and mutually satisfying. But sex with someone you've known your entire life?

It changed everything.

So yeah—what the hell had they done?

"If you scratch my skin any harder, you'll be scratching organs," she murmured with a hint of humor.

His hand instantly stilled as he realized his mind had wandered. "Sorry." Kissing the top of her head, Carter waited to see how she'd respond.

Emery pulled back and looked at him and his heart kicked hard in his chest.

She was beautiful.

Her hair was in disarray, her skin was flushed, and she took his breath away. He wanted to tell her—to say all of that to her—but…it felt awkward.

And that's when he saw it. Right before his eyes, her expression changed. Fell. Reaching out, he cupped her cheek. "Hey," he said softly. "What's wrong?"

"You're having regrets," she said sadly. "I can see it in your face. You're looking at me and…and I can see you're uncomfortable." Carefully, she rolled away from him, taking the sheet with her. "Just…just give me a minute to get my clothes on and—if you don't mind, don't watch. I'll go and—"

He never let her finish. In a flash, he pulled her back and had her beneath him. Her eyes sparked with anger, then confusion, before she finally settled and waited him out.

"I wasn't having regrets," he explained. "You leaned up and I was looking at you, and all I could think was how beautiful you are. I wanted to say it—wanted to tell you—but…"

He sighed and rested his forehead against hers. "I wasn't sure how you'd react to me saying that to you."

The smile she gave him was full of relief before turning impish.

He was almost afraid to ask why she was looking at him that way.

"You were afraid to tell me you thought I was beautiful?" she said lightly, playfully.

"I wouldn't say afraid, exactly…"

The look she gave him told her he wasn't fooling her at all. Her hands smoothed up his arms and into his hair. "Uh-huh."

The only way to shut her up was to prove her wrong. "You're beautiful," he said gruffly. "Utterly and completely beautiful."

Her soft gasp preceded a dreamy smile and he was suddenly at a loss for words.

Emery slid one foot up the side of his leg and let it rest on the small of his back, repeating the move with the other. Once her legs were wrapped around him, he felt his arousal stirring back to life.

He congratulated himself on the quick recovery time.

Clearly, Emery had noticed it as well because she squirmed beneath him in a very sexy move that took him from the first stirrings of arousal to ready to go in the blink of an eye.

Beneath him, she let out a sexy little hum. "Why, Carter…do you have something for me?"

Most. Loaded. Question. Ever.

He canted his hips back and forth and grinned down at her. "I don't know. You tell me."

Her laugh was husky and she pulled him closer to kiss him soundly. "It definitely feels like you do." Another kiss.

"Is that okay with you?" he asked, suddenly feeling a little concerned that he was overenthusiastic in his need for her.

She let out another little laugh that turned into a breathy sigh as she rubbed against him. "Mmm-hmm. In fact…" She moved again and gasped as he hit a particularly sensitive spot.

"In fact…" he prompted.

"Dammit, Carter, you know what I want…" Her head fell back, her throat arched, and her eyes closed as she continued to show him with her body exactly what she wanted. "Don't make me beg."

Rather than torture them both any longer, he was more than willing to forgo the begging.

It was well after nine in the evening when they finally sat down to dinner. It wasn't the massive Christmas feast that Carter was supposed to make—they'd opted to hold off until tomorrow—but were enjoying some omelets he had whipped up.

And eating on the living room floor in front of the Christmas tree.

He wanted to be disappointed that he hadn't prepared all the fabulous food he'd been thinking about for days, but he couldn't. Not when he had a scantily clad Emery sitting beside him with a big smile on her face. She looked like a kid on Christmas morning as she gazed up at the tree, telling him about all the decorations she normally put on hers and why they held significance for her.

"Honestly, my mother cringes every year when she comes over," she was saying. "We never had a personalized tree. Every ornament was perfectly placed and we were never allowed to touch them." She shuddered. "The first Christmas I was on my own, I went a little wild. I bought ornaments every time I went shopping and then had a hell of a time trying to find a tree to fit them all!"

He laughed with her. "And did you?"

She nodded excitedly. "That was another great thing—I bought a real tree that year. Going to a tree lot was a little out of my comfort zone, because I had no idea what I should be looking for, but the owners—a really nice elderly couple— let me ask a ton of questions and then helped me find one." She smiled dreamily. "It was the perfect tree. But I almost destroyed it."

"How?"

"They tied it to my car for me and I drove away feeling so happy, planning how I was going to decorate and when I was going to do it…" She paused and took another bite of her dinner. "Then I got home and realized I had to get it from the car and into my apartment by myself!"

Carter could only imagine how she must have freaked out when the realization hit her at the time. "So what did you do?"

"At first I figured I could handle it. After all, how heavy could a tree be, right?"

It felt safer not to answer that question.

"I got it down off the car and made it all of five feet before I tripped and fell on top of it." She laughed and it made him relax. "So there I was, sprawled out in the middle of my complex's parking lot and wondering what in the world I was going to do. Fortunately, there were a couple of teenagers who lived in the building walking by and they offered to help me." She grinned at him. "I was so relieved that I tipped them a ridiculous amount of money."

"How much?" he asked with amusement.

"Let's just say it was enough that they asked me every day for about six months if I needed help carrying anything." She rolled her eyes. "Still, it was worth it. That tree was spectacular by the time I had it set up and decorated."

He didn't doubt it for a minute.

"What about you?" she asked. "How do you normally decorate for Christmas?"

Taking a bite of his omelet, he shrugged. "I don't do a whole lot. I have a team that takes care of the trees and decorations at the restaurants, and because I'm usually traveling, I don't put one up at home."

She studied him for a moment. "And where is home for you?"

Another shrug. "I have a couple of places—all close to my restaurants—but the one in New Orleans is probably the one I'd call my home base."

"Wow." It sounded more like disappointment being than impressed.

For some reason, he felt the need to explain himself. "At some point I'll cut back on the traveling and settle into one place, but with the business still growing, this is the way it has to be."

"How much more are you looking to build? This

restaurant you're building here in Montauk is going to be your fourth, right?"

He nodded.

"So what's the end goal, here? How many places do you need to open?"

For some reason, her question struck him as odd. Most people asked how many places he wanted to open, not needed to. He wondered if she meant to ask him that.

"I'd like to have six," he replied casually, waiting to see how she'd respond.

"And that will satisfy you?"

Yeah, she'd meant it.

But he didn't want to examine it, because the implication was that he was doing this—creating his restaurant empire, such as it was—out of ego.

If this conversation had come up before they'd crossed the line into his bedroom, he'd be ready to kick up one hell of a debate with her, but right now he didn't want to ruin the moment.

"Sure," he said with a smile, reaching for his glass of wine. Not the best combination to go with eggs for dinner, but it was what they'd opted for.

Emery's plate clanking on the floor snapped his attention to her. The look of annoyance on her face confused him. "You okay?"

"No, I'm not okay, Carter," she snapped.

Carefully, he put his plate on the floor and turned to her. "What's wrong?"

"You're acting weird!"

His eyes went wide, but before he could comment, she was speaking again.

"For twenty years we've had conversations where we banter back and forth. Sometimes it gets heated, but neither one of us ever backs down the way you just did!"

"How did I...?"

"'Sure'," she mocked, imitating his voice. "I mean, what the hell was that?"

He was too relaxed to take the bait, so he shifted until his back was against the sofa. "It was an answer to your question."

"It was bullshit," she countered. "You want to know what I think?"

"I'm sure I already have a good idea," he murmured, reaching for his wine again.

"I think you're sitting here trying to change the dynamics of who we are and it's insulting. A few days ago—hell, a few hours ago—you would have gone into a lengthy discussion about why you need to open more restaurants and then bragged about how you were going to do it. Instead, you gave me a meek little 'sure' and dropped the subject!"

"There really wasn't that much to it. You asked how many I planned on, and I answered. I'm feeling good, I'm relaxed, and I'm enjoying our dinner. It didn't seem like a big deal."

Clearly, that wasn't quite what she wanted to hear because he could practically feel the tension rolling off of her. But rather than come back at him, she picked up her plate, stood, and walked to the kitchen.

He figured they were done—or at least this part of the conversation was done—but when he heard her put her plate in the sink and she didn't come back, he got suspicious. Sure enough, when he turned he saw her coming out of his bedroom with the rest of her clothes, going up the stairs.

What the hell?

Jumping to his feet, he went after her. "What are you doing?"

She was halfway up the stairs when she glanced over her shoulder at him and kept going. "I'm going to take a shower and go to bed."

It wasn't hard to catch up to her. At the top of the stairs, Carter reached out and grasped her arm and spun her toward him. "What is going on with you?" he demanded. "We were having dinner and conversation, and then you just storm off?"

"I was done," she said. She said it through clenched teeth and was glaring at him, so he knew to be prepared for a fight.

"Oh yeah? Well, I'm not," he said, his voice a low growl. He hauled her in close and then did exactly what he'd sworn he wasn't going to do.

He took the damn bait.

"When I opened my first restaurant, it was all I wanted. All I needed," he added for clarity. "I hadn't planned beyond that because it consumed me day and night. But once everything settled and I was open for a while and it became successful, everyone was asking about when I was going to open the next one. So I did. And it was more successful than the first.

"After the second one I was exhausted and a little burned out, but I had someone constantly breathing down my neck—telling me how it could all go away at any moment if I didn't keep up, keep changing," he added with a snarl, "so

I opened a third one. That one was a no-brainer, because we simply copied the first two. But this new one? This one here in Montauk? It's damn near killing me, because I want to break the mold. I want to do something new and different and I'm scared as hell to do it! I don't want it to fail. I can't fail!"

And then he released her and found he was breathless and disgusted with himself. He didn't look at her as he turned and walked down the stairs. "I'll see you in the morning," he muttered, all but sprinting away from her.

He stomped across the living room, threw the sliding glass doors open, and walked outside. It didn't matter that he was still only in a pair of boxers or that the air was chill; he needed to cool off anyway.

What was so damn wrong with him not wanting to fight? How did that make him the bad guy here? After spending the better part of the day in bed exploring one another and sharing some of the most incredible sex of his life, why would Emery get pissed off because he wanted to keep the peace for a little longer? If anyone got to be annoyed in this scenario, it should be him, considering she wasn't willing simply to enjoy the truce they had called!

Pacing beside the pool, Carter shivered. It was much cooler out than he'd anticipated, but he'd be damned before he'd go back inside this soon. To distract himself from the temperature, he put his focus back on why he was so angry.

Emery.

And her damn tendency to pick fights with him at the most inopportune times.

Like after a day of making love.

Ugh…I did not just think of it like that, did I?

It was pointless to argue with himself there. He did think of it like that because that's exactly what had happened.

Emery wasn't a casual hookup and she wasn't a one-night stand. Well…he hoped she wasn't going to be a one-night stand.

Muttering a curse, he turned and walked back into the house, hating how she had him so tied up in knots that he had to chase after her in his own house in order to give himself a little peace.

She wanted him to fight with her? Disagree with her?

"Your wish is my command," he said, storming back into the house. Taking the stairs two at a time, Carter threw open her bedroom door without knocking and found the room empty. He looked around in utter confusion for a moment before the sound of the shower running registered with him.

A slow smile spread across his face at the thought of walking in and finding Emery in the shower—warm and soapy and no doubt still spitting mad.

Good, he thought. Because he was too.

Pushing open the bathroom door, he heard Emery's gasp. She turned to look at him and her expression instantly became hostile. Slamming the door closed, he walked close to the glass. They stood like that for several moments, staring at each other. The room was steamy, and as much as he had to say, nothing came to mind as she stood naked and glorious before him.

After what seemed like an eternity, she reached out and pushed open the glass door and then took a step back.

She did what he was too scared to do.

Silently, he slid his briefs off and stepped under the hot

spray as he backed her up against the tiled wall. Without a word, he leaned in and kissed her—softy, tenderly, lovingly. He kissed her until she wrapped her arms around him and she melted against him. When he finally lifted his head, he scanned her face. "I'm sorry," he said quietly.

"Me too." Her hand caressed his cheek. "I shouldn't have pushed. I don't know why I did."

Chuckling softly, he mimicked her movements, caressing her cheek. "Because you're a pain in the ass and it's one of the things I have always appreciated about you."

The look on her face told him she wasn't amused. "In my defense," she said, "you're usually a pompous jerk."

His laugh was a little heartier this time. Placing a kiss on the tip of her nose, he replied, "And none of that is going to change because we spent the day in bed together." After kissing her again, he rested his forehead against hers. "And I don't want that to change. Arguing with you is some of my favorite memories of my life growing up. But it's not all there is to us—obviously."

She blushed and it was sexy as hell. When she tried to look away, he gently nudged her. "But sometimes it's okay not to want to fight. Believe it or not, I was really enjoying our conversation while we ate. I loved hearing about your Christmas tree."

Her expression turned a little sad. "I'm sorry I ruined that. Believe it or not, I was enjoying it too."

"Then why…?"

Shrugging, she said, "I don't know. It just sort of came out. I wasn't thinking and…I'm sorry."

He kissed her then with a little more heat than he had a minute ago. It didn't take long for things to escalate.

Pulling back, Carter reached for her shower gel and poured some into his hands while explaining in great detail all the ways he was going to touch her and please her, but how she would have to wait until he had her back in his bed before he would love her again.

And again and again and again. All night long.

The house was dark and quiet, and Emery knew that opening the bag of chips could quite possibly end up sounding like firecrackers, but she couldn't help it. She was hungry and feeling a little stressed and needed a snack.

Well…that and the fact that she and Carter had Olympics-quality sex for the last several hours had helped her work up an appetite.

Tiptoeing out of the kitchen and up to her room, the first thing she did was grab her robe and put it on. The second was to curl up in the oversized chair in the corner and slowly open the bag.

"I'm ridiculous," she murmured as she was carefully reaching into the bag to keep the noise down. That first bite of crunchy saltiness went a long way toward helping her relax.

What have I done?

Yeah, now that it was dark and quiet and Carter was asleep, her mind was going into overdrive. As much as she wanted to stay in his luxurious and monstrous bed, she feared he'd be able to hear each and every one of her thoughts because they were so loud in her head. It was safer to get up and leave the room. Now, upstairs and curled up in the corner, Emery felt like she could finally wrap her brain around all that had transpired today.

She'd started doing that earlier in the shower before Carter had shown up and joined her.

And that was the moment that had changed everything. Not that it hadn't already been changed by their earlier multiple romps, but it was a perfect time for them to simply say *"Oops—that was fun, but…"*

But they hadn't.

Instead, Emery had seen the look on his face when she turned toward him and read every emotion there. It was becoming a blessing and a curse how she could do that with him. She read every bit of anger, frustration, and need he had, and instead of going the safe route—the path that they always took of fighting it out—she had chosen to wait. To listen. And ultimately, to comfort.

Their honest admissions to one another felt natural and terrifying at the same time. In that moment, she couldn't examine it, but now that she was alone with her thoughts, she could say without a doubt that it was the defining moment for them.

With a sigh, she ate another chip.

With nothing but time on her hands for well over a month now, Emery had come to several conclusions about her life. First and foremost, she was done letting her parents dictate how she was supposed to live and who she was supposed to be with. That part of her life was over. Next was her job. She'd been on a leave of absence since moving into Eliza Montgomery's condo in Manhattan, and not once had anyone reached out to her to see if she was all right or because they might have some questions for her about her accounts. And that raised several questions in her mind: After working with those people for two years, did she really mean so little to them that no one was concerned about her well-being? On top of that, she was clearly easy to replace, since whoever was covering for her was doing such a bang-up job that they didn't need to reach out.

Another chip.

Maybe it was time for a change. Maybe it was time to take a deeper look at herself and try to figure out what *she* wanted to do and not what everyone was expecting her to do.

"There's a first time for everything," she said and turned her attention to the window. Outside, the moonlight was reflecting off the ocean, and even with the windows closed, she could hear the sound of the waves crashing.

It went a long way in helping her relax.

This house, this setting, was the best kind of therapy.

The amazingly sexy man asleep downstairs was merely a perk.

Sure, if that's what you need to tell yourself.

Yeah, that was something else that required some serious thinking. Her and Carter. This…whatever it was they'd started.

Another chip.

No man had the right to be so damn sexy, she thought. And as much as she wanted to hold it against him—like the old Emery would do—she couldn't. There was so much more to him than just an adversary. He was a man who loved his family and wanted to make his mother happy. He was a man who was passionate about his career. He was a man who was still fighting some demons.

Something she ached to help him with.

Not that he'd let her. She saw that earlier and figured out pretty fast that this drive he had to succeed wasn't something he was fully in control of. And the weird thing was she didn't take it personally that he wouldn't share it with her. She had a feeling he didn't share it with anyone.

And that's why he was so quick to snap at her over it.

Letting out a long breath, she tried to think of what she could do to help him. Unfortunately, she was fighting to keep her eyes open, and after one last chip, she was more than ready to crawl into bed. Carefully rolling the top of the bag down, she placed it on the side table and stood to stretch. Looking out the window one more time, she yawned. It really was peaceful here and there were far too many things she needed to work through that weren't going to be answered tonight.

When she turned around and stared at the bed, she paused. Was she supposed to sleep up here or go back down to Carter? He'd been sound asleep when she left, so he really had no idea she had ever gotten up. It wouldn't be hard to slide back in bed with him.

Shaking her head, Emery decided the bed five feet away was just fine. She'd deal with his disapproval tomorrow. Right now, the thought of sliding between the sheets and resting her head on a soft pillow was too strong to fight.

Within minutes, her robe was on the floor, her head was on the pillow, and she was fast asleep.

The next time she opened her eyes, the room was bright with sunlight and there was a very warm, very hard male wrapped around her. She stiffened slightly and then relaxed.

"Care to tell me why I'm up here rather than downstairs?"

he said sleepily in her ear. Her back was pressed firmly against his chest and their legs were tangled together.

"I would imagine it's because you walked up here," she said around a yawn.

He chuckled softly behind her. "Okay, let me rephrase that—care to tell me why I had to come up here to find you in the wee hours of the morning?"

She felt bad about that now. At the time it didn't seem like a big deal. She figured he'd think she'd just wanted to sleep alone and wait to talk to her about it when they met up for breakfast.

"I couldn't sleep," she admitted after a moment. "I got up to have a snack and I didn't want to wake you, so I came up here."

"You have a secret stash of food up here?" he teased.

Playfully, she elbowed him in the stomach. "No. I grabbed a bag of chips, realized it was going to sound like I was setting off fireworks or something when I tried to open the bag, and opted to come up here to be quiet." Saying it out loud had her feeling more than a little foolish, but luckily Carter didn't say anything. "By the time I had a few, I couldn't keep my eyes open and this bed was much closer than going down the stairs."

Then she held her breath and wondered what he was going to say next. The fact that he was here in her bed told her that yesterday and last night wasn't a fluke. That he wasn't relieved to find her gone.

"Did you consider coming back to bed with me?" he asked quietly, and because she knew him so well, Emery could hear the vulnerability in his voice.

Rolling over, she faced him and stared in wonder at his handsome face. Even first thing in the morning, with bed-head and quite a bit of scruff on his chin, he was absolutely magnificent to look at.

She didn't even want to think about her own appearance.

Looking Carter right in the eyes, she said, "Yes. And if I wasn't so tired and afraid of falling down the stairs and breaking my neck in the dark, I would have been right back there under the blankets with you."

Her words seemed to please him, because a slow smile crossed his face before he maneuvered them so she was lying beneath him. "I missed you when I woke up."

Her heart kicked hard in her chest at his admission. No one had ever said anything like that to her.

Ever.

"I'm sorry you had to come looking for me." She paused, reaching up to caress his jaw and then down to his strong shoulder.

His smile only seemed to grow. "You weren't too hard to find."

He shifted and Emery's legs immediately wrapped around him. She loved the feel of him, the weight and warmth of his body on top of hers. "Now that you've found me, what are you going to do?" She couldn't believe the words had come out of her mouth—and sounded remotely flirty, because that wasn't something she normally did.

Yet she had.

And it felt really good.

"Everything, Em," he said, sipping at her lips. "I had big plans for us this morning, and leaving my bed wasn't part of them."

Now she felt *really* bad about not going back downstairs last night. Her guilt didn't last long, however, because Carter was the king of distraction. His hands seemed to be touching her everywhere along with his lips. They went from lazy movements and kisses to urgent in the blink of an eye.

Which was totally becoming their thing.

And that felt really good too.

There were so many things they needed to do today—there were a ton of dishes to prepare to get them back on track with the cookbook—and they couldn't afford to spend another day in bed together.

But as Carter quickly whipped their blanket off and hauled her from the bed to over his shoulder, cooking became the furthest thing from her mind.

"Carter!" she shrieked even as she laughed. "What in the world are you doing?"

"All of my plans involved having you in my bed," he said, heedless of them both being completely naked as he carried her down the stairs and across the living room. "My bed, Emery. That's where I want us to be. And not just right now. But tonight, it's where I want you to be and where I want you to stay. All night."

Tossing her on his bed, he grinned down at her. "And if that means I have to keep a basket of snacks next to the bed to keep you here for the entire night, then that's what I'm going to do. Okay?"

Only Carter would come up with something that was so ridiculous and yet so incredibly sweet. Reaching out, she grasped his hand and tugged him down beside her, laughing as he bounced on the mattress. Lightning-quick, she moved to straddle him.

"Promise to get the potato chips with the ridges and some chocolate, and we have a deal."

Chapter 6

"C'MON. JUST TASTE IT."

"No."

"You're going to love it, I promise."

"That's what you said about the other gross things you made me taste."

"It was escargot and it was fabulous," Carter chided. "And you said you'd had it before."

"I lied."

Honestly, it was like dealing with a petulant child.

A week had passed since they had decorated the house for Christmas and begun this new phase of their relationship. The house was still decorated, and he had cooked enough meals to feed everyone during the dinner hours at one of his restaurants.

And Emery wasn't impressed with most of it.

Sadly, it stung.

Maybe it was just ego, but no one had ever *not* enjoyed his cooking. Whether he was concocting something new or following a recipe he'd found someplace, people raved about it. Sure, there was the occasional critique about something needing a little more or a little less of a specific spice or ingredient, but that went with the territory. But the way Emery reacted to most of his meals? It had him seriously second-guessing his career.

Letting out a long breath, he crossed his arms over his chest and studied her. "What's wrong this time?"

She was peering into the pot, her nose wrinkled with distaste.

"It smells funny."

He pinched the bridge of his nose and counted to ten. "Funny how?"

"Like..." She groaned with annoyance. "I don't know, Carter! Can't you just make something normal for dinner? Does everything have to be pretentious?"

"Pretentious?" he mocked. "Em, this is a simple carbonara sauce and it's delicious. It's a very popular dish. You said you wanted Italian for dinner tonight, so I made you something Italian!"

Rolling her eyes, she walked across the kitchen to the pantry, where she moved things around on the shelf before turning to face him.

While holding up a can of crushed tomatoes.

"When I said Italian, I figured you'd make a normal red sauce! Maybe some spaghetti and meatballs or some baked ziti! Did you think to ask if I'd want something with... with... What the hell is that in there?" she yelled.

"Pancetta."

"Pan-whatta?" she mocked.

Walking over, he took the can of tomatoes from her and placed it on the kitchen counter. "Will you just trust me on this? Please? Taste it and if you don't love it, I'll whip up a quick red sauce for you."

There wasn't a doubt in his mind that if she just stopped fighting him on this food thing, she'd actually find new dishes to enjoy. He wasn't going to whip up another sauce because he wasn't going to need to. Once he mixed the sauce with some linguine and added a healthy dose of pecorino romano cheese and some black pepper, she'd be thanking him.

"Seriously, what is pancetta?"

"It's like bacon," he explained. "And it is so flavorful, I know you're going to love it." He gave her a loving tap on the tip of her nose. "And I know how much you adore bacon."

"Not on my pasta," she murmured.

"Emery…"

She growled again and stormed across the room. "I'm going to try your damn bacon pasta stuff because I know you'll just keep hounding me until I do, but I have some stipulations too."

Unable to stop himself, he laughed. "Oh really? This I can't wait to hear."

That only seemed to rile her up more.

"If I eat this crap—which I am vehemently against—then for the next three nights, you have to make food that I like," she said firmly.

"So popcorn and nachos for dinner?" he asked sarcastically. "Done."

Myriad emotions played across her face but she didn't lash back at him. Instead, she calmly walked around to the opposite side of the kitchen island and said, "Comfort food. I want meatloaf and mashed potatoes, pot roast with carrots, maybe some chili or homemade chicken soup, and"—she leaned across the island, her eyes narrowing at him—"spaghetti and meatballs. You know, normal food."

His mind was already spinning with some great stuffed meatloaf recipes as well as some meatballs he'd eaten in Sicily that were made with pine nuts.

"Oh no!" she cried, pointing at him. "I can see it

already–you're going to put your Carter Montgomery spin on those meals and that's not allowed! You have to cook them in the normal, regular, everyday kind of way. No crazy ingredients! Do you understand?"

Carter had always known he was passionate about food—about cooking it, creating it, and eating it. Apparently, Emery was equally passionate—but in a completely different way.

Nodding, he agreed. "Dinner will be ready in twenty minutes."

It was her turn to nod. "I'm going to look over those pictures we took this morning of the breakfast foods and see if there are any we can use. Call me when you're done." Then she turned and walked up the stairs.

This morning he had baked cinnamon rolls from scratch and made seafood benedict for them. Well, it was for the book, but they definitely benefitted from it. They'd been cooking so damn much over the last week and Emery had been taking pictures and getting some great shots with the holiday décor in the background. His mother was giddy with the results and this morning they had decided to host a mock Christmas dinner at her place with their extended family—or as many of them as they could wrangle up—to do a photo shoot. This time with a professional photographer.

When he had called his mother and talked to her about the idea, she had squealed with delight. Within the hour she had confirmed Uncle William and Aunt Monica would be coming in, as well as Aunt Janice and Uncle Robert. Megan and Alex were going to fly in, and apparently Christian and Sophie too. Beyond them, it was anyone's guess as to how many of their cousins would make it. After all, it wasn't as if this was happening at Christmas—it was just for the purpose of a couple of photos. Hell, they probably could have hired strangers to come sit and pretend to be family without making so many people fly across the country for a meal. But his mother assured him it was always a good thing to get everyone together and she was thankful for the excuse to do so for a happy occasion.

Even if it was fake, he thought.

So he'd been working on finalizing the menu while at the same time trying to work on the menu for the new restaurant. Nothing was fitting there, not like it was with the book. He wanted something different, something you couldn't find on the menus at his other restaurants, but his mind was a complete blank. He'd thought all of this cooking would inspire him, but it hadn't.

And it was frustrating as hell.

The only thing keeping him sane, ironically, was Emery.

In the kitchen and while they were working, she could be a complete pain in the ass, but once they were done and moved on to any topic other than food, she was amazing.

And that didn't include the way she had completely worn him out and blown his mind on a nightly basis.

He kept waiting for things to get awkward, or maybe just to cool down. But they didn't. If anything, with each day he found more about her to like, more he wanted to know, and he was craving her more than he'd thought possible. For all the years they had known each other, it had been relatively superficial. But now they were talking about their lives and sharing things and he realized how little they really knew about one another.

And he was enjoying everything he was discovering about her.

They had one more week here at the house, and then it would be time to return to their normal lives. He had to get back down to New Orleans, and Emery…well, she still seemed up in the air. She mentioned going back upstate and returning to work, but she'd shared how that wasn't as appealing as she'd once thought. His heart went out to her. Her entire life had been thrown for a loop and it left her at loose ends.

This cookbook project had been a great distraction, and once they went to his mother's for the weekend, they would be done. Come Sunday night, he was leaving and he had no idea where Emery was going.

Probably should talk about that…

And why weren't they talking about it? Because he didn't want to think about it. Didn't want to think about the time when he was going to have to say goodbye to her. Not that it would be forever, but it would certainly be a while before they would have time to be together again. He had to settle back into his schedule and buckle down on this new menu, and she had things of her own to figure out. The time apart could be a good thing for them—a chance to see if what they had right now was real.

None of this was going to come up tonight over dinner, that was for sure. She was already feeling a little hostile about what she was eating, no need to add to it by forcing her to talk about topics she was clearly avoiding.

This was new and foreign to him—talking about feelings and the future. The relationships he usually had were casual, and Carter had always used work as an excuse to keep from getting serious. It wasn't really an excuse, it was how his life was. He was always busy and his time wasn't his own. Getting the restaurants off the ground and making money involved long hours in the beginning. But now? The reality was that his three existing restaurants ran well without him. He'd hired the best staff and had excellent managers in place who handled everything. He was merely a figurehead—the face of the restaurant. His presence wasn't particularly necessary. And after he went back to New Orleans for a few weeks— which was more for him than anything else—his time was going to be spent here in Montauk for the foreseeable future.

And that made him freeze for a moment.

He was going to be here in New York.

For a while.

Then he pushed that aside because being here in the same state as Emery wasn't the same as being near her. It was a five-hour drive, six by train, to where she lived. It wasn't as if they'd be close enough to go out to dinner on the spur of the moment.

But they could have their weekends together.

That was something, right?

With a sigh, he raked his hand through his hair and put his attention back on their dinner. Now that he knew just how much she wasn't enthused about the meal, he wanted to do what he could to make it appealing. While waiting for the water to boil for the linguine, he whipped up a caesar salad because he knew she loved those. He picked out one of her favorite wines. He set a beautiful table and turned on some soft music. Even if she didn't enjoy the food, she would enjoy the atmosphere—and this house and its view provided some incredible atmosphere. He'd already talked to his real estate agent about getting the house again when he came back in a month and although the homeowner did have some other renters interested, Carter had negotiated like the shrewd businessman he was and managed to get the extended lease. He had fallen in love with the place and knew Emery had as well. It would be nice for her to have it to come to on the weekends.

Should she want to.

And man oh man, did he hope she wanted to.

Clicking on the last picture on her laptop screen, Emery smiled.

She'd done it. She'd gotten this cookbook done. The pictures were perfect, and once they did a final shoot with Carter's family, it would be ready to go to the formatter, who had everything ready and just had to plug the new files in. Eliza was thrilled. Attaching the pictures she'd just edited in an email to Carter's mother, she hit Send and sat back, stretching. She'd had no idea this project would feel so fulfilling. It was silly, really—it seemed like such a simple thing when she'd first been approached about it, but now that it was done, she could say honestly it was one of the best accomplishments she'd ever experienced.

She'd learned so much about cooking and the amount of time and prep work that went into it. Not that it made her want to cook, but it was interesting. Carter made it all look easy, but it was part of who he was—it came as naturally to him as breathing. But she'd like to think the reason these recipes came easily to him or this project finally came together was because of her. She wanted to believe they worked well as a team and wanted him to see it too.

Would she sound stupid or needy if she asked him?

At the end of the week they'd head back upstate to his mother's house and do a meal with his family. They had no idea how many Montgomerys were going to show up, but at last count at least a dozen. She laughed softly. No doubt it would be a loud and boisterous affair and so completely different from anything she'd ever experienced with her own family. No, the Monaghans were very reserved. Even when her sisters came home for the holidays with their families, it wasn't fun or relaxing like she was certain Carter's family was going to be. Not that she had anything to go by; it was just something she knew because she'd been around Carter and listened to his stories for the last several weeks.

She envied them their closeness, their laughter, their ability to put joy into simply being together. So for that one weekend when she would get to play a part in the family meal and photo shoot, she would take it all in and keep it with her when her own family holidays threatened to depress the hell out of her.

It was just one of the many things she'd take away from this time with Carter.

Sunday night he was leaving and she was going back to her own home for the first time in close to two months.

And not looking forward to it one bit.

Besides the usual stuff most people dreaded about going home—laundry, sorting through mail, etc.—Emery had to deal with sorting through her life.

Amazingly enough, things had been anticlimactic after her refusal to show up at court for Derek. Of course she had taken away his lawyer's threat by simply not being at the address he was going to leak. Her mother had called and left multiple voice messages regarding her own disappointment in Emery's behavior, but that wasn't anything new. After the fourth one, Emery hadn't heard from her since.

Morbid curiosity had her going to a news site and looking for the latest on Derek. It surprised her to see how he had—only days ago—made a public confession of his wrongdoings and was going into rehab for alcohol, prescription drugs, and sex addiction. Swallowing hard, she scrolled down the page to a video clip of his statement.

"But most of all, I'm sorry for letting my family down," he said solemnly. He looked impeccable, as always. Not a hair out of place and wearing a three-thousand-dollar suit. "My behavior has ruined so many lives and that's not something I can ignore. To my parents, I hope you know how much I love you. To my colleagues and the public who trusted me, I apologize for breaking that trust. And to Emery," he said, looking directly at the camera, "I regret how our relationship ended."

No apology.

And no real regret in his damn voice.

Slamming the laptop shut, she let out a shuddery breath and stood, going over to the window and looking out at the beach. Then she spun, quickly went down the stairs, and walked outside with nothing more than an "I'll be back in a few minutes" to Carter. In the distance, she heard him call out to her and ask if she was all right, but she needed to breathe.

By the time she hit the edge of the backyard and her feet touched the sand, her eyes stung with tears and she didn't care if they fell or what a mess she would end up looking like. Taking off in a sprint, she ran down to the edge of the water, bent at the waist, and waited to get sick.

Strong arms suddenly came around her, gently holding her while she shook and forced herself to breathe normally. When she straightened, she turned and buried her face into his chest, his hands slowly, rhythmically, rubbing up and down her back. He didn't say a word, although she knew he had to be curious what had happened. She had no idea how much time passed before she finally felt a little more in control of herself. Pulling back slightly, she looked up at him and offered a weak smile. "Thank you."

His expression was firm. Fierce. "You okay?"

Shaking her head, she whispered, "No."

He waited, not pushing her to talk until she was ready.

Letting out one last shaky breath, she stayed in the circle of his arms and explained about the article she'd just read and Derek's statement. "He apologized to everyone. Every. One. Except me." She paused. "I knew our relationship wasn't perfect. Hell, it wasn't even good by the time the news story broke. But to think I invested two years in a relationship with him—was prepared to marry him—and he didn't have the decency to apologize to me publicly the way he did to everyone else?"

The trembling was back and Carter pulled her in close again. They were practically cheek to cheek right now and—not for the first time—she was thankful for his presence. Those first few weeks she hadn't had anyone she could draw comfort or support from. Not like this. Right now, she just wanted someone to listen to her—to hear her without offering some ridiculous platitude about how things weren't as bad as they seemed.

Bull. Shit.

They sucked.

They were worse than what they seemed and this press conference video proved it.

Derek's career was over for the time being, but she had a feeling he'd be back in office eventually. Maybe he wouldn't go as far as he'd once dreamed, but politics was in his blood. His family had very deep pockets and they'd do whatever it took to get him back in the game when the time came.

Just the thought of it made her sick.

The only silver lining to this was how she had been spared having to stand there in the media circus with everyone looking at her with pity. When she got home, maybe the bulk of it would have died down and she could quietly slip back into her life, going back to work and even going to the grocery store without everyone wanting to talk about Derek and the whole debacle.

She doubted it would be that simple, but for now she had to cling to the hope that the worst was over. All she had left was this anger.

With one last heavy sigh, she stepped out of his arms. "Thank you."

"I didn't do anything."

"Believe me, you did everything. More than you'll ever know."

His expression didn't change. Didn't waver. But he held out his hand to her and together they walked back into the house. Once inside, he let go of her and walked over to the stove, turning the burner back on before checking the pasta. The look on his face told her he wasn't disappointed with what he found. Clearly, dinner wasn't ruined.

Dammit.

Then she let out a low laugh and walked over to join him, pouring them each a glass of wine. He was tense, she could see it in his movements, and knew she needed to defuse the situation.

"So dinner isn't ruined, huh?"

He shook his head.

"Well, damn. I thought for sure I had created the perfect foil for your bacon pasta." And when he looked up at her and laughed, she knew her plan had worked. Stepping closer to the stove, she watched as he whisked the sauce and then added the pasta to it. It didn't smell half bad, but she wasn't going to tell him that. More than anything Emery was determined to get him to cook some of the things she liked rather than constantly pushing his frou-frou food on her.

"Pretty clever trick," he teased. "For a minute there I thought there was really a problem. Adding theatrics seems a little drastic just to get out of eating a five-star meal."

"Five star? Someone's awful confident in his cooking skills."

That had him laughing heartily. "Sweetheart, I think we both know I'm confident in *all* of my skills." The heated look he gave her left nothing to her imagination. He knew exactly where her mind would go with that innuendo and he was right—he was confident in everything he did. But more so in the bedroom.

And with good reason.

"Well, since we've already established your confidence in the kitchen, how about we move on to something else," she said silkily, motioning over her shoulder toward his bedroom.

He seemed amused as he plated their dinner. "Nice try,

Em. You're not getting out of this meal until you try at least one forkful of my carbonara."

Muttering a curse, she followed him over to the table with their wine glasses and took her seat. Staring at her plate, she asked, "And what else is in this? You know, other than the pancetta-bacon stuff?"

"Cream, butter, pancetta, onions, grated cheese… Just taste it before you start making that face again, please."

"Fine." Picking up her fork, she pushed her food this way and that before finally steeling herself against her distaste at the thought of it. Twirling the pasta on her fork, she picked it up and noticed Carter staring at her expectantly. "I'm not going to eat while you stare at me, Carter. So knock it off."

Without a word, he took a forkful of his pasta and put it in his mouth—and made a sexy as hell yummy sound.

Damn the man.

With a dramatically loud huff of breath, she tasted it.

Oh, that's good.

Double damn the man.

Don't make a yummy sound. Don't make a yummy sound…

Placing her fork down primly beside her plate, she chewed and noticed Carter glancing at her while he pretended to be busy twirling his own pasta. Next, she picked up her napkin and gently dabbed at the corners of her mouth.

"Well?" he finally asked, impatient.

"It's not bad," she forced herself to say. "But—"

His expression fell and she hated that she had hurt his feelings. "But…?"

And she couldn't do it. Couldn't let him believe he'd done anything wrong. "It's good, okay?" she snapped. "There. Happy now? It's good. Really good. I still would have preferred a red sauce, but this is very good." Slouching down in her chair, she pouted.

Reaching across the table, Carter took her hand in his and brought it to his lips, kissing it. "That wasn't so difficult, was it?"

"Yes. It was incredibly painful because now I know you're not going to make the stuff I want. I'm going to be deprived of the foods I am practically fantasizing about because of this."

"You've been fantasizing about food? Seriously?"

"Food is my comfort, Carter. I have a food for every mood and you haven't let me have most of them."

He sat back and studied her. "Really? A food for every mood?"

Nodding, she explained. "There's the usual everyone has—when I'm not feeling well, I love a good bowl of soup and maybe some grilled cheese. When I'm stressed, I enjoy a good meatloaf with mashed potatoes and gravy. If that stress is really getting to me, I love french fries with extra salt. On a lazy Sunday afternoon, there is something about smelling a pot roast slow-cooking in the kitchen."

"And you make all these things yourself?"

"Hardly," she said with a small laugh. "My grandmother used to cook—my dad's mom. She made the best pot roast ever. I haven't had one like it since she passed away about ten years ago, but I always try it when I see it on a menu. You know, if I'm in the mood." Then she sighed, realizing she hadn't thought of that in a long time. "Going to her house was a comfort to me and I guess that's why I associate some of those foods with my emotions. When things were tense at home or the pressure of school was getting to me, a weekend with Grandma used to go a long way in making me feel better."

"Most people do equate food with good memories. That's why this cookbook was so important to my mother. She wanted to convey that feeling. I'm not sure we did exactly what she wanted, but I think we came pretty damn close."

"We did a great job, Carter. Well, you did. You did all the hard work."

He squeezed her hand. "It was a team effort, Em. I couldn't do it without you." He squeezed again. "Thank you. Thank you for doing something that meant so much to my mom. I know she's thrilled with everything you did."

"She made it easy. I wanted to make her smile."

The look on his face showed how much he appreciated her words.

"I'm not sure if this is the right time to bring this up, but... she seems to be doing well," Emery said cautiously. "I know losing your father so suddenly was awful. They were married for so long and I know she struggled a lot with it. But lately, it's like she's coming back into her own, you know?"

Carter nodded and took a sip of his wine. "I feel the same way." Then he laughed softly. "Actually, I knew she was when she started nagging me about this project. There was always guilt involved—she's a master at throwing that around—but more and more, I'm seeing signs of the old Mom. She's always been a bit feisty, but my father used to try to—" He stopped himself and seemed to regret his words.

Emery waited for him to continue or move on to another topic, but instead he went back to eating. "You know," she began gently, "it's okay to say when something about your father bothered you. I know people say it's not nice to speak ill of the dead, but it's also not a good thing to pretend the things they said or did were all perfect."

The silverware clanked down loudly against his plate, but he wasn't looking at her. "Whenever Mom and I had time together one-on-one, she was always so happy. She'd make jokes and had a wicked sense of humor. But when my father was with her, she was always stiff and reserved, and I used to hate that. When I'd try to get her to say something snarky or comment on something she might have said to me and my father was there, he would cut us off and tell us to stop acting ridiculous." His expression turned fierce for the barest of moments before going neutral. "Eventually, I just gave up. I figured if that's how she wanted to live, then who was I to rock the boat."

"You're her son! Did you ever confront your father about it?"

This time his laugh was mirthless. "Believe me, I confronted my father about a lot of things. Not that it ever did me any good." He shrugged and reached for his glass again. "But I had it easy. Well, easier than my brother. By not working for the corporate Montgomery machine, I at least had some distance. Christian never stood a chance. I'm glad he's finally getting to live his life the way he wants to."

Before Emery could react—could wrap her brain around his words and how harsh they were—Carter hung his head and she could see how he was struggling with his admission. When he looked at her, his expression was devastated.

"That was awful, wasn't it," he said flatly. "It sounds like I'm glad he's dead so our family can have some peace." He muttered a curse, swiped a weary hand over his face. "What kind of person does that make me?"

"An honest one. Not every person who dies is a martyr and not everyone gets remembered fondly. We all have our faults, Carter."

"But he's not here to defend himself," he said quietly.

"And if he was, would anything be different? Would you suddenly not feel this way about him?"

He stared at her for a long moment before he said, "No. No, I would still feel this way." He paused. "Right before Dad died, Christian and I had a long talk and we both decided we were tired of the way he treated us. For so many years, we each kept our struggles with the old man to ourselves and finally we were going to band together and try to put an end to all of the negativity. But we never got the chance."

Reaching across the table, she placed her hand over his. "I'm so sorry, Carter."

"We'll never know…we'll never know if things could have changed. We each craved his approval even when it was unhealthy. Christian did until it became an obsession that almost killed him." He let out a long breath. "We all have peace now—but also a sense of unfinished business. There will never be any closure."

Emery knew Joseph Montgomery had died suddenly after complications from a stroke. But hearing this side of the story—how his death not only affected his family due to the suddenness, but also the way he had treated all of them—broke her heart. While her parents weren't exactly the warm and fuzzy types, she realized things could have been a lot worse.

Although…

"I learned early on that the way to gain my parents' approval was through doing well in school," she said softly.

"It wasn't as if I set out to have it be that way, it's just how it turned out. I remember how excited I was when they first started bragging about me and how good my grades were. Up until then, it was my sisters who were getting all the attention."

"They were good in school?"

She shook her head. "No, but they took ballet and gymnastics, and we were always going to recitals or competitions. I know my mother enjoyed it and they tried to get me into it as well, but...let's just say I wasn't as graceful as my sisters."

Carter's eyes went a little wide. "I find that hard to believe. You were always...well, whenever I thought of you—particularly when we got older—you reminded me of Audrey Hepburn." His lopsided grin made her heart skip a beat. "To me you always exuded grace and confidence. More so than any other woman I've ever met."

Wow.

"Carter, I..." But she didn't know what to say. There weren't words to convey how much his description of her meant.

"It's true," he said tenderly, turning her hand over and linking their fingers together. "I look at you and I'm a little in awe. And intimidated. All those years where we competed against one another, it was because of that." His grin was back. "Plus it was fun watching you get all flustered."

Laughing, she pulled her hand away. "And now you ruined it."

But he was faster and had not only grabbed her hand back but managed to tug her out of her chair and into his lap. "You're one hell of a woman, Emery. Always remember that."

And then he kissed her, and all talk of food and families was over.

It was late and Carter couldn't sleep. Beside him, Emery was out cold. Quietly, he slipped from the bed, pulled on a pair of shorts, and walked out to the living room, closing the door behind him. Staring at the room, he chuckled. It was still decorated for Christmas. At first he thought it was crazy to keep it all up, since the pictures and book were done, but they'd decided to wait a few more days and have it all removed the day before they headed to his mother's.

Grabbing a bottle of water, he walked back out to the living room and turned on the tree lights before sitting on the sofa. As a kid, he remembered staying up late and enjoying staring at the Christmas tree while it was all lit up and no other lights were on in the house.

Just like now.

Feeling a little nostalgic—and a little emotionally raw after their conversation over dinner—Carter decided to call his brother and reached for his phone on the coffee table. With the three-hour time difference, it shouldn't be too late in California and Christian should still be up.

"Please don't be calling with bad news," Christian said as he answered the phone.

"Why would you so much as think that?"

"The last time you called late at night, it was to tell me Dad died, remember?"

Honestly, he hadn't. But after a moment he said, "It was much later than this. Unless you're such an old man now that nine o'clock is past your bedtime." He laughed as he got comfortable on the couch.

"It is when my beautiful wife is already there and waiting for me," Christian replied lightly.

"Oh…uh, well if now isn't a good time, you can… I mean, we can talk some other time," he stammered, hating how he hadn't thought about what his brother and his new bride might be up to.

Christian's bark of laughter brought him out of his thoughts. "Oh, good Lord, relax, Carter. I was joking!"

Whew! "Ha ha. Very funny."

"Yeah, well, I hate to admit it, but when I saw your name on the screen, my first thought was that you might be calling to tell me something happened to Mom."

Damn. "That sucks," he stated. "And it's unfair—it was one bad news call in, like…thirty years. I don't want you feeling dread whenever you see my name." He paused. "And might I remind you I've called you plenty of times between then and now and you never reacted like this."

"I know. I can't explain it. It was a knee-jerk reaction. Sorry." He could hear his brother moving around a bit and then telling Sophie who he was talking to on the phone before he spoke again. "So what's up? Kind of late where you are, isn't it?"

"Couldn't sleep. I'm feeling a little restless and figured I'd give you a call to distract me."

"You should open the windows and doors and listen to the ocean. It goes a long way in helping me relax. Although it's probably a lot colder where you are right now."

Carter laughed softly. "Just a bit. And yeah, you were spot on about that. I can't believe how much it has helped me over the last month."

"How's the new restaurant coming?"

"Great," he said quickly, though he didn't quite mean it. "Construction is coming along, and every day I have calls with the designers and there's progress, but...I don't know, I'm still not feeling it."

"What's going on? You've never had this much trouble before. What's bothering you?"

Sighing, he raked a hand through his hair, his head falling back against the cushions. "I wish I knew. I've been planning on having this place out here for so damn long, but nothing is gelling in my head about the specifics. So what I have—or what I'm going to have very soon—is the shell of a restaurant with no real design, interior, or menu in mind. And they all go together. If I can just figure out one, the rest will fall into place."

"Which one is the most important?"

"The menu."

"So what's the problem? Food has always been your thing. This should be a breeze for you. If anything, I would have thought the menu had to be done before you broke ground."

"It was," he admitted, "but then I kept changing it and changing it until I threw the whole concept out. I want something different for this place, but I have no idea what that is."

"You mean like having one kind of cuisine—like Italian or French, something like that?"

He shook his head even though his brother couldn't see him. "No, it's just—" He muttered a curse. "It's like it's right there just out of my reach. It's frustrating, and no matter what I do or how hard I try to work it out, nothing's coming to me. I've been cooking up a storm for this damn cookbook project for Mom, and while it was fun, it didn't inspire me all that much."

"Maybe you're thinking about it too hard and trying to work it all out yourself. Why not go out into the community and see what type of place they're looking for? Ask around and see what's missing?"

"I did all the market research more than a year ago. I know what will work here, it's just… It's not what I want to do. I'm not passionate about it."

"And that's important to you?"

"Of course it is!" he snapped and then instantly cringed. No need to wake up Emery. His voice lowered, he went on, "When I open the place, I'm going to be there every day for the first three to six months. I need to be passionate about what I'm cooking, and the name of the restaurant and the décor all need to reflect what I'm trying to say with the food. It's a vicious circle and I can't seem to get anything to stick."

They were quiet for a moment before Christian asked, "What are you looking at right now?"

Carter chuckled. "You wouldn't believe me if I told you."

"Try me."

"A Christmas tree."

Now it was Christian's turn to laugh. "Seriously? It's not even Thanksgiving yet."

Carter explained Emery's thought process for decorating the house and how much it had helped them get started on the book. "We got some good pictures and I have to admit, the place looks great. All of this stuff should have come down days ago, but we can't seem to make ourselves do it."

"So…you and Emery, huh? I mean, she's great and I always thought that, but knowing the history between the two of you? It just seems weird."

"Wait—how did you… I mean, I never said…"

Christian found that hilarious. "Dude, really? Every word you just spoke about her said it all. In all the years the two of you have known each other, you've never talked about her like that. That's number one. Number two, there's no way you would have brought her out to Montauk with you if there wasn't something going on, so don't try to deny it."

He sighed. "Okay, fine. But I wasn't going to deny it, I just wasn't going to share, that's all."

"Well, that's stupid. You made me talk about my feelings with Sophie. What makes you think I'm not going to do the same to you?"

Swiping a hand over his eyes, he wearily replied, "Are you?"

"Of course I am! Hell, I'm practically giddy right now knowing how the tables have turned!"

Great.

"So why are you sitting alone looking at a Christmas tree in the middle of the night when you no doubt have a beautiful woman in your bed?"

"I already told you I couldn't sleep."

His brother made a *tsk*-ing sound. "And there was no other way to exhaust yourself than leaving the warmth of your bed and sitting in the dark looking at a tree? Really?"

There was no way he was going to share just how much he and Emery had exhausted one another already tonight, and how that still wasn't enough to make him sleep.

"Remember when we were kids and we'd sneak downstairs after Mom and Dad were asleep and play with the train under the tree?"

Christian was quiet for a moment. "Oh yeah. Holy crap, I haven't thought about that in years. Maybe Sophie and I will get a train for under the tree this year."

Carter studied his. "Yeah, this tree doesn't have one either, but maybe I'll do the same at home."

"What made you think of that?"

"This whole project was supposed to be low-effort— throw some recipes down, write a couple of sappy blurbs, and be done with it."

"But…?"

"When I arrived in New York and found Emery at the condo, she began poking at me to put more thought into it, more effort. She made me think about the holidays we spent when we were growing up, and…I don't know—it wasn't all bad, right? I mean, not all of our memories of our childhood were bad."

He heard Christian sigh. "No. No, they weren't. In fact, there were probably more good times than bad. It was just easier to keep the bad ones front and center when we got older because of the way Dad treated us." He paused. "But the holidays were always different. He was different."

This was why he'd called his brother—Carter needed the reminder of how life growing up with his parents hadn't been so bad.

"I remember him getting things for me at Christmas that I wanted but never mentioned to him or Mom," Christian was saying. "It was like they overheard my thoughts some-how, and it always amazed me."

"How do you know it wasn't Mom?"

"Because it was always stuff he and I could use together and—believe it or not—he was always excited to talk with me about it. Stuff like model cars and airplanes, new ski equipment… It was the things I was too afraid to ask for because I figured they'd think it was frivolous. And yet each year there was always one gift like that."

Now that Carter thought about it, it was the same with him. Unfortunately, he'd assumed the gifts were all his mother's doing. "Maybe we should ask her about that when we're there next weekend." He paused. "Which, by the way, thank you for being willing to come. I know it seems crazy."

"It's not a big deal. Sophie and I were trying to find the time to visit Mom and couldn't seem to decide, so this was the perfect excuse to go. It will be nice to see everyone again for something fun. I was talking to Megan and she said Summer and Ethan may take the trip too."

"Really? That would be great. It seems like the only time we all get together anymore is for big events like weddings and funerals. Which sucks. It's going to be great to have something low-key where we can catch up and relax together."

"Tell me about it. And I think it will be nice to take work talk off the table," Christian added.

"That was always Dad's thing. You know that. Uncle William and Uncle Robert were never the ones to bring up anything work-related."

"Well, now that there's no one for Uncle William to play matchmaker to, he might be looking for something to talk about!"

That had them both laughing. "No way. By now he's got grandkids to brag about and then that's going to turn all the attention to you and when you're making Mom a grandmother."

"Oh no."

"Oh yeah. And I'll sit back and take it all in, feeling no pressure at all," Carter teased. "It's gonna be awesome."

"Not so fast, little brother. Now that you're involved with Emery, I can easily sway the conversation toward you and when you're going to settle down. How would you like that?" Christian challenged.

"Don't upset the chef. You wouldn't want me distracted and ruining dinner, would you?"

Christian burst out laughing. "Leave it to you to find a loophole. Nice."

"I do what I can."

"So what are you making? Sticking with the usual traditional menu or are we getting something with the famous Carter Montgomery flair?"

"Actually, this project had me remembering the Christmas menus from when we were little and we used to have a houseful of people. It was more of a buffet than a sit-down affair. I'm making a selection of foods from back then."

"Oh wow! That's going to be awesome!"

"We're planning two big meals—the big dinner on Saturday night, and then a traditional holiday brunch on Sunday before we all leave."

"Speak for yourself. Sophie and I are leaving on Tuesday, and I think Megan and Alex are doing the same. No doubt Summer and Ethan will leave with them. You're seriously heading out on Sunday?"

"Um…that was the plan," he said hesitantly. "I've been away from home for a month and need to get back."

"So what's another couple of days? C'mon. We never get to hang out and relax. It will be fun."

In that moment, Carter knew his brother was right.

They didn't get together and visit with one another nearly enough. And really, what was another couple of days in the grand scheme of things?

"You know what? You're right. I'll change my flight to Tuesday. What time are you flying out?"

"We're leaving Mom's after breakfast on Tuesday— sometime around ten. Our flight out is at one. Same with everyone else. We're taking a limo to the airport." While they discussed travel arrangements, Carter went to the kitchen and wrote it all down so he could change his plans in the morning.

Now as he made his way back toward the sofa, he realized he felt good. Relaxed. And more than likely would be able to fall asleep.

"This all sounds good, Chris. Thanks."

"What about Emery? Is she heading back with you?"

Just thinking about it—about how she wasn't and they were going to be apart—had him rubbing his chest. He sank back down on the couch. "No. She's heading home to straighten everything out." He shared the story about Emery's ex and—even though he figured his brother must have heard some of this from their mother—Christian listened without interrupting. "I hate that she has to deal with this. She has no idea what's going to happen when she gets back home—how people will react, if her job will be waiting for her...it's a damn mess. And the worst part is how her parents are still backing that scumbag."

"Damn. That's got to hurt."

The image of holding Emery in his arms out on the beach earlier came to mind and he had to fight back the wave of anger he had toward her family and her ex for making her feel like she didn't matter.

Because she did.

And if they were all foolish enough not to realize that—not to be grateful every day for the amazing woman they had in their lives—then they didn't deserve her.

He was getting wound up and knew if he didn't cut himself off right now, he was going to be wide awake again. "I wish she was coming with me rather than going home."

"Have you asked her to go with you?"

"No," he replied wearily. "I know she has to do this. She's tired of hiding out and putting her life on hold. What she has to go back to, though, sucks." As he said the words, a war was waging within himself. From everything she'd shared with him—which still wasn't much—no one was on her side. No one was protecting her. And he feared that when she went back home, she was going to get a lot of grief because of her absence. Carter wanted nothing more than to protect her from all of it—to stand up to all those people and demand they apologize to Emery and leave her in peace.

Somehow, he doubted she'd appreciate him going all Neanderthal on her family and friends.

Didn't stop him from wanting to, though.

"So...this is serious, huh?"

"What is?"

"You and Emery. This isn't just a way to pass the time. You're crazy about her."

It wasn't a question and Carter didn't hesitate. "I am." A nervous laugh followed that simple statement. "In a million years I never saw this coming, but for some insane reason, this works."

"And how does she feel?"

I wish I knew.

"We haven't really talked about…you know—"

"Feelings?" Christian finished for him, humor lacing his voice.

"Exactly. In case you haven't been following along, we've had a lot on our plates."

"Can I offer one piece of advice?"

"No."

After a snort, his brother's reply was, "Too bad."

Sighing dramatically, Carter said, "Go ahead. I'm about ready to crash, so drop whatever pearl of wisdom you've got so I can go to bed." He said it lightly but knew his words could also come off as a little snarky.

"Don't wait to talk to her," Christian said, his tone serious and a little somber. "Sophie and I lost a lot of time because I didn't want to talk about how I was feeling—and not just about her, but about everything I was going through after Dad died." He paused. "If you really care about her and see this relationship going somewhere, don't be afraid to talk about how you feel."

Yeah, this wasn't news to him, but…

"You know the relationship we've always had," Carter said. "We were opponents, rivals, and at times enemies. We have this snarky banter and sometimes it's—it's awkward. Like when one of us is being serious, it's not always obvious. More than once we've offended each other because of the way we react. It's hard to undo years of snark and animosity, you know?"

"Unfortunately, I don't. I've never been in that situation and I certainly don't want to make light of it. Just… don't wait, Carter. This weekend is going to be loud and boisterous and out-and-out crazy. You've got a long drive to Mom's. Use that time to make sure she's going to be okay and that she knows how you feel and you'll be there if she needs you."

Unable to help himself, he yawned. "I don't want to fight with her in the car."

"No one said fight, Carter. Talk. I know you can do that."

"But what if… What if she doesn't need me?" And man, did that hurt to say out loud.

"I wish I could answer that. I don't know Emery all that well, but I'd like to think she needs you just as much as you clearly need her."

It was too much for Carter to wrap his brain around at this hour. When he finally said good night to his brother, he tossed the phone down on the sofa, turned the lights off on the tree, and slowly made his way back to the bedroom. Emery was still sound asleep, sprawled diagonally across the bed.

She was a bed hog.

Chuckling, he walked around to the opposite side of the bed and stripped down before sliding between the sheets. It was slow work, but he managed to maneuver them both so she was spooned against him, her back to his front. His favorite position for them to sleep in. He kissed the top of her head and breathed her in. She was warm and soft and… Yeah, he was crazy about her.

"How did we get here, beautiful girl?" he whispered.

Of course she didn't respond, but that didn't stop him from imagining her response.

She'd remind him of all the facts first—she was always logical. Then she'd try to make light of it all and blame it on proximity before lightly putting herself down and questioning his taste in women.

There was nothing wrong with her, and there certainly wasn't anything wrong with his taste. She didn't give herself enough credit. Ever. And that more than anything bothered him. She'd always been the most intelligent, the most confident woman he'd known, and to see how this whole situation with her ex had stripped her of that? It filled him with rage. He wanted that confidence back. Wanted her to try to outsmart him and everyone around her just because she could.

Over the last several weeks, he'd created situations specifically to make that happen. If she was aware of it, she didn't say anything. No doubt she'd be pissed. Still, every time he caught a glimpse of the girl he used to know, it made him smile.

And how twisted was that—arguing with her and being yelled at by her made his day!

This was probably the most dysfunctional relationship he'd ever been in, but it was also the most fulfilling and exciting. He enjoyed the challenge. And more than anything, he enjoyed knowing they were equals in every sense of the word.

He kissed her again as he closed his eyes. Beside him, she hummed softly in her sleep.

"You can argue all you want, but I'm not letting you go," he whispered. "This is where you belong."

Chapter 7

"WHAT IF I JUST ADD—"

"No."

"But it will add so much flavor! We could just—"

"*No!*"

Sighing, Carter looked at the ingredients in front of him. Bland meatloaf. Bland mashed potatoes. And—"I'm sorry, did you say you wanted *corn* with this?"

Beside him, Emery nodded, her smile going from ear to ear. "That's right. Corn. Not creamed, not grilled, not anything but good ol' corn with a little bit of butter." The look she gave him was downright impish. "It's killing you, isn't it?"

It wasn't, but he wasn't going to admit it. This was the third night of him making comfort food for her. The first night, he'd made fried chicken and mashed potatoes. He was finding that mashed potatoes were a big thing to Emery. If given the opportunity, she'd have them at every meal.

Not on his watch.

Last night, he made spaghetti and meatballs.

And the ways she had thanked him afterwards made him blush just thinking about it.

Neither of those meals had been particularly challenging, but they were extremely satisfying. It had been so long since he'd made something so simple and gotten such pleasure from it.

And not just from Emery.

When he glanced over at her, she was looking at him expectantly. Oh, right…she'd asked him a question.

"I wouldn't say killing me, but I just have some ideas I wish you'd let me experiment with."

She sighed loudly, crossing her arms over her chest. "You're going to ruin this, aren't you?"

"How can you say that? I haven't told you what I'm thinking."

The eye roll was her only response.

"I was thinking of stuffing the meatloaf with bacon and cheddar cheese," he stated, gauging her reaction.

None.

"The bacon would be cooked first and be extra crispy— just the way you like it."

She blinked. Her expression could only be described as bored.

"I could do a barbecue sauce glaze. It would be like a barbecue bacon cheeseburger and—"

"Say what, now?" she asked, leaning in a little closer— almost as if she were suddenly very interested in what he had to say.

The way to this girl's heart was definitely through her stomach.

Leaning on the granite counter top, he gave her his most charming smile. "That's right. I can make your beloved meatloaf taste like your favorite barbecue bacon cheese-burger. That is…if you'll let me."

Her beautiful eyes narrowed. "You're not going to put anything weird in there, are you? Just the bacon and cheese, right?"

"Define weird," he challenged. "Because even a basic

meatloaf requires some seasonings. I don't want you freaking out when you see me adding garlic or onion to the mix."

"I'm aware of the use of seasonings, Carter. I'm not completely clueless when it comes to cooking."

He shrugged. "I wouldn't know, considering you've yet to cook anything other than frozen pizza and microwave popcorn."

Watching her expression turn fierce was practically a turn-on at this point. There was something a little twisted about how much pleasure he got out of making her mad and then making love to her, but not twisted enough to make him stop.

"Bastard," she snapped before storming around the island and launching herself into his arms. The kiss was brutal and full of raw need and emotion. Her legs wrapped around his waist as his hands gripped her ass.

They'd done this enough times where it shouldn't be this exciting—this frantic. And yet it still was. Hell, every time she was near him, he felt like this. He kissed her like he couldn't get enough and she clung to him like she wanted to crawl inside of him.

Dishes crashed to the floor, but it barely registered. Placing Emery on the countertop, he rained kisses across her cheek as his hands snaked under her shirt and whipped it over her head. She bit his shoulder, and he bit her back, both of them laughing in between the madness because this was them and it was *fun*.

Sex with Emery was fun.

It was crazy and wild and sometimes completely out of control, but it was always fun because they took the time to be playful with one another.

Kicking aside a baking dish that was now broken in half,

he said, "There goes dinner. And I was really looking forward to that meatloaf."

"You can think about food right now?"

Pulling back, Carter laughed heartily. "You can't? Oh my God, did we finally find the *one* thing that keeps you from thinking about food?" He feigned surprise, placing his hand over his heart. "I never thought I'd live to see the day!"

She swatted at him playfully right before reaching a hand into his hair and bringing his lips back to hers. "Smartass."

The woman kissed like she did everything else—completely. She consumed him and left him feeling a little weak, and while he did his best to give as good as he was getting, there was no doubt he was the one being seduced here.

And that was more than all right with him.

Clothes shifted—they weren't going to the bedroom. Carter had learned to be prepared at all times where sex and Emery were concerned and as he tossed her panties over his shoulder, he was thankful he'd learned that early on.

It was all breathless sighs and moans of pleasure. It was fast and hard and a little frantic.

It was perfect.

Minutes later, when his legs threatened to give out and Emery was draped over his shoulder, that's exactly what he told her.

Couldn't stop himself from damn-near gushing about it.

"You're perfect, Em. So damn perfect," he said, his voice a soft whisper against her skin.

Slowly, Emery lifted her head and gave him a very satisfied smile as she gently cupped his cheek in her hand. "I think you're perfect too, Carter."

The kiss was soft, lazy. He rested his forehead against hers as he waited for his heart rate to return to normal. And once it did, he helped her down from the counter. As they both fixed their clothes, he looked around at the mess everywhere.

"I think there's another baking pan we can use," he said, looking inside the cabinets.

Emery came and crouched down beside him. "We could order takeout if there isn't one."

Turning his head, he looked at her. "No way. I promised you these dinners and I'm not backing out on the last one. We're going to be on the road most of the day tomorrow and I want to do this for you."

Her smile was grateful and he saw the emotion in her eyes that said more than any words ever could. This was his opening—this was the time to take his brother's advice and talk to her about what was going to happen after the weekend. Where were they going and where did she see them a week from now? As much as he wanted to know, there was a part of him that was afraid of the answer.

Looking back into the cabinet, he pulled out a glass loaf pan and held it up triumphantly. "Here we go. This will work just fine." Then he stood and held out a hand to help her up and cursed himself for being a coward. "How about a little wine?" he asked, hoping to distract them both for a few minutes until he got his thoughts under control.

"How about a beer?" she asked from across the room. "Somehow, I wasn't envisioning wine with meatloaf."

Amused, he responded, "A good wine can go with anything, but I'll have whatever you're having."

She handed him a beer with a wink. They gently tapped

bottles and then Carter put his attention into prepping the meatloaf. Within minutes, bacon was frying and he was seasoning the ground beef, while Emery sat on one of the bar stools at the kitchen island with her laptop.

"Whatcha looking at?"

"I got a rough draft of the cookbook back and I'm looking it over to see what else we may want to add."

They worked in silence and it was very comfortable to Carter. He was used to working in a kitchen that was loud and chaotic, but he found it equally comfortable to sit in companionable silence with Emery.

Color me surprised…

Once he placed the meatloaf in the oven, he turned his attention to prepping the mashed potatoes, quickly peeling and cutting them up and getting them on the stove. When that was going, he made quick work of cleaning a couple of ears of fresh corn and blanching them before cutting the corn off the cob. Emery had claimed that frozen corn was fine, but he had his standards. This meal was already something he would never have thought to make on his own, so there was no way he was going to use frozen products when he knew how much better the fresh version was.

He wondered if Emery would be able to tell the difference.

Looking up at her, he smiled. She was biting her lip, her expression serious as she studied her computer screen. It didn't matter that this project was nothing more than a fundraiser; she was treating it as if she was editing the next *New York Times* bestseller.

Not that he expected anything less. Emery Monaghan always gave one hundred percent to everything she did.

And now that things were a little less contentious between them, he found it to be something he loved about her. And the fact that she was doing this to help his mother made him love her even more.

At the sound of her sighing, he asked, "Everything okay?"

His voice seemed to startle her. "What?" She paused. "I mean, yeah. I guess." And then she was studying the screen again.

Carter walked around the island and came to stand beside her. She quickly shut the laptop and stared at him.

"What's going on, Em?"

"Nothing." Jumping up from her seat, she went over to the oven and glanced inside. "This smells fantastic. What kind of glaze did you end up doing?"

He knew a distraction when he heard it. Going to her, Carter took one of her hands in his and led her back to her seat. "It's barbecue and you know it. Now what's going on?"

This time her sigh was full of frustration. "You really want to know?"

"I wouldn't have asked otherwise," he said mildly.

Exhaling, she began, "Okay, this cookbook? The charity your mother is chairing? They're having a big dinner gala the first Saturday in December for it."

"O-kay…"

"My parents are going to be there."

It wasn't that she never shared much about her relationship with her parents, but she'd shared enough for Carter to know they were still a bit of a sore subject for her in the light of recent events.

"Of course I'm going to go," she explained, "and right

now, they have no idea I'm helping with it or how I've kept in touch with your mother. I'm trying to figure out how to explain it to them without it turning into another uncomfortable conversation."

Seemed to him any conversation she had with them was going to be uncomfortable. "Em, there isn't anything wrong with what you're doing here. You needed to take a leave of absence from work—at your boss's request, not your own. I would think they'd find it commendable that you found something to do for a good cause."

"You would think," she murmured.

Taking her hand back in his, he said softly, "Hey, don't let them minimize this or make you feel like you did something wrong. If anything, they're the ones who should feel bad about how they've spent their time. Instead of supporting you—their daughter—they put their support behind the man who caused all the problems!" His voice rose with every word. "You shouldn't be feeling anything but proud of yourself."

Her eyes were wide and she looked a little shocked by his outburst. "You don't understand—"

"Yes, I do!" he cried, releasing her and taking a couple of steps back. "Do you know how successful I was when I opened my first restaurant? It was an overnight success! I had food critics praising me in every publication and yet my father made me feel like I had made a mistake. Why? Because I didn't do things *his* way! I struggled for years with it. He made me second-guess myself and my passion because he never once said he was proud of me. And even after I achieved success, he still wouldn't give an inch. It wasn't until my second place opened that he finally unclenched enough to show a little bit of approval. Not too much, mind you." Now he began to pace.

"That's why I sort of phoned in the third restaurant. I mean, why mess with success, right? It was a carbon copy of the other two and it was a no-brainer. But this place? I want the feeling I had when I first started. I want to know I'm creating something new and fabulous and original. Yet all I can seem to focus on is the fear I had—of being that kid who still wasn't enough to please his father." Slamming his palms down on the granite, he looked her fiercely in the eye. "Don't make my mistake, Em. Stand up for yourself!"

"Carter, I... It's not that easy! They have a way of speaking to me that just... It makes me want to just cringe and hide and...I don't know!"

Tears welled in her eyes but he didn't back off. "You need to go to that gala with your head held high and show them that you can do anything! You walked away from the life they talked you into—they should be apologizing to you. You went your own way and you did something incredible!"

Her shoulders sagged. "It's just a cookbook, Carter. It's not like I went out and found the cure for cancer."

"No, but you helped contribute to the hospice foundation. And that is something no one can take away from you and that thousands of people are going to remember. You're making a difference in the lives of people who need it. Unlike your parents, who seem to just want to latch on to someone else's success or ride someone else's coattails. I say shame on them!"

They were both silent for a long moment before she gave him a weak smile. "You're pretty fierce, Carter."

His hand reached out and cupped her cheek. "When I'm

passionate about something, I am." He moved closer. "And right now, I'm feeling very passionate about you."

She laughed softly. "Dinner's almost ready. But I'm sure we could have a repeat performance of our pre-dinner show."

He didn't laugh.

Didn't even smile.

"I'm not talking about sex here, Em. I'm talking about how I feel about you. Period." He swallowed hard—it was time to go big or go home. "I'm crazy about you. I still don't know how we got here or why it took so damn long for me to open my eyes, but…now that we are, I don't want to go back. I'm not looking for this to end."

"Carter…"

"I know I have to go back to New Orleans next week and you're going back upstate, but…I don't know, we need to talk about where we see ourselves going." Resting his forehead against hers, he added, "I know where I see us, but I need to know where you do." Closing his eyes, Carter held his breath and waited for her response.

And waited.

And waited.

And just when he was about to prompt her, she finally responded. "I've been afraid to think about it."

"Why?" he whispered.

Emery pulled back and looked at him sadly. "Because I wasn't sure what you were thinking. I was afraid this was all one-sided and…that this was something you normally do." When he looked at her curiously, she clarified, "I know you always dated a lot of women. I don't remember a time when you were ever single. I thought maybe we were just—"

He didn't let her finish. His anger burned bright, but he quickly pushed it aside. "I've been single more than you'll ever know," he said gruffly. "And for the record, I've never done this. I've never felt the need to be with someone the way I need to be with you. I've never lived with a woman, and I think we can both agree that's what we've been doing for the last several weeks. And it was never weird and there was never a time when I wished you weren't here."

"Carter—"

"I'm serious, Em. Even before we started sleeping together, I genuinely enjoyed being with you." He caressed her cheek. "The thought of going back to work next week has me in knots, and that's never happened before. I've never taken this much time away from my restaurants."

"You've been busy with the construction here," she reasoned and Carter couldn't help but smirk. "What? Why are you looking at me like that?"

"If you think the only reason why I'm still here is because of construction, then you're crazy."

Her brows furrowed a bit before she seemed to understand. "Well, that and the cookbook project."

But he shook his head. "Wrong again, brainiac," he said softly, teasingly. "*You're* the reason I'm still here. You're the reason I haven't gone home. And you're the reason I'm still working on this damn book. I could have had it done weeks ago and I would have been okay with the guilt my mother threw at me over it." He paused, scanning her beautiful face. "The only reason I'm still here instead of in one of my restaurants is you."

Her eyes went a little wide again as she gasped softly. "But...I don't... We never..."

Confusion was an adorable look on her, he thought. "It doesn't matter what we did or didn't do before. I'm only concerned with what we do from now on." He swallowed hard, unable to believe just how terrifying talking so honestly about his feelings could be. "I know we both have jobs and commitments that aren't anywhere near one another and I have no idea how to make it all work yet. What I do know is that I want to figure it all out with you."

"I want that too, Carter. I really do," she said, her voice no more than a whisper. "Are we crazy? Is this just too bizarre for us to think about?"

Shaking his head, he told her, "No. It's not crazy. It makes perfect sense. We've never been able to stay away from each other—not while we were younger, not while we were competing against each other for everything when we were in school. It just took us a while to figure out what to do with all those feelings." He pulled her in close. "Personally, I'm a big fan of what we've been doing with them lately."

Her laugh wrapped around him and had him smiling. "Me too. But—"

Now he laughed. "I knew you were eventually going to find something to argue."

"I'm not arguing."

"But...?"

Before answering, she gave an exaggerated eye roll. "But you can't possibly think this has been going on since—since high school. That's crazy."

"You're wrong. I mean, I'm not gonna lie to you, Em. You made me crazy with all the competitiveness, but what you never knew was, well..." *Just tell her.* "I always wished things could have been different. There was a time when I tried to ask you out and—"

"Oh my gosh!" Her hands flew to her mouth before she stepped away from him. "You're just saying that. I would have remembered if you—"

"I tried," he persisted. "We were working on the history project in Mr. Winslow's class, junior year. I came over to your house because it was quieter than the school library. There were pages and pages of notes scattered all over your kitchen table and we were eating—"

"Brownies you picked up on the way over," she finished for him.

He smiled because she remembered. "That's right. You mentioned how much you loved the bakery over on South Main, so I stopped there and picked up a couple of brownies for us. For a few minutes we sat down and talked—not about the project or school or anything serious. It was the first time we'd ever done that and I kept thinking…I wanted to do that more with you."

"Then why…?"

He shrugged. "I chickened out. I was afraid you'd laugh at me and tell me I was being a jerk or…I don't know. Something."

She was quiet for several moments before admitting, "I probably would have thought you weren't serious or that you were teasing me. After all, why would the most popular boy in school want to ask me out?"

"Why wouldn't I?"

"Oh, come on, Carter. Be serious. You dated all those… popular girls." She shuddered. "It was borderline cliché."

"Hey! That's a little unfair. And you were popular too, Em. Don't try to pretend you weren't."

"It wasn't the same!" she countered. "I was studious, not sexy!"

This wasn't an argument he was going to win.

But he had one more thing to say.

Stepping in close to her again, he said, "Believe it or not, it was your intellect that was the most appealing. You've always been beautiful. Whether you want to believe that or not is up to you, but it's the truth. You just never tried to use your looks to get attention."

And before he could say anything else, one of the timers beeped and he needed to pay attention to their dinner—to make it the best one yet for her.

Because, he was finding out, there wasn't anything he wouldn't do for Emery.

Even if it meant preparing an ordinary meal like meatloaf.

"That was amazing!"

"I know, right?"

"I mean, I knew it all smelled really good, but it was so much better than I imagined."

"I can't believe you're surprised."

"Well, trust me. I am."

Emery laughed. "Carter, you can't seriously be this surprised! You know you're an amazing chef, so stop fishing for compliments!"

Standing, he tossed his napkin on the table and walked over to the refrigerator to grab a bottle of water. "I'm not fishing! I'm genuinely…surprised!"

And honestly, so was she.

For weeks she'd watched her cocky chef swagger around the kitchen, boasting about whatever it was he was making, and not once had she seen the look of pure delight on his face like she was seeing right now.

"You know, if this was on the menu in one of your restaurants, I'd be tempted to eat there."

His bark of laughter was infectious. "Right. Because that's what I should do—a junk food and comfort food restaurant. I mean, that would be..." The words trailed off and he instantly sobered before practically sprinting over to the living room to grab his notebook.

"What are you doing?"

He shushed her as he took his seat and began making notes. He'd done this several times before that she'd noticed—he'd get an idea and then go deep into thought while he wrote it all out. No matter how many times she encouraged him to use his laptop and type it, Carter was old school and seemed to take great pleasure in hand-writing his thoughts.

Crazy man.

Without disturbing him, Emery stood and began to clear the table. While she went about cleaning up the rest of the kitchen, she snuck glances at him to see if he had so much as lifted his head.

He hadn't.

By the time everything was cleaned and put away, she wasn't sure what she was supposed to do with herself. The decorator and her crew were coming back tomorrow to take the Christmas decorations away, so while Carter was busy writing, Emery decided she would get a head start.

For an hour, she worked on packing up the decorations in the dining room before moving into the living room. The tree was too big of a project and part of her really wanted to leave it up as long as possible, so she worked on the miscellaneous decorations from the mantel and coffee table.

The temperature outside was cool, but once she was done and Carter still hadn't surfaced from his work, she opened the sliding doors that led to the deck and slipped outside. The sound of the surf always relaxed her and rather than walk down to the beach, she moved over to the fire pit and started it up.

"Thank you, inventor of the gas-flamed fire pit," she murmured, sitting down on one of the large chairs flanking it. Curling her feet under her, Emery hugged herself to stay warm until the heat reached her.

Resting her head back, she looked up at the starry sky and sighed. This was their last night here and the thought of leaving was unappealing. Carter's admission earlier weighed heavily on her mind. She had almost resigned herself to their relationship coming to an end after their weekend at his mother's. Knowing he wanted to keep seeing her made her happier than she was comfortable admitting to herself.

It should have been too soon to consider getting involved with anyone again. She was still getting over Derek's betrayal and their breakup. Was she foolish to jump into another relationship so soon?

Am I ready for another relationship?

Her immediate answer was *yes*. The truth was, her relationship with Derek had been failing for a long time. The only reason she'd stayed in it as long as she had was because of her parents.

The sound of the sliding glass doors opening had her turning her head. Carter stood there smiling at her, and suddenly she felt all the things she'd never felt with anyone but him.

Tingly.

Excited.

And very, very needy.

When he looked at her with one of his lopsided grins, Emery felt like she was looking at everything she ever wanted. Then he turned and motioned to the room behind him in surprise.

"I thought we weren't taking anything down until tomorrow."

Shaking her head, she laughed softly. "While you were over there no doubt getting a hand cramp, I decided to get a bit of a jump start on dismantling Christmas."

Carter walked slowly toward her until he was sharing the chair with her. "I hate to see it all go. I think it looked great around here and it put me in a better mood. It inspired me."

Relief washed over her. "I'm glad it helped."

Kissing her on the forehead, he said, "You helped. All the rest was just a small perk and made for a nice background. Everything else was all you."

So many thoughts raced through her head—things she wanted to say, ways she could respond—but for the life of her, she couldn't utter a single word.

After a few minutes, he turned off the flame and led her back into the house. "But if this is our last night with the tree," he said, oblivious to her thoughts, "then I say let's set up camp out here tonight and sleep under the twinkly lights. What do you say?"

At first, she thought he was crazy. There was an amazingly comfortable bed in the next room and he wanted to sleep on the living room floor? "Umm..."

"When we were kids, Christian and I would camp out in the living room at least once while the tree was up. Our parents had no idea—at least, I don't think they did—and we'd sit up and talk about everything we thought was under the tree."

Her heart melted a little as she imagined a young Carter doing such a thing. "Did you ever get any of them right?"

He chuckled. "Only because we knew we'd always get new pajamas on Christmas Eve and at least three new sweaters. My mom is the master at using odd-shaped boxes so we couldn't guess what was inside. One year she used empty cereal boxes and shoe boxes to confuse us."

It totally seemed like something Eliza would do. "That's very sweet."

He shrugged. "What about you? Ever try to guess what was under the tree?"

"Honestly? No. There was never any...whimsy about the holiday. We gave our parents a list of what we'd like and we got it. There were never any boxes under the tree until Christmas morning."

He pulled back with a look of utter shock. "Seriously? Not even a few for decorative purposes?"

"Nope. My mother thought it always looked like clutter, and she hates clutter."

Dark brows furrowed as he studied her. "How did you turn out the way you did after growing up in that environment?"

Emery knew it wasn't an insult. "I just knew that wasn't

how I wanted to be and I vowed that once I was out and living on my own that I wouldn't be. Turns out it wasn't as easy as I thought."

Taking her by the hand, he led them over to the sofa, where they sat. "What do you mean?"

"For all my talk about making my own way, I let them dictate way too much of my life. At the time, I wasn't aware it was happening, but now that I've had some distance, I can see it. It's what I was thinking about while I was sitting out by the fire."

He kissed her temple. "I'm sorry, Em. I really am. I hate that you have to deal with all of this, and I hate it even more that you have to go back there alone."

She shrugged. "I have to do it eventually. I need to. Even if I decide to sell my place and quit my job, they're still my family and I'm going to have to talk to them too."

Then he pulled back even further. "Are you?"

"Am I what?"

"Are you thinking of quitting your job and selling your place?" It almost sounded hopeful.

Letting out a long breath was her first response. "My gut reaction is to say yes, but the reality isn't going to be quite that easy."

"Why not? You can find a job doing anything you want, anywhere you want! We could—"

"No!" she quickly interrupted, placing her hand on his knee. "I don't want you or anyone helping me with this. It's how I got into this whole place I'm in now. It's time for me to do something on my own without any interference or help from anyone."

"Em, everyone needs help. There's no shame in it."

"For me there is. I've let that happen too many times in my life and now I have to take a stand and do what I need to do, the way I need to do it."

His expression was intense, but he didn't say anything. She knew if she asked, he'd not only have a job for her tomorrow but a place for her to live and everything she could need. It wasn't that she resented it, but it would be too easy to let him do it. For far too long she'd let people do too much for her—to the point that she didn't recognize herself or the life she was living. She still had no idea how it would all go or how she was going to make the changes that needed to be made; all Emery knew was that it was time to sink or swim on her own. And at the end of it all, she hoped Carter would understand and be there for her.

With a sigh, she looked at him and offered a small smile. "You have already done so much for me. But when the weekend is over and you head your way and I head mine, there are things I have to do by myself. I hope you understand."

He nodded. "It doesn't mean I don't want to be there to protect you."

Reaching up, she put her hand to his face—reveling in the feel of his stubbled jaw. "And I'm sure there will be times when I wish I had let you," she admitted. "But the fact remains that until I learn to stand up for myself and face the fallout, I'm going to be stuck in this self-destructive pattern."

Carter's expression didn't change, but his voice was gruff when he said, "You're the strongest woman I know. And when you go home, you need to remember that and not let anyone try to convince you that you're not. You're strong and smart and beautiful, and they're all intimidated by that. By tearing you down, they make themselves feel stronger.

Show them what you're made of, Em. Prove to them how wrong they are."

His words made her want to jump up and do it all right now, but it wasn't possible. Not when they had more important things to do.

"So are we going to move a mattress out here or something?" she asked, giving him a sexy grin and hoping he wouldn't mind the abrupt change of subject.

His laughter was infectious. Standing, he grasped her hand and pulled her to her feet. "If that's what you want, then that's what we'll do."

Together, they went into the bedroom and clumsily made their way back to the tree, pulling the king-size mattress. Sofas had to be moved, along with a coffee table and end table, but eventually they made it all fit. Next came the pillows and blankets, and by the time everything was in place, they were both breathless.

"That was a bit more of a workout than I was planning on," she said, collapsing on the bed. Carter was still standing and looking down at her with amusement.

"How about I make us some popcorn to eat while we relax?"

Her eyes went wide, just like her smile. "Really? We're gonna eat in bed?"

"Not only that, but I'll get you a glass of extra-fizzy Coke if you'd like."

Now she was practically giddy. Pushing up on her elbows, she asked, "Are you having some too?"

"I'm having a glass of wine, but I'll definitely have popcorn with you." His smile was sweet and wonderful, and just as she was about to get up, he held out a hand to stop her.

"You just sit here and get comfortable. Five minutes and I'll be right beside you."

He turned away, but Emery jumped up anyway and ran into the bedroom to change. Most nights, they ended up naked, but tonight she was going to put on what she normally slept in when she was home alone—her boy-shorts and a tank top. When she left the bedroom a few minutes later, Carter was walking toward the bed, but stopped in his tracks when he spotted her.

She saw him swallow hard as his eyes raked over her. Unable to resist, she struck a sassy pose. "I thought I'd get a little more comfortable."

"The first time I saw you at the condo, you were wearing something like this and that image is burned on my brain. I always thought you had a great figure, but that night confirmed it."

After everything they'd shared since meeting up again, Emery thought she'd be used to him saying things like that. But she wasn't. His praise of her, his compliments, always made her blush. Without a word, she climbed onto the mattress and made herself comfortable. When she was settled and sitting up against the pillows, she held out a hand to take the bowl of popcorn from him. Once she set it down, she reached for the glass of soda he'd poured for her. "Thank you."

A curt nod was Carter's only response before he walked back to the kitchen to grab his glass of wine. When he was back by the bed, he placed it on the floor before stripping down to his boxers.

And Carter looked really good in his boxers.

Slipping into bed beside her, he made himself comfortable before putting an arm around her and pulling her in close, balancing the bowl of popcorn on his lap. They sat in silence for several minutes, staring at the tree and eating their snack.

"If there were gifts under the tree right now, what would you hope was there?" he asked.

Humming softly, Emery considered her options. It had been a long time since anyone had surprised her with anything and the gifts she normally found for herself under the family Christmas tree tended to be of the more practical variety.

"Nothing practical," she blurted out and then instantly covered her mouth and giggled. Carter's dark brows arched at her response and it took her a moment to explain her theory. "Sometimes it's nice to get something other than clothes or office supplies."

"We always get new pajamas," he said with a serene smile, grabbing a handful of the kettle corn. "I swear, we used to hate it, but now I look forward to it every year. It's not Christmas without them."

"What else do you normally get?"

He playfully tugged on her hair. "Oh no. We were talking about you. Now focus. Look at the tree and imagine there are dozens of beautifully wrapped gifts under it. What are you hoping is there for you?"

The mild huff of annoyance was out before she could stop it, but then Emery focused on the tree. "I would love a cashmere robe," she said after a long moment. "Something so soft and warm and completely impractical, considering the only one seeing it is me."

"I wouldn't say that."

"And I'd love to get some of those really great-smelling bath sets. You know, bath bombs and lotions and all that fun stuff. I love soaking in a nice hot bath after work some-times." She turned her head and grinned at him.

Nodding, he commented, "But you haven't used the tub in the master bath. How come?"

Grabbing her own handful of popcorn, she shrugged. "Probably because every time I mentioned going to take a bath or shower, you showed up and dragged me into the shower with you." It was said lightly—she didn't want to offend him—but yeah, it would have been nice to soak in that big glorious tub at least once.

Carter kicked the blankets off and went to stand up.

"Wait, what are you doing?"

"Going to draw you a bath," he said casually. "I know there's no bath bomb, but I'm sure we can improvise with something and at least get you a bubble bath."

Emery was instantly on her feet, knocking popcorn all over the bed as she reached out to stop him. "Carter…"

He looked at her like she was crazy. "What? You can't tell me you don't want to take a bath because there're no bombs, Em. That's ridiculous. Come on, let me do this for you."

Grimacing as she stepped on some kernels, she quickly hopped off the mattress. "That wasn't what I was going to say. I would love to take a nice hot bath, but…later. With you." Her hands came up and splayed across his chest as she looked at him. "I was really enjoying sitting here and talking about hypothetical Christmas gifts and…well, I was curi-ous to hear your answers too."

Carter's expression was full of tenderness as he looked down at her.

Not so much when he looked at the popcorn mess on the bed.

With a not-so-subtle sigh, he said, "Scoot. Let me clean this mess up while you go make another bag. Then we'll *carefully* crawl back in here and talk some more. And then later..."

Up on her tiptoes, Emery planted a kiss on his lips. "Later we soak," she said playfully and skipped off happily to the kitchen.

Five minutes later they were back under the blankets and she felt like this was perfect—this little cocoon they were in that she didn't want to leave.

"So, cashmere robe and smelly bath stuff," Carter said blandly. "What else?"

"Excuse me, I don't think smelly is the word I used," she argued lightly, but was laughing just the same.

"What else has Santa put under the tree for you?" he asked, rather than acknowledging her comment.

"Hmm...let me think." Munching on popcorn, Emery thought about some of the things she'd always wanted but never got. When she giggled, Carter looked at her again. "Roller skates."

"Um...what?"

"Uh-huh. Roller skates. I always wanted them when I was growing up and never got them. Remember the roller rink next to the middle school? Oh my goodness, I went to so many birthday parties there and I always wanted my own pair of skates, but my parents thought it wasn't a necessity, so I never got them." She pouted. "That and an Easy-Bake Oven."

Carter immediately began to choke after hearing her admission, and it took him a minute to catch his breath. "Excuse me, but did you seriously just say you wanted an Easy-Bake Oven? Aren't you a little old for that?"

"I'm sorry, are you ever too old to want to bake a tiny cake for a snack?" she asked sarcastically.

"Em, you're an adult. You can go to a bakery and get all the cake you want. Why would you want to go through all the trouble of making one yourself that cooks with the help of a light bulb?"

Huffing, she pushed him away. "Now you sound just like my parents. Between the lack of tiny cakes in my life and the fact that I never got NSYNC's *No Strings Attached* on CD, is it any wonder I have issues?"

He found that hilarious. "Don't tell me, you were a Justin Timberlake fan, right?"

She gave him the side-eye. "Carter, we're *all* Justin Timberlake fans."

He laughed harder. "I hate to admit it, but you're right. The man has some serious talent."

"And he's extremely yummy to look at."

"Hey!"

"Deal with it," she said, popping more kettle corn into her mouth. "JT is the total package. He can sing, dance, act, and is so handsome he makes me want to cry."

His expression bordered on horrified. "Seriously? Cry? That doesn't make sense!"

She shrugged. "To me it does." Then she reached for her soda and took a long drink.

"I swear, I will never understand women," he said, taking a sip of his wine. "I enjoy an attractive woman as much as the next guy, but no supermodel has ever made me want to cry."

"Sure they haven't."

"What? It's true!"

"Uh-huh," she said mildly, resting her head on his shoulder as she ate more popcorn.

"Why would I lie about that? Guys don't cry over a beautiful woman! It's ridiculous!"

"I think I'd really like a dog too," she said, no longer paying attention. "Once I decide where I'm going to live and whether or not I'm going to stay with my job, I'm definitely going to get a dog." She munched on a few more kernels. "What's the best kind of dog, do you think?"

"Have you ever had a dog?"

She shook her head. "My sisters are both allergic."

"And you're not?"

"Nope. And Derek never wanted any pets, so I just figured it wasn't meant to be, but now—now I can." She looked up at him and smiled. "I used to wish we'd get one when I was little. Like I'd wake up on Christmas morning and there would be this adorable puppy sitting obediently under the tree with a big red bow as a collar and my sisters would miraculously be cured of their allergies."

Rather than say anything, Carter kissed her on the top of her head. "Sorry."

"Yeah. Me too." She sighed. "Nothing says I can't do that now, though."

"Probably won't be in the scenario you just described. After all, if you go and adopt the dog, it's hardly a surprise on Christmas morning."

"It would still be worth it." They sat in silence for a few minutes before Emery looked at him and said, "Your turn. What are you hoping for under the tree?"

He didn't say a word, instead he moved the bowl of popcorn onto the floor and then pushed his wine glass farther away. Emery thought he was done with them and was about to comment on how she might have enjoyed finishing what was left in the bowl, but before she could utter a single word, he was maneuvering them until she was flat on her back and he was sprawled out on top of her.

"This," he said, his voice low and gruff and oh so sexy. "This is what I'm hoping to find under the tree. You." His eyes scanned her face. "Only you'd be wearing tiny scraps of red silk and lace, stilettos, and a Santa hat."

If he hadn't looked so intense and serious, she might have laughed. "You've clearly put some thought into this."

He nodded. "Yes, I have. Ever since the tree went up. Every time we're out here, I can picture you dressed like that and it makes me crazy."

"Had you said something sooner, I could have fulfilled that fantasy for you," she said, her own voice low and husky.

Carter ran a finger across her cheek and then his hand sank into her hair. "You've already fulfilled so many of them. And I don't need the silk and lace or any of that. It's you I want. Right here. Just like this."

And when he kissed her, there was no room for doubt.

But in the back of her mind, Emery knew she'd love to surprise him anyway. After everything he'd given her—done for her—she'd find a way to do this one thing for him.

Soon.

Chapter 8

CARTER HAD ALWAYS ENJOYED DRIVING.

When he traveled, however, it was rare that he took the time to drive himself. It was more important to multitask and let someone else drive while he took calls or worked on his plans for new endeavors. So the fact that he got to not only enjoy driving from Montauk up to Albany but have Emery beside him singing completely off-key to the Taylor Swift song on the radio had him feeling pretty damn good.

They'd packed up the house early that morning, and Emery having taken down most of the Christmas decorations the night before made for less work today. Once the decorator and her team had come and gone, they had walked through the house and made sure everything was ready for the cleaning crew. And as they loaded the car and closed the door behind them, he knew they were both sad to be leaving.

Carter knew it would be a long time before he would forget all they'd shared there. After making love to Emery in front of the Christmas tree last night, he'd made good on his promise and drawn a bubble bath using shampoo to make the bubbles. They could have gone outside and sat in the hot tub, but it didn't take long for him to find the pros of the close confines of the bathtub.

By the time they'd crawled back into bed after midnight, they were both exhausted and slept deeply.

Something else he found he was enjoying since he and

Emery started sleeping together: he was actually sleeping better. He loved having her next to him—or sometimes wrapped around him like some sort of cuddly boa constrictor. It didn't matter. Just knowing she was there in the bed with him made him sleep better. In all honesty, he couldn't remember ever being this well-rested.

Going back to work in five days would be a reality check he really wasn't looking forward to.

The frantic pace, the long hours on his feet, the constant demand on his time… It was the sort of thing he normally enjoyed, but now that he'd finally taken some time to himself, Carter wasn't the least bit anxious to get back to it.

His plan was to put in a couple of weeks in New Orleans, then check on his places in LA and Orlando before coming back to Montauk to put the finishing touches on the restaurant there. Hopefully while he was traveling, he'd be able to pin down exactly what he was going to do with the place. Last night he had been inspired with an idea for the menu. He hadn't shared it with Emery and she hadn't asked about it, but he had a feeling when he showed it to his investors, they were going to think he'd lost his mind.

And maybe he had.

Only time would tell.

Beside him, Emery pulled a bottle of water from the small cooler they'd placed in the back seat. "Want one?" she asked.

"Sure."

"Are we going to stop someplace for lunch?"

He laughed softly. "We ate a late breakfast and packed enough snacks for a cross-country trip. I thought we agreed we'd be okay until we got to my mom's."

"Oh. Right." She shot him a grin and all he could think

of was how it didn't seem possible for her to be so obsessed with food.

"My mother wanted to take us out to dinner tonight, but I told her exactly what to buy and I'm going to cook for us," he explained. "I hope you don't mind."

"Are you kidding? Your mother lives close enough to my parents and my place that the thought of going out anywhere was giving me a little anxiety. If we can postpone letting me out in the wild for a few more days, I'd greatly appreciate it."

"Out in the wild?" he repeated, laughing. "What does that mean?"

"Just what it implies—I'm not quite ready to start going out around town yet. You know, like in my natural habitat."

That just made him laugh harder. "You certainly have a way of painting a picture, Em."

"And don't you forget it."

The conversation flowed as they drove on and they covered every kind of topic—current events, sports, movies, music, and then, of course, his family. While Emery had known his family since elementary school, she didn't really know his extended family. At last count, Uncle William and Aunt Monica were definitely going to be there this weekend, along with Uncle Robert and Aunt Janice. Then there was his cousin Summer, her husband, Ethan, and their daughter Autumn, who were bringing their dog, Maylene.

When Carter had questioned why the dog was traveling with them, his mother had said how sweet it was and how Maylene was a member of the family.

He'd rolled his eyes at the thought.

His siblings and their spouses were going to be there, and

last he'd heard, they were still waiting to hear whether Zach and Gabriella could make it. Not that it mattered; a few more seats at the table was always a good thing, and it would be loud and boisterous and crazy because that's what his family was like and he wouldn't trade them for all the world.

It wasn't hard to tell that Emery was a little nervous—not so much about spending the weekend with his family but just about going home in general. Honestly, she didn't need to stay at his mother's house with him—her own place was less than thirty minutes away—but she never brought it up and neither did he. Their time together was already close to coming to an end, and as crazy as it still seemed to him, he was reluctant to see it happen.

Meeting up with Emery again hadn't been all that surprising.

Finding out just how perfect for him she was? Yeah, *that* was the surprising part.

With each day that passed, Carter was still a little dazed by it all. How was it possible to know someone for so long—and to *dislike* someone for all that time—and then find out they're your ideal person? Quite possibly your other half?

And more than likely, *the one*?

With his heart racing, he glanced over at her and she was singing, again, to the song on the radio. This time she was adorably dancing in her seat and looked so happy and so relaxed that it had him feeling the same way. Emery was like a breath of fresh air in his life with her crazy off-key singing, her awful taste in food, and the way she embraced the things she did with such abandon.

Reaching over, he placed a hand on her thigh and chuckled when she gave him a sassy wink without missing a beat in her singing and passenger-seat choreography. He loved her sassiness, her silliness, and most of all her sexiness. Emery Monaghan made for one incredibly appealing package.

And she was all his.

Hopefully, she'd stay that way.

Carter couldn't help but wish that she could just say "screw it" and walk away from it all. She could come to New Orleans with him, and he'd help her find a new career where she could travel with him and...

Wait—why couldn't he?

Don't do the same thing her family did to her, dude.

Oh yeah. That.

It was maddening!

There weren't any answers right now, and as much as he hated it, Carter knew there would be enough distractions this weekend to keep him busy. Along with cooking all the food, he would spend some time catching up with his aunts, uncles, siblings, cousins, and their dog. He laughed at the thought.

But most of all, he smiled because he was blessed with an amazing family, and in a little while, he was going to get to introduce Emery to all of them.

———————

There were Montgomerys everywhere.

Every. Where.

It was like they were in every room, every nook and cranny of Eliza's house, and there was no place for Emery to hide.

And right now, she kind of wanted to.

This was all just a little too…much. Not that anyone was rude or mean to her, they were just all so larger than life that it intimidated the heck out of her.

Everyone was laughing.

Everyone was smiling.

And everyone had hugged her and treated her like she was part of the family.

What was wrong with them?

Of course, she shouldn't be surprised. Just because her own family was less than affectionate didn't mean everyone else's was. And she had been around the Montgomerys enough—well, Carter's immediate family—to know they were definitely warmer than her own. But this extended group seemed almost too good to be true.

Too nice.

Too friendly.

Too…everything she'd always wanted.

Damn, she was falling in love with the whole family just as much as she was falling in love with the man.

When she and Carter had arrived the previous day, his siblings were already here. Emery knew them and it had been a comfortable setting to step into. Eliza had taken the idea Emery had used at the beach house and had the entire place decorated for Christmas.

Except the tree.

That was something they had done together as a family last night.

Stepping closer to the tree, Emery examined some of the ornaments and remembered Eliza talking about why she had picked certain ones for her kids and the meanings behind them. As she had spoken, Emery had fought back tears, because it was the exact same thing she'd wanted to have when she was growing up and had finally decided to do on her own. But someday, she hoped to have a moment like that with her own kids. Maybe even…hers and Carter's.

A strange noise seemed to be getting closer and Emery looked around trying to figure out what it was. It wasn't until she felt the scratching on her leg that she realized the tiny pug was the one making all the racket. Good Lord— she breathed and snorted like a freight train! But she was as cute as could be, and just like the rest of her family, she was extremely friendly.

"Hey, sweet girl," Emery cooed as she squatted down to pet the dog who was frantically dancing at her feet, her little tail wagging, trying to lick her face. "Oh my goodness! You are so excitable, aren't you?"

"You don't know the half of it." Emery looked up and spotted Carter's sister, Megan, walking over. "She looks all sweet and adorable, but she has enough energy for ten dogs twice her size." As if sensing they were talking about her, Maylene scampered over and began scratching at Megan's legs for attention. After petting the dog and kissing her head, she looked back up at Emery. "So? How are you holding up? Did we scare you? Is that why you're hiding out here in the den by yourself?"

Why deny it? With a nervous laugh, Emery said, "Maybe. Just a little."

Megan stood and gave her a smile. "Sorry about that. I swear we don't realize how overwhelming we can be."

"It's not a bad thing. I'm just not used to so much…"

"Everything?" Megan asked with her own laugh. "Believe

me, they're my family and I love them, but they overwhelm me too."

That had her letting out a sigh of relief. "Okay. Good to know."

Megan studied her for a moment. "You know, it's kind of awesome that you're here."

"Really? Why?"

Gracefully brushing her long hair over her shoulder, Megan sat down on the arm of one of the sofas and smiled. "Because you made this possible." She motioned toward the rest of the house and all the noise and chaos coming from the other room.

"Me?" she squeaked. "I didn't do anything!"

"Oh, please. You totally are responsible for this and it's the best thing to happen to our family in a long time." She paused. "After my dad died, it seemed like we all scattered. This is the first time that we're back together since his funeral. And I know it's not all of us—I have a lot more cousins who I wish could be here—but it's a nice start."

"It's funny how the family that lives the furthest away are the ones who made it here."

"I know, right? Go figure." She shook her head. "Honestly, it was easier for all of us to travel together. Uncle William sent the Montgomery company jet to pick us all up, so it made things even better. Especially with the kids and the dog." Once again she reached down to pet Maylene. "Summer was very upset at the thought of either leaving Maylene at a kennel for the long weekend or having her go in cargo on a commercial flight. Having use of the company plane put her at ease."

"I'm sure."

"Anyway, back to you," Megan said as she made herself comfortable. "All of this would never have happened if you weren't involved."

"Megan—"

"It's true! You not only got my brother to step away from his precious restaurants for a little while, but you got him to do something for someone other than himself." Then she frowned. "I know that sounds terrible, and we're all workaholics in this family, but because Carter chose a career that was so different from the rest of ours, we never see him. But with this project, you sort of reeled him in and got him to do something that meant a lot to my mom, so…thank you."

Damn, there must be something in the air here, she thought, because she was on the verge of crying again! "Your mother went out on a limb for me, so if this was something I could help with, then—"

"Maylene! Maylene, where are you?"

"She's in here, Summer!" Megan called out.

Emery looked up to see not only Summer walking into the room, but Carter's cousin Zach's wife too. What was her name again?

"There you are," Summer said as she bent down and picked up the dog. "You better be behaving yourself."

The gorgeous dark-haired woman married to Zach looked at her and smiled. "I'm Gabriella," she said, reaching out a hand to Emery. "We met in the midst of all the chaos earlier. I'm sure it was a lot of names to remember."

Feeling instantly at ease, Emery returned the smile. "It was. Normally, I'm pretty good with that sort of thing, but it was like you all walked in at once and…"

"No need to explain," Gabriella said. "I had a lot of years

working with Zach's family, and for a while there it was hard for me to keep some of them straight."

"You're such a liar," Summer said, chuckling. She sat on the sofa with the dog curled up in her lap. Turning to Emery, she explained, "Gabriella is the queen of organization. Don't let her fool you. The only time she's ever forgotten a name was when my brother was distracting her." Then she winked at Gabriella.

"That is not true," Gabriella argued lightly. "There are a lot of you—particularly the male side of the family. And you're all so damn good-looking it was hard to keep names straight at the beginning, because all you can see is sexy… Montgomeryness."

"Sexy what?" Summer asked, laughing.

"Ugh, please don't let any of them hear you say that," Megan chimed in. "Their egos do *not* need to be stroked."

"Who's getting stroked?" Zach asked as he walked into the room, handing a glass of water to his wife. He smiled at all of them briefly before his attention returned to Gabriella. "You doing okay?"

She nodded and Emery had a feeling there was a little more going on here. When Gabriella glanced her way, her smile turned serene. "We just found out we're pregnant again." Zach wrapped an arm around her and kissed her on the cheek. "So far this pregnancy hasn't been quite as easy as the first, so—".

"She vomits all the time," Summer stated and then sighed. "Of course, she still manages to look great."

They all laughed and as soon as he confirmed that his wife was all right, Zach returned to the rest of the family in the other room.

"Congratulations," Emery said. "A new baby is always exciting."

"Thanks. We're very excited." Then she looked at Summer and Megan. "And one of you better be working on getting pregnant soon. You know how I want all our kids to be close."

"Well," Summer said sweetly, "I just thought I'd let you go first this time. You know, since Autumn and Willow are so close together."

"Wait," Gabriella said, straightening in her seat. "Are you saying…?"

Summer's finger went to her lips to keep everyone from reacting. "We were going to announce it at Thanksgiving, so everyone has to keep it quiet. Got it?"

They all agreed and Emery found herself giddy at being included in this exciting little secret. She caught Megan's eye and noticed she was grinning widely too.

"Since you're all already keeping one secret," Megan whispered, "I hope you won't mind keeping two."

It was almost too much! Not only finding out that this already large family was about to grow even more with the next generation, but also that she was actually being included in this little secret sisterhood thing.

Unable to help herself, Emery craned her neck toward the kitchen and spotted Christian's wife, Sophie. Turning back to the group, she asked, "Does Sophie know? I feel bad that she's not in here for this."

Megan jumped up and hugged her before calling out to Sophie and motioning for her to join the girls. Once they were all seated and Sophie was sitting next to Summer, she looked at the group and frowned. "What? What's going on?"

Summer leaned in close and whispered the group news. When Sophie gasped and made to cry out her delight, Summer immediately placed her hand over her mouth and shushed her. "Did you not get that it was a secret by the fact that I whispered it?" she teased.

"Oh my gosh!" Sophie said quietly but excitedly. "This is amazing! I can't believe it! All the babies at one time!" She fanned herself as her eyes welled with tears. "Now I wish I had taken the test before Christian and I flew out here!"

"*What?!*" they all cried.

She nodded vigorously and gave them all a watery grin. "I haven't told Christian yet, but I think…well, you know."

"Clearly, there's something in the water," Emery said with a giggle, wiping away her own happy tears.

"Better watch out," Gabriella said to her. "You could be next!"

And instead of panic washing over her or any kind of denial, Emery found the thought of getting pregnant with Carter's baby wasn't the least bit scary.

That had to be a sign, right?

"Oh, don't scare her," Megan chided, reaching over and hugging Emery. "Even though she and my brother have known each other forever, their relationship is brand new."

With four pairs of concerned eyes on her, Emery knew that not only was she good at keeping a secret, she was pretty good at sharing one of her own.

Leaning forward conspiratorially, she quietly said, "Don't worry, I don't scare easily." And when everyone relaxed, she added, "And being part of this family would be amazing."

"So the family, huh?" Summer teased. "More so than Carter?"

Emery could feel herself blushing. "Especially Carter." And then she did something she hadn't done since she was a teenager.

She sighed dreamily.

"I still can't believe we're together," she admitted. "All the years of animosity and competing against one another…"

"It sounds like twenty years of foreplay," Gabriella said with a wink. "Good for you!"

And honestly, Emery couldn't agree more.

It was good for her.

"Merry Mock Christmas," Carter said as he raised his glass at the massive dining room table.

"Merry Mock Christmas!" everyone echoed.

It was the first time this many Montgomerys were together in his family home since his father's funeral, and because he'd been the cook, his mother had asked him to take the seat at the head of the table.

His father's seat.

Uncle William should be sitting here, he thought. When he tried to make that point to his mother, she had smiled and waved him off, pointing to his uncle who was sitting at the other end of the table.

As much as he tried not to dwell on it, it wasn't easy. Taking his seat, Carter looked around the table and couldn't help but smile.

This was Dad's view. Did he appreciate it?

How could he not? It seemed a little surreal to be seeing the faces of so many people he loved sitting down to a meal together. Especially one he prepared. Conversation flowed and platters were passed around, though it took a while before he felt at ease enough to take his first bite. His mother sat to his left and Emery to his right.

When he finally took a bite, his own meal tasted like sawdust in his mouth.

Pushing back from the table, he murmured, "Excuse me," before fleeing the room. He was outside on the back deck when he heard the glass doors slide open. No doubt it was Emery coming to check on him, but he wasn't quite ready to talk to her—mainly because he had no idea why he was having this mild panic attack.

Without turning around, he said, "Sorry to leave you in there with my whole family. I just…I needed a minute."

But it wasn't Emery who came to stand beside him. It was his Uncle William.

Leaning on the wooden deck rail, his uncle looked out over the yard and smiled. "Those were some pretty big shoes to fill, huh?"

Mimicking the pose, Carter looked at his uncle but didn't say anything.

"She thought of asking Christian to sit at the head of the table—he's the oldest—but decided you deserved the honor since you created the feast." William turned to face him. "I swear, every meal you make is better than the last."

"Thanks," he said quietly before turning his attention forward again.

"You miss him."

It wasn't a question.

"I don't think it hit me until I sat down. Crazy, right? I mean, it's a chair. It shouldn't be a big deal and yet all I could think about was how it was his spot, his view, his—" The words stuck in his throat. For years, he had been angry with his father—most of his adult life, if he were being honest—but in the past year Carter thought he'd found peace with his father's death.

Yet here he was.

His uncle placed a warm hand on his shoulder and squeezed. "It's okay to be emotional, Carter. This is the first time we're all together and the first real celebration we're allowing ourselves in your father's house."

"Everyone must think I'm mental or something."

A bark of laughter was William's first response. After a moment, he cleared his throat and rested both his arms on the rail again. "Who cares what any of them think? You're entitled to feel how you feel, and if you needed a moment to get a little air and settle your thoughts, then so be it."

"Maybe."

"No maybe about it." He paused. "Emery's a great girl."

Just the mention of her name made Carter smile. "Yeah, she is."

"Had a nice conversation with her this morning while you were prepping in the kitchen."

Carter knew his uncle enjoyed talking to people and Emery was always very sociable, so it was no surprise the two of them had hit it off.

"She was telling me about her education and her job before all of this happened." He shook his head. "No doubt she'll land on her feet when the dust settles. A smart woman like her would be an asset to any company. Montgomerys included." He paused again. "And it was definitely nice to see her again."

"Again?"

"I met her at your father's funeral," he said, his voice going a little softer, as if the memory of his brother was just as hard on him. "Met her sorry excuse for an ex, too."

Carter frowned but didn't move.

"I was surprised to see her here because...I remembered her from your high school graduation."

That made Carter turn his head. "Really?"

William nodded. "I was sitting next to your father in that massive auditorium with the lousy air-conditioning. I mean, really, it was an expensive private school and they couldn't crank up the cool air?" He laughed. "But I digress. I was sitting next to your father and you had just finished your class president's speech, and then Emery came up to the podium. The two of you walked right by one another, bumping shoulders and giving each other the side-eye and your father was grinning from ear to ear."

It was hard to imagine his father ever ginning, but just the thought of it had Carter doing it too. "Why? Why was he smiling?"

"He nudged me on the shoulder—a very un-Joseph-like move—and said, 'You see that girl? The one at the podium?'" He seemed to be remembering it fondly. "Your father looked at me and said, 'That girl has been knocking my son on his ass for years and she's the greatest thing ever to happen to him!'" William paused and shook his head. "I think he would love how the two of you are together now."

"Somehow, I doubt it. I don't think my father approved of anything I did. And just because he liked Emery a dozen years ago doesn't mean he'd like her now." He hated how bitter the words sounded even as they came out.

"I wouldn't be so sure about that." Straightening, his uncle turned to face him head-on. "Here's the thing, Carter. Father-son relationships are complicated. It doesn't matter who we're talking about."

His uncle gave him a sad smile. "I wish things could have been different for you. For all of you. It kills me that the memories you have of your father are negative ones more than positive and joyful ones." His hand went back to Carter's shoulder as he leaned in a little closer. "Just remember this— your mother is counting on you kids now more than ever and she feels terrible that she didn't do more to change the way Joseph was with all of you. You need to go in there and sit at the head of the table and celebrate this milestone with your family with a smile on your face." His expression turned fierce. "Don't make the same mistakes he made, Carter. Don't let your career and ambition take over your life. You have a beautiful woman in there who you can have a future with, and you have a family who loves you. That's what's important."

Then he ruffled Carter's hair just like he used to do when he was a boy and walked into the house, leaving Carter wondering how to make his own way back to the table without drawing too much attention to himself. Hanging his head for a moment, he took a steadying breath and went inside.

At the table, he sat down and saw the relieved smile on his mother's face. Reaching out, he took her hand and kissed it before turning his attention back to his plate. After the first bite, which tasted better than it had before he went outside, he caught Emery's eye and winked at her.

And yeah, she definitely looked relieved too.

His uncle was right—Carter was surrounded by the family he loved, sitting next to the woman he loved, and what could be better than that?

Well—he could actually *tell* Emery he loved her.

Soon, he thought. Very soon.

"So, Eliza," Aunt Monica began from across the table, "tell us about the gala for the charity! Have you gotten a big response? Are people excited about the cookbook?"

"Oh my goodness, as soon as I started telling people that Carter was doing it, they all clamored to reserve their copies! Honestly, the book isn't even done and we have over a thousand orders already."

"That's amazing!" Monica cried. "Good for you!" Then she looked at Carter and gave him an endearing smile. "You did a very good thing, Carter. And if the recipes in the book are what you used for this meal, then I can guarantee those orders will be doubled in no time at all. This is all delicious!"

"Eliza," his aunt Janice chimed in, "remember when we used to celebrate Christmas Eve like this? It started out as a potluck when the kids were little and our men were starting up their business, and now look! Your son took a tradition that was full of such good memories and gave it back to us." She looked at Carter with love in her eyes. "You have no idea the number of holidays when you kids were small that were so much fun. They meant so much simply because we were all together. Thank you, Carter."

His mother smiled at him as she clasped his hand. He saw the tears in her eyes and knew she was remembering it all too. And before he found himself too overcome with emotion, he leaned over and kissed her on the cheek. "Love you, Mom," he whispered. "This is a good day. A really good day."

When he straightened in his seat, he reached for his wine glass again and raised it. Everyone turned to him, the voices quieted down, and their expressions turned a little curious.

"When Mom asked me to help her with this project, I figured all I needed to do was write down a couple of recipes and call it a day." They laughed. "Clearly, I was wrong. And believe it or not, I've never been gladder about that. You see, if it hadn't been for me being lazy, we all wouldn't be here today, celebrating this mock Christmas." He smiled and looked at each and every face around the table, ending with Emery. "You wouldn't be here," he said softly. "I may have made the food, but you made this possible. You pushed me, you challenged me, and you made me remember the good times I had with my family. You made me remember what was important."

"Carter..." Emery whispered, seeming a little embarrassed at all the attention.

He faced his family again. "Most of you know my and Emery's history with each other, but I'm so glad we were able to push past that and start something new. Something...well, something more than either of us ever imagined." He raised his glass a little higher. "So I'd like to propose a toast—to Emery. Thank you for making all of this possible and for bringing us all together for this incredible weekend and giving us something to celebrate. To Emery!" Then he looked at her and smiled before tapping his glass to hers. Leaning toward her, he brushed his lips against hers and said, "To you."

It was just after eleven when Carter closed the bedroom door behind him. Emery was already in the bed and reading on her tablet. When she looked up at him, she could see how tired he was.

"Long day for you, Chef Carter. You sure you're going to be up for doing it all again tomorrow for brunch?"

He peeled his shirt off before doing the same with his shoes, socks, and trousers. When he was down to his boxers, he slid under the sheets beside her. "Brunch is much easier. I spent the last hour prepping."

"So what's on tomorrow's menu?"

"I've got a couple of quiches, a French toast loaf, a massive fruit salad, and we're going to make Belgian waffles because...my dad used to love them. That was our traditional Christmas morning meal and we thought we should incorporate it."

"That's very sweet, Carter," she said softly, resting her head on his shoulder.

"I know it's not particularly gourmet and it was probably the most common recipe we put in the book, but it holds a special place in our family holiday tradition, so..."

"You don't owe me an explanation. Besides, I love Belgian waffles." Lifting her head, she grinned at him. "Any chance there'll be some whipped cream, peanut butter, and bananas?"

He laughed and took the tablet from her hands before setting it on the bedside table. "Why would you ruin perfectly good waffles like that?" he asked, shifting them until Emery was on her back beneath him.

"Ruin them? I'll have you know they're delicious, and you should know better than to knock it before you try it. Remember how much you enjoyed the meatloaf?"

"Don't remind me."

She swatted at him playfully. "Oh, stop. Don't be such a snob."

He looked like he was about to argue, but leaned down and kissed her instead. Which was more than fine with Emery. All day and certainly all night she'd missed this.

It was totally worth the wait.

When he raised his head a few minutes later, she reached up and caressed his face. "Rest, wonderful man. You need some sleep."

"I need you more," he whispered, placing kisses on the tip of her nose, her cheek, her chin.

"Carter…we can't do that here in your mom's house. Your siblings are—"

"In their own rooms and probably doing the same thing I'm trying to do. Probably succeeding too."

Laughing softly, she relaxed and wrapped her arms around him. "You think so, huh?"

He gently nipped at her shoulder before saying, "Definitely." And just when she was about to give in, there was a knock on the bedroom door. Carter sighed heavily and rolled off of her. "Come in!"

Eliza tentatively peeked around the door. "Sorry to disturb you…"

Carter sat up and adjusted the blanket over his lap, and Emery had to hide a grin. Not that she was dressed any more appropriately, but it was still cute to watch him cover up. "Everything okay, Mom?"

Nodding, she stepped into the room and stopped near the foot of the bed. "I just wanted to thank you both," she said, her voice thick with emotion. Emery could tell she had been crying and wanted nothing more than to get up and hug her.

If she had pants on.

"In my mind, I knew this was going to be a good thing—having everyone get together and having a practice Christmas dinner," she went on. "But you both made it so much more."

"Eliza," Emery said, unable to hold back. "I think you and Carter did all the work. I'm just glad I was here to celebrate it with all of you."

Waving her off, Eliza moved closer and sat on the corner of the bed. "Just as Carter said in his toast, you were the reason we got to take this whole project to the next level." She gently wiped at her eyes. "I can't wait to see some of the photos Drew took tonight. Sometimes I forgot he was there!"

Both Emery and Carter nodded.

"The thing is, I wasn't...well, everyone said this Christmas would be easier since it wasn't the first one since Joseph died, but they were wrong. Last year, you kids came home and it was wonderful having you all close, but I think we were all still a little shell-shocked. This year, I feel like it's finally sunk in that he's gone and I'm having to make my way on my own. Taking on this project for the charity was a great distraction, and having you both help me with it turned into such a blessing."

"That's not what you were saying a month ago," Carter teased.

"You were being a brat a month ago," his mother reminded him.

Emery laughed quietly and when Carter glanced her way, she said, "What? It's the truth!"

"Still," he muttered, "she didn't need to say it."

"Poor baby," she cooed.

"Anyway," Eliza continued, "it felt really good to have everyone here and for you to remind us all of a simpler time in our family history. It was perfect. You did something I never imagined, not only for the project, but for me." Her tears came in earnest now. "It's not like I don't miss your father or that I'm saying that I'm over losing him." She paused. "But tonight was such a precious reminder of all of the good things in our lives, so…thank you."

Glancing at Carter, Emery could see the way he was fighting to keep his own emotions under control. She didn't think he was a man who was afraid to cry, but she did think he was the kind of man who wanted to be strong for his mother.

It didn't matter that she was in nothing more than her boy-shorts and a tank top. Emery kicked the blankets off and walked over to hug Eliza, holding her close as she cried a little more. Her own emotions were too close to the surface to stop and soon she found herself sobbing too. And just as she hoped, Carter took advantage of the distraction to stand and slip his pants back on so he could come around and comfort Eliza too.

Then Emery stood and grabbed her robe, slipping it on. Lucky for her, because another knock came on the open door and she turned in time to see Megan standing there.

"Everything all right?" she asked, stepping into the room.

Eliza wiped away some tears as she pulled back from Carter. "I was just telling Carter and Emery how much today meant to me and I got a little emotional."

Megan walked over and sat on the bed next to her mother and smiled at her brother. "It really was a great day. It felt like those Christmas Eves when we were kids. I had forgotten about the eclectic menu we used to do."

Carter nodded. "I'm sure I forgot a dish or two, but the ones I made were the ones I remembered, so…"

"Hey, what's going on?" They all raised their heads to find Christian standing in the doorway. He looked at his mother and his siblings, then Emery. "Everyone okay?"

Eliza explained the situation again, so Christian sat next to his sister; Emery felt like the fifth wheel, but didn't know how to go about giving them a moment without being obvious about it.

But she didn't need to, because Christian's wife, Sophie, and Megan's husband, Alex, soon entered the room and the whole lot of them were sitting on Carter's bed. It was a bit comical at first, but Emery found herself being gently tugged onto Carter's lap.

"Don't think you can hide," he whispered in her ear. "You're family."

Nothing he could have ever said to her would have affected Emery more. Burying her face in his neck, she took a moment to get her emotions under control as Christian pulled Sophie into his lap and Megan and Alex switched places so they could be there on the bed too.

"Probably should have moved this to Mom's bed," Megan said with a laugh. "At least she has a king-size mattress and we all would have fit a little bit better."

"What?" Christian teased. "You mean you don't like feeling this cozy with your family?" He nudged her with his shoulder and they all felt the effect of it and started to laugh.

Even Eliza.

"Nonsense," Eliza said after a moment. "This is perfect." She reached out to try to get her arms around everyone. "I'm feeling incredibly blessed tonight. Thank you for being willing to come home and indulge me in this little endeavor."

"No need to thank us, Mom," Christian said. "And we know Carter's going to do it all again in December—"

"Wait, wait, wait," Carter quickly interrupted. "I didn't say that."

"Really? After all the praise you've been getting?" Megan quipped. "You're saying you're willing to break your mother's heart by not making Christmas dinner when it's actually Christmas?"

Emery lifted her head from his shoulder and caught the bewildered look on his face. "Yeah, Carter," she said to egg everyone on. "You mean to tell me you're not willing to come back and do this all again? What in the world?" Her smile was pure mischief and when he pinched her, she cried out before bursting into a fit of giggles.

By the time they calmed down, it was decided that Carter was, indeed, coming home for Christmas and making dinner for however many people happened to show up.

"Glad that's decided," Christian said, standing with his wife in his arms. "Now if you'll excuse us, we're going to bed."

Alex stood with Megan in his arms and grinned at them. "Same here. Good night!" Megan waved while grinning from ear to ear as they walked out the door.

When it was down to just the three of them, Eliza rose and kissed them both on the cheek. "Thank you again," she said softly. "Get some sleep. Brunch is in less than twelve hours." With a small wave, she was gone, closing the door behind her.

They sat on the corner of the bed for a minute before Carter got up holding Emery in his arms and took them to her side of the bed. "Carter, what in the world?"

"Seemed like the thing to do," he said mildly. "Everyone else did it."

"You also said everyone else was having sex earlier and see how wrong you were?"

Slowly, he let her slide down his body before untying her robe and slipping it off her shoulders. "Well, I'm confident they're doing it now. Trust me."

She rolled her eyes but wasn't about to debate with him.

Then his lips were on hers and his hands were holding her hips. Carter was the master of seduction and it didn't take much. She was more than a little needy for him. The urge to be close to him and loved by him was growing stronger by the minute.

When he lifted his head, he had a triumphant look on his face—like he could read her mind.

He knew her well enough by now that he probably could.

He tugged her closer and she could feel just how ready he was. "You know we're going to have to be quiet," she whispered against his lips. "And we have no idea how squeaky this bed can be."

"The headboard might bang against the wall between us and the laundry room," he said, raining kisses along her jaw before lightly biting her earlobe. "But if it makes you feel better, we can stuff a towel or something between it and the wall to buffer the sound a bit."

She couldn't help it.

She giggled.

Carter pulled back and looked at her as if she was crazy. "What's so funny about that?"

Emery shook her head and laughed a little more. "It just struck me as comical—like we're kids sneaking up to your room to fool around. We're adults!" Now she had to wipe away tears of mirth. "I mean, it just seems crazy."

"Em…"

"Although, knowing you, you did this a lot when you were growing up. Go ahead, admit it. You did this with a lot of girls, right?"

She knew she was teasing and they were just joking around, but part of her really didn't want to know the answer. It wasn't hard to remember how many girls Carter had dated in high school, and she had hated each and every one of them. Thinking about that now wasn't helping with the mood, but…

Carter's hands left her hips as he reached up and cupped her face. "Never," he said fiercely. "You may not believe this, but you are the first and only woman to be in this room with me."

Gasping softly, she looked at him with disbelief. "But… how? I mean…why?"

But really, it didn't matter, and she didn't want to know— and it seemed as if Carter didn't want to talk about it either.

This time when his lips claimed hers, Emery was more than willing not only to let him take the lead but for him to take her to bed and have his way with her.

Quietly.

Perfectly.

Chapter 9

CARTER STOOD ON THE DRIVEWAY TUESDAY MORNING and watched as the cab carrying Emery pulled away.

A cab.

After multiple heated discussions, he had finally agreed to her ridiculous request that he not drive her home. She wanted to say her goodbyes here at his mother's and go back to her place alone. From the moment she'd first mentioned it, he'd hated the idea. So much so that they were barely speaking when she left.

"We were taking bets on whether or not you were going to haul her out of the cab before it pulled away."

Carter turned to face his brother and nearly growled.

Christian wasn't deterred. He stepped up next to Carter and stared at the end of the driveway, just as Carter was doing. "You knew this was going to happen. Why are you fighting it so much?"

Now he did growl as he raked both hands through his hair. Turning toward Christian, he snapped, "Because it isn't right! There is no one waiting there for her—there are no good memories for her to go back to! Why would she want to face all that alone?"

And damn if he wasn't breathless by the time he got that out.

He and his brother were alike in so many ways, but right now, their differences were blazingly obvious. Where

Carter was looking frazzled and out of control, Christian was the picture of the mild-mannered gentleman.

"I know you're not really looking for an answer—because you think you know what's best for everyone—but I'm going to tell you why," Christian explained mildly.

"Dude, come on."

"Maybe she's ready for a little alone time. Ever since you went to the city and brought her out to Montauk with you, she hasn't had a moment to herself. I mean, think about it." He paused briefly before continuing his theory. "And while there's no doubt it's going to be hard for her, you can't say there aren't any good memories for her at her place. It wasn't like she was living with her ex there. The house is hers and hers alone, and while it may not be her dream house—I'm completely theorizing here—it's not like the house itself is the reason for all of her troubles."

"Okay, I get that, but—"

"And most important…"

Carter exhaled loudly at the interruption, but let his brother speak.

"You forget that Emery was a fiercely independent woman at one time. The last several years have done a number on her, between this scandal with her ex and her overcontrolling parents, but…dude, you can't tell me you wouldn't want to take control of your life back if you were in that situation."

"Maybe."

"No maybes about it," Christian argued. "There was a time not so long ago when we were all about going and confronting Dad about the way he treated us. Are you telling me you would have been okay with someone doing it for you?"

Now he was beyond frustrated. "If memory serves, Christian, we never got to do that, so it's kind of the same thing, isn't it?"

Rather than argue, his brother laughed. A full-blown, hearty laugh. When he finally stopped, he looked at Carter with a smug grin. "You know what? Yeah, it is kind of the same thing, except we are never going to get the chance to stand up for ourselves or have our voices be heard. We got our way by default, and believe me, that was a bitter pill to swallow."

Carter remembered how hard that reality was on his brother and felt bad for bringing it up. However…

"We would have had each other's backs, given the opportunity, Chris. Emery has no one. She's all alone, going in there to fight with these people who have proven that her feelings don't mean a damn thing to them! Someone should be with her!"

Rather than agreeing or disagreeing, Christian placed a hand on his shoulder and gave him a small smile. "I think it's great you want to fight this battle for her, but in order for her to move on and have some peace, you're going to have to let her do this her own way, on her own terms."

"But what if…what if it goes badly? What if they convince her to go back to this guy or…or…?"

"Carter, are you afraid she's not going to come back to you?"

Yes.

That realization was so hard and so painful that his chest actually hurt.

"I'm going to be fifteen-hundred miles away," he said sadly. "I can't hop in a car and be there if she needs me. And because I know how damn stubborn she can be, I don't know if she'd tell me if she did."

"The two of you have known each other for a long time, and this new part of your relationship has got to be a bit tricky," Christian said carefully. "You talked to Emery. She knows how you feel. Now you just have to trust."

"It's not her I don't trust."

"I think it is," he countered. "You don't trust her to be strong enough to stand up for herself. You don't trust her to go back there and keep on being the woman you brought out in her." He paused. "I'm going to ask you something and you need to be honest."

It was on the tip of his tongue to be difficult, but he opted against it.

"Fine."

"Do you love her?"

"Yes." There was no hesitation. Carter knew he loved her, only…he still hadn't told her. There never seemed to be the right time, and now? Now he regretted not saying it.

"Does she know that?"

He shook his head. "I kept thinking I needed the perfect moment, that the timing had to be just right."

"To be fair, it was chaotic this weekend. Between the mock Christmas dinner, the brunch, the girls going out all day yesterday…I get it. But sometimes there isn't a perfect moment. Sometimes you just have to put it out there!"

They stood there for a long moment without saying a word. Finally Christian placed his hand back on Carter's shoulder and gave it a reassuring squeeze. "Faith. You have to keep the faith." Stepping back, he pulled his phone out of his pocket and looked at the time. "Our ride will be here in fifteen minutes. You sure you don't want to share?"

But Carter shook his head. "My flight isn't until four and

I figured I'd hang out here a little bit longer with Mom and Uncle William and Aunt Monica."

"All right. But call me if you start to freak out—before you take it out on Emery, okay?"

"I'm not going to freak out."

"Carter, you're already freaking out and her car left five minutes ago. So promise to call me when you're feeling stressed."

Agreeing was easier than continuing this conversation. "I promise."

With a smile and a curt nod, Christian turned and walked back into the house, leaving Carter alone in the driveway.

Not that he stayed that way for long.

Surprisingly, it was his aunt who came out and stood beside him. She gave him a big hug and a kiss on the cheek. When she pulled back, her smile was one of total peace and happiness.

Oh, how he envied her in that moment.

"You're missing her already, aren't you?"

It was pointless to pretend he didn't know who she was talking about.

"Yup."

"You know it's not a bad thing to have a little time apart, right?"

He nodded.

"I watched all three of my sons let the women they loved walk away," she said with a bit of a sigh. "And not like what you just did here with Emery, but let them walk away because of their own stubbornness. Learn from their mistakes."

"I don't think I'm being stubborn, Aunt Monica," he said casually.

"Not yet. But trust me, you will. I think it's genetic." She gave him a sassy wink before kissing him on the cheek and going back into the house.

"Wow. That was…short and almost painless," he murmured to himself as he went inside.

Within minutes, Sophie and Christian were saying goodbye and Megan and Alex were right there with them doing the same. In a matter of weeks they'd all be together again for Thanksgiving—this time in Portland with Megan hosting this year. She'd already asked Carter to come a few days early to help with the menu and he'd agreed. Emery had said she'd like to go with him, but hadn't firmly committed.

That also had come up during the last few days' discussions.

The thought didn't get to take hold fully because he got swept up in seeing his siblings off and then he was with his aunt, uncle, and mother all chatting incessantly about what was next for all of them. They were determined to include him in the conversation no matter how hard he tried to get a few minutes to himself.

But maybe it was for the better. At least this way he was focusing on the positives and not the possibility of all that could go wrong in the coming weeks.

———

Emery stood on her front walkway and stared up at the home she hadn't stepped inside of in nearly two months and felt…nothing. There were no *It's good to be home* or *Can't wait to sleep in my own bed* feelings. Just…nothing.

Pulling her suitcase behind her, she walked up to the

door and let herself in. The house definitely needed to be aired out and there was a bit of an unpleasant smell—it seemed fitting that this was what would greet her.

Diving right into action, she opened windows and then dragged her suitcase into the laundry room to start her first load. After that, she went to the kitchen and began making a list of all the things she'd need from the grocery store.

"Going to have to cook for myself," she murmured, writing down some of her usual picks. As she wrote "frozen pizza," she laughed softly. No doubt Carter would have a fit when she told him she was back to eating that. Then again, Carter had been having a lot of fits over the last several days over a lot of things. She knew he was only doing it because he cared and he was worried about her, but it bothered her that he didn't seem to think she was capable of taking care of herself without him.

Well, considering her history in the last couple of years, could she really blame him?

Yes. Yes, she totally could.

With another laugh, she finished making her shopping list. Once that was done, she weighed her options—go shopping now and call her parents when she got back or call them first and then go shopping.

Knowing there were going to be harsh words, she opted to buy groceries first and save the aggravation for later.

Out in her garage, her car took a little while to start up and she was thankful she didn't have to call anyone to give her a jump.

Driving through town, Emery felt a little uneasy. There was a good chance she'd run into someone she knew and then the questions would start and then... It was so tempting to turn the car around, go home, and order take-out to be delivered.

"No," she said firmly. "I'm done hiding. I want my life back."

Or at least a new life where she was more in control.

A life like she'd had with Carter. Or the life they'd had over the weekend with his family, where she was accepted by everyone and loved and encouraged the way she'd always wished for.

It was all possible. She'd been living it. So why should she have any fear about pushing her old self aside and letting this new version of herself—the one she'd always wanted to be—out? While Emery knew there had never been anything wrong with her, it was the way she let other people make her feel that was her biggest weakness. Now that she could see it so clearly, she was ready to release herself back into the world.

Carter had been so worried about her—but the only way for her to do this and do it right was on her own. He would be waiting for her when she was done. When she was ready. And then they could be together on a more level playing field—one where she wasn't hiding and he didn't need to watch out for her so much.

Although…she liked the way he took care of her. No one had ever done that for her before. No man had ever made her feel so safe and secure. No man had ever accepted her, warts and all, without looking to change her. Carter had accepted who she was, and though he'd tried to change her eating habits, that was the worst of it—and really, what was wrong with that? He was right! She made terrible choices in food and he'd spoiled her for the last month by feeding her gourmet home-cooked meals! And when she'd fussed at him—for no other reason except to be difficult—he'd caved and made her some of her favorite dishes! She loved the meals he made for her. She loved how he didn't try to change her or tell her she was wrong for the things she felt. She loved *him*.

So why hadn't she told him? Wouldn't it have helped them these last couple of days? Wouldn't it have put his mind at ease when he was freaking out over her coming here alone? Maybe, maybe not. For all she knew, it would have made him more adamant about coming home with her. And no doubt she would have stood her ground and done what she needed to do, and he would have been right there encouraging her and offering her support.

It was sweet, and it was wonderful how he wanted to do that for her, but deep in her heart, Emery knew she needed this for herself. When she saw Carter again, she wanted to be able to go to him free of her insecurities and emotional baggage. It would be good for them, but it would be great for her.

Her own peace of mind was what was most important here. Carter was going to love her no matter what the outcome was.

All the more reason she was in love with him.

Her foot pressed a little harder on the gas pedal, and by the time she pulled into the shopping center and parked, she was almost giddy with the thought of running into people. "Bring it," she said, reaching for her purse.

Unfortunately, she didn't get a chance to test her theory or her newfound bravery, and grocery shopping was as uneventful as it ever was. But she refused to let it get her down. Back at home, she changed the laundry, put her food away, and finally did what she'd been avoiding for weeks.

Grabbing her phone, Emery let out a long breath. "I am woman, hear me roar," she declared as she pulled up her parents' number and hit Call. Her mother answered on the third ring.

"Emery! What a surprise! It's been weeks since you deemed me worthy of a phone call," her mother said in a tone that was perfectly sweet though her words were tart.

Don't let her psych you out.

"Hey, Mom," she said with equal sweetness, walking over to sit down on her couch, then ultimately thinking better of it and pacing. "How are you?"

"Fine, dear. Just fine. And you?"

Ugh…she hated pleasantries. "I'm good. Really good," she added for emphasis. "And I'm home."

"You are?"

"Uh-huh. Just got back today, in fact." She paused. "I went grocery shopping, started my laundry, and now I'm airing out the house since it's been closed up for so long, but yeah. I'm back."

"It's about time, Emery. I mean, honestly, it must be nice to shirk your responsibilities and only worry about yourself."

And amazingly enough, that snarky comment was the opening she had been waiting for.

"You know what? It *was* nice," she replied with a bit of an edge. "You see, I had to worry about myself because nobody else was!"

"Now, Emery—"

"Do you know what it's like to have your whole world

come crashing down and your heart broken and find out the people who are supposed to love you—the people who you count on most in this world—don't give a damn about you or your feelings? Do you have one tiny bit of a clue what that feels like, Mom?"

"Well, I…um…"

"Not only did I find out that the man I was supposed to marry was a cheating dirtbag, but I had to find all that out with the news media watching!" she cried. "And instead of helping me, you told me to go out there and smile for the cameras so Derek didn't look bad. You were more concerned with *his* image than your own daughter!"

"Emery, I…it was—"

"It was awful and horrible and so damn wrong of you!" Emery interrupted. "My whole life I wanted nothing but to please you and Dad. I was a good student, a good daughter, and when I needed you both the most, you opted to be on Team Derek. And for what, huh? Because you wanted so badly to be part of some sort of political dynasty! You wanted it so badly you sold out your own child! And to that I say shame on you!"

She was breathless and found she was wandering from room to room the entire time. Was there some response she was waiting for? Yes—an apology! A logical explanation! Anything! But after a full minute of her mother saying absolutely nothing, Emery decided to keep unleashing.

"I had to go into hiding to get some peace. Do you have any idea how humiliating that was? None of my friends around here wanted to take me in because they didn't want the media attention, and you only agreed to let me stay if I played by your rules and went to stand by my man. Well, you know what? Derek's *not* my man! He never *was* my man. And he never will be my man. That is over and you need to accept that!"

Silence.

For all Emery knew, her mother had put the phone down and walked away, but that didn't mean she had to keep quiet.

Oh no—there was plenty more to say.

"Then there was Derek's lawyer tracking me down and trying to blackmail me into going to court. Did you send him there? Did you tip him off to where I was?"

"Don't be ridiculous, Emery. I had no idea where you were. You said you were going to Martha's Vineyard."

"Then tell me, Mom, how did he find me? How did he know where I was? You were the only one I had talked to!"

On the other end of the phone, she heard her mother sigh. "Derek's attorney hired a private investigator. They have one on retainer. He was the one who found you in Manhattan. You wouldn't answer most of my calls, and I did try to warn you—or at least I was going to try to warn you. If you had simply answered your phone, Emery, we could have avoided having anyone show up on your doorstep! And really, the Montgomerys? You went to the Montgomerys for help? You hate their son. That...Carter. Eliza's a very nice woman and we were sorry to hear about her husband, but they're nothing to you! Why would you go to them for help?"

"I didn't go to them, Eliza reached out to me, and I am so happy she did," she explained with an almost maniacal laugh. "I had no idea where to go and what to do. You weren't helping me and I had no place else to stay. I had camera crews on my front lawn, I couldn't leave, couldn't go to work, and Eliza Montgomery's call was like an answer to a prayer! I never knew someone could be so kind and selfless!"

Her mother exhaled loudly. "Yes, I'm sure Eliza's a saint in your eyes—a little attention and suddenly she's the hero. Well, your father and I have been here holding things together after you made things awkward."

She almost choked. "Um…excuse me? After *I* made things awkward? How is it that I did anything? Why aren't you looking at what Derek did as awkward? Why is it that he was a known womanizer, with videos of him going in and out of hotels with random women, not considered awkward? How is it that multiple women accusing him of sexual harassment is not considered awkward? How is it that he apologized to everyone in the whole damn world except me not considered awkward?" she all but screamed. "Explain that to me—*please*—because I am dying to hear how you can possibly put that kind of spin on it!"

"No one's saying what Derek did wasn't…unfortunate," she reasoned. "But you not showing up or making a statement made things difficult for everyone."

"I hate to break it to you, but if I had stayed and made a statement, it wasn't going to be in his favor. If anything, I can guarantee you I would have made things a lot worse for him and his perfect image because I would have backed all those women. I would have backed each and every one of those accusers and told all the attorneys just what a pathetic and disgusting man Derek is."

"And yet you were going to marry him," her mother replied smugly. "You would have come off as a sad and bitter woman."

At that point, Emery was almost speechless. It was hard to believe this was her mother, the woman who had given her life, and who now…was this cold and heartless person. When had that happened? When had she started to change, and why hadn't Emery noticed it until just recently?

"I guess it all goes back to me thinking I was being a good daughter. Unfortunately, that made me naive. You see, I thought my parents had my best interests at heart. I'm glad I found out how big a mistake I'd made before I said 'I do,' just how horrible of a mistake I'd made. My ego may be hurt, but I'll get over it. As a matter of fact, I already am."

It was on the tip of her tongue to mention Carter and their new relationship, but she didn't. Her mother didn't deserve to know about the wonderful relationship she was in, and there was no way Emery would give her ammunition to turn it into something ugly and twisted. Now wasn't the time for that. Right now, she needed to stand her ground and make sure this pattern of behavior ended here.

"Here's the thing, Mom," she began after taking a steadying breath and letting it out slowly, "you're my mother. If you can't see the extent of the damage your support of Derek has done to our relationship—then I feel bad for you. If you're so willing to turn your back on your own child for a man who has no use for you—or anyone, for that matter— then that's your decision. I'll be here when you're ready to apologize to me, and you know what? I'll forgive you, because that's what family does. If you want to stand beside Derek through this public-relations nightmare, you go right ahead. But leave me out of it."

She let out a shaky breath and finally walked over to her sofa and collapsed down on it.

They were silent for a long moment.

"Are you done?" her mother finally asked.

Emery replied, "Yes. I believe I am."

"It goes both ways, Emery. I'll be here when you're ready to apologize. I'm your mother and your little speech was hurtful and disrespectful. And when Derek is cleared of these false charges, maybe I'll be able to convince him to take you back."

Letting out a mirthless laugh, she said, "Mom, it will be a cold day in hell when I even *think* about that. It's never going to happen. And if that's still all you can think of, then I'll just wish you well and say goodbye."

And without waiting for a response, she hung up the phone. Placing it on the sofa cushion beside her, she waited to feel something. Waited for the tears to come.

But they didn't.

If anything, she felt completely…free. Taking several deep breaths, Emery realized that for the first time in years, there was no weight on her shoulders. No pressure on her chest. There was a lightness to her entire being that felt unfamiliar and yet…wonderful! How was it possible that after yelling and screaming at her own mother she could feel like this?

Her next thought was that she should call Carter, but when she looked at the time, she realized he was on his flight back to New Orleans. He'd promised to call when he landed, so she could share it all with him then.

But oh, how she wished she had someone to talk to right now! She felt…invigorated! Powerful! And as she stood up and looked around, Emery knew it was only the first step in reclaiming her life.

"I can't stop now," she said, walking across the room and heading into her home office. "There's so much more to be done!" The first thing she did once her computer was booted up was pull up a real estate site to get an estimate on what her townhouse was worth. She lived in a sought-after community, and no doubt she'd be able to get the place ready and on the market fairly quickly. Once she did a little research, she pulled up the site for a local agency and made an appointment to have someone come out and meet with her the following day.

"Well, that wasn't so hard." Looking at the time, the next call was to her boss. They'd only talked twice during her time away, so now was the time to really get to the heart of the matter—did they really need her back, or was her replacement already in her job permanently? During her absence, Emery had dreaded asking that question, but considering she had just stood up to her mother and started the process of putting her house up for sale, this seemed like a piece of cake.

Fifteen minutes later, she was reading the email officially terminating her employment.

Leaning back in her chair, Emery let out a long breath and smiled.

Okay, now that she was out of work, she was going to have to find something else. Fast. Her savings were almost gone and selling the house would go a long way to keeping her going, but that wasn't the pattern she wanted to fall into. She wanted a job, wanted to work.

"Might as well get started on that now too!" she said almost giddily, pulling up a couple of local job search sites. And then something hit her—she didn't have to stay local.

Hell, she could pick up and go anyplace she wanted to right now! There were no limits! She was a well-educated and intelligent woman who could very much find a job anywhere in the country and simply go! Now estranged from her parents, there was no longer anything holding her to this area.

Of course, there was a potential job offer on the table that she was keeping to herself...

"Dammit, Carter," she cursed. "I wish I could talk to you about this."

And that was true. Not that she was going to let him tell her where she should look for a job or where she should move, but she would love his input. His job kept him on the move, so there was no way for her to choose a location that would work for him or for them to be together.

That made her pause.

Because being with Carter was what she wanted most right now. It was the only thing she wanted. They had danced around the topic and said what they wanted without ever *really* saying what they wanted, and that had to stop.

For two people who always spoke their minds and never shied away from an argument, it seemed like they had spent the last couple of weeks doing just that. Each afraid of disrupting the new balance they had found. In doing so, they hadn't really solved anything; all they'd managed to do was delay the awkward conversation.

What if there wasn't a way for this to work? What if Carter wasn't able to settle in one place? And if that was the case, where did it leave her? It wasn't as if Emery was opposed to traveling, but if she was going to work, she'd have to move and settle in one city, right? Sure, there were jobs where she could work remotely, but she wasn't sure how to go about doing that.

"I'm getting ahead of myself here. Talk to Carter, then freak out if you have to."

Easier said than done.

And then she had an idea—a spur of the moment, totally unlike her kind of idea.

With a grin on her face, she made a few more calls to put her plan into action.

His flight had been diverted due to bad weather, so his five-hour trip had ended up taking almost double the time to land in New Orleans. During the entire time, he hadn't been able to reach Emery due to his own stupidity—not charging his phone or packing his charger in his carry-on.

Stupid.

When the first leg of the flight touched down in Atlanta, he figured he'd be able to get off the plane and run in to one of the tech shops inside the airport and grab a charger. That wasn't the case. They had been held on the plane because there weren't any gates available, and when there finally was one, all they had time for was refueling before they were lining up to take off again.

It was maddening.

Now it was after two in the morning and he was angry at himself and exhausted, and wanted to crash as soon as he got home. Well, he'd texted Emery as soon as his phone had reached one percent battery life and then he'd crashed.

When he woke up the next morning, the sun was shining

and it was almost eleven. The morning was already gone! Cursing, he got up and showered, and as soon as he was dry, he grabbed his phone and saw that Emery hadn't responded to his text. Thinking it was odd of her not to, he called her.

"Hey, you've reached Emery. Leave a message and I'll get back to you as soon as I can. Have a great day! Bye!"

Muttering a curse, he did as her message asked. "Hey, I'm sorry I missed you—again. I can't believe I forgot to charge my phone. The whole day was a damn nightmare and I was hoping to hear your voice. Call me. I miss you." He paused. "Bye." Placing the phone down, he swore again. Already his life felt awkward and out of control because she wasn't with him, and he resented it and was just plain angry at himself for that. He'd managed to live just fine for thirty-something years without her and now, after barely a month, he couldn't seem to function at all.

I need to get back into my regular routine, that's all. Get over to the restaurant and meet up with the staff and I'll feel like I'm back on level ground again. No big deal. And by the time the dinner crowd arrives, it will be like I never left. He realized he didn't feel nearly as confident as his words sounded in his head. Refusing to think about it, he made himself a cup of coffee and got dressed. By noon, he was in his car and on his way.

By one, he was laughing with his staff and getting caught up on what had been going on—which wasn't much. This particular restaurant ran like a well-oiled machine.

It was both comforting and a little anticlimactic.

"So what do you say, Chef," his manager, Rocco, asked. "You've got a pile of mail a mile high on your desk and you have an appointment with our wine guy scheduled for two

o'clock. Why don't you get started on the mail and I'll prepare you something to eat, deal?"

"That would be great. I'm craving some jambalaya, if
there's any ready," he requested. "And if not, surprise me."
After thanking the staff, he let them all get back to work and
went to his office.

The mail took a little time to go through, but his assistant had already sorted it out so only things that required his
attention or his signature were left for him to handle. Lunch
was delicious and the meeting with the wine distributor was
pleasant. By the time he left, Carter was growing concerned
that he hadn't heard from Emery yet. He knew she had a lot
to handle when she got home, but he had hoped it wouldn't
mean she would go radio silent on him.

Pulling out his phone, he called her.

"Hey, you've reached Emery. Leave a message and I'll
get back to you as soon as I can. Have a great day! Bye!"

With a growl of frustration, he left a message. "Em, I'm
getting a little concerned now. I know you're busy settling
back in, but call me. Soon. I'm going to need you to call me,
otherwise I'm getting on the next flight back to Albany and
coming to check on you in person." Hanging up, he tossed
the phone on his desk with frustration. Where the hell was
she? Had her parents given her grief? Was she back at work?
Had something happened to her? His mind was swirling
with every sort of scenario and he was just about to pull up
flight options when there was a knock on the door.

"Come in!" he barked and opted to search flights anyway.

"Sorry to bother you," Rocco said, peeking into the
room. "But we've got a situation out here and—"

"You'll have to handle it. Something's come up and I

need to leave," he snapped, his eyes never leaving the computer screen. It would take him an hour to get to the airport if he didn't stop at home to pack, and then there was security to get through. In all honesty, the earliest he could get on a flight was around 7:00 p.m. and even that would be cutting it close. Cursing, he pushed himself away from the desk, raking a hand through his hair.

"You're leaving? You just got back," Rocco said, confusion lacing his words.

"And you run everything so efficiently that I'm really not needed," Carter said, finally looking over at the man. "And I'm not saying that to be snarky, I'm actually very thankful for you, Rocco. It's just…there's something I need to take care of back in Albany."

Rocco smiled. "Well, before you go, there's someone here to see you."

"Really, Roc, I don't have the time. Can't you make an excuse for me? I need to book this flight and—"

Suddenly the door opened wide—almost slamming against the wall behind it—and Emery stepped into the threshold. "Don't you dare book a flight back to Albany," she said with all the sass and attitude he loved about her. "This is my first time in New Orleans and I'm not leaving until you show me around properly." She paused, still not stepping fully into the room. "Plus someone once dared me to come to one of his restaurants because he was confident I'd be so wowed by his cooking prowess."

With a small smile, Rocco waved and walked away. Once he was gone, Emery stepped into the office and closed the door behind her. Carter was certain his jaw was hanging on the ground and that he was hallucinating. She couldn't be here. It wasn't possible. She was back in Albany taking care of her life. How…? Why…?

Finally, he forced himself to speak. "What are you doing here?" Standing, he walked around the desk and slowly made his way to her—as if he was afraid she would leave. He prayed she wouldn't—she looked more beautiful than he remembered. Had it really only been twenty-four hours? In all the years they'd known each other and in the last month where they were together every day, he'd never seen her look like this.

With a shrug, Emery stood her ground and waited for him to come to her. "I was hungry and figured I should come and eat at one of your restaurants." She grinned at him—one of her smartass ones that he knew so well. "I almost went to the one in Orlando because…you know, theme parks and all that, but then I figured there'd be time for that later. I've never been to New Orleans, so here I am." She took a step toward him. "So—what's on the menu here? Anything normal?"

Then she was in his arms and he was kissing her, because the only way he knew to stop Emery from talking food was to keep her quiet like this. Her arms wrapped around him, and if he could, he'd devour her right here, right now, in his office.

And why couldn't he?

Maneuvering them over to the desk, he had her pressed against it when she broke the kiss and started to laugh.

"Nice try, Montgomery. But you've been boasting and bragging about how awesome your restaurants are that you're not going to distract me this time. Feed me now and then you can have your way with me later."

And damn if that wasn't a good deal, he thought.

"Fine, but just…don't get too close to me, because I've been out of my mind missing you and now that you're here, there are so many things I'd rather be doing than sitting down to a meal."

Her husky laugh wrapped around him as she grabbed his hand and walked toward the door. "And I promise you'll get to do them all. After I eat."

It took a few minutes to get through the kitchen because he introduced her to everyone. She had his staff eating out of the palm of her hand as she talked about what foods she liked and disliked, and Carter knew she would convince his chef to prepare some sort of specialty dish just for her.

He showed her around the restaurant, explaining his décor choices before choosing a table in the back corner. Lunch hadn't been that long ago, but he knew whatever food was brought out for her, there'd be enough for the two of them to share.

And really, the sooner they ate, the sooner he could take her home.

Once they had drinks in front of them and were finally alone, he asked, "So seriously, Em, what are you doing here? I thought you had a lot to do."

Some of her vibrancy faded and her shoulders hunched a little before she shifted in her seat to look at him. "I got home, aired the place out, did laundry, and food shopped," she explained, playing with the straw in her drink as she spoke. "Then I called my mother."

"And how did that go?"

She let out a small, bitter laugh. "Depends on who you ask, I guess."

"What do you mean?"

She shrugged. "I said my piece and explained why I thought her stand on this entire situation was wrong, and she disagreed. I told her I'd be there when she was ready to apologize, and she said she'd be waiting for me to do the same."

His eyes went wide. "Wow."

She nodded. "I know." Quiet for a moment, Emery took a sip of her drink before going on. "It's not like I'm completely surprised, although I was hoping she'd at least try to see my side of things, but she didn't. When I got off the phone with her after getting everything off my chest, I felt relieved. Maybe more so than if she'd apologized. I think this way I can have a good reason for keeping my distance. I said what I had to say and...that's it."

He knew what she was doing—she was making an excuse for her mother's bad behavior, because it was easier than admitting how much it hurt. Reaching out, he took her hand and kissed it.

"Right before my father died, Christian and I had talked about confronting him about the way he treated us. Well, mostly Christian, but I told him I'd be right there with him to stand up for him."

Emery looked at him oddly. "And what happened?"

Letting out a long breath, he shook his head. "It never happened. He had the stroke before either of us could say anything to him." He paused and studied her hand in his. "The thing is, I think it would have gone exactly the way you just described. I think Christian would have spoken his mind, I would have backed him up and told my father how much his disrespect of my career choice hurt, and he wouldn't have been affected at all."

"You don't know that for sure, Carter. He might have surprised you."

He shook his head. "Unfortunately, I don't think so. Over the years I'd argued with him enough to know he never wanted to admit he was wrong—never believed there was any other way except his way."

"I'm so sorry."

"It was harder for my brother. Our father was always harder on him, and when Dad died, Christian felt the loss the most because there was unfinished business. He never had the opportunity to tell my father what he thought or how he felt." Then he looked at her. "I'm glad you got to do that. You didn't let this go on for years and fester. You took a stand and I only wish it had gone better for you, that she had respected your words and apologized for the pain she caused you."

"On some level I knew she wouldn't, but I didn't let it stop me, so I'm proud of myself."

He kissed her hand again. "You should be."

"After I hung up, I was feeling pretty empowered and relieved and just so many different emotions, so I decided to keep up the momentum and reached out to a real estate agent and put my place on the market!" she said excitedly. "I met with them yesterday evening and started the process. Actually, the original appointment was for today, but I called them back and asked them to come over ASAP and they did."

"Wait, what? You put your place up for sale already?"

She nodded.

"But…where are you going to go? What are you going to do?" Then he realized what he wanted her answer to be—where he wanted her to be.

"Well," she began coyly, "that's kind of why I'm here. To talk to you about it."

How he loved this woman even as she frustrated the hell out of him. "And you couldn't do that by phone?"

She shook her head. "Nope. I thought it best if we were face-to-face for this conversation."

Leaning back in his seat, he motioned for her to continue. They were interrupted by the arrival of their food—a plate of bronzed salmon with fried oysters and an herbal brie cream. Honestly, he couldn't believe Emery had agreed to it, but the look of delight on her face at the plate of food proved that maybe he didn't know her as well as he'd thought.

And that delighted him far more than it should have.

A caesar salad for two, per her request, was also placed on the table, followed by a large plate of french fries.

Carter looked at her and then the fries and then back to her. "Really? How did I miss that order?"

She was grinning broadly as she reached for one of the fries. "Guess you weren't paying attention." After one bite, she moaned happily. "So. Damn. Good."

"You also thought the fast food place had great fries."

She swatted his hand away when he tried to grab a fry. "Uh-uh, none for you. These are all mine and they're so good, I may have to go back and ask the chef to marry me."

Even though he knew she was kidding, he couldn't help the overwhelming sense of jealousy that he felt. "I taught everyone back there how to cook," he snapped, taking a fry and biting into it before she could stop him. "So if you're proposing to anyone, it's going to be me!"

Her eyes went wide as she gasped at his words. "Carter, I was... I mean, it was just..." Then she paused and seemed to consider him for a long moment. Twisting in her seat again, she faced him. "This all goes back to why I'm here," she said calmly.

"It is?" Holy crap. Was she really here to talk marriage with him?

And that annoyed him because she was beating him to the punch—just like she used to do in school.

Nodding, Emery happily munched on a few more french fries before replying. "You see, I realized that by selling my townhouse, I could live anywhere."

"What about your job?"

"Oh yeah!" she said excitedly, slapping her hand down on the table. "I totally forgot that part of the story—I have been let go from my job. Isn't that great?"

For a moment, Carter had no idea how to respond, and felt like maybe Emery wasn't completely comprehending everything she'd just done, how her entire life was upside down again, but this time all of it her own doing.

"Um, Em, are you sure that's good news? I mean, in the span of an afternoon, you lost your job, put your home up for sale, and stopped talking to your parents. I know I'm not the best one to give advice, but…this all seems like a bit much. Are you sure you know what you're doing?"

Fork in hand, Emery took a taste of the salmon and hummed with delight before acknowledging him. "I'll admit, it does seem like a lot, but I've been thinking about it for months now. It was just finally time to put it all into action." She handed him a second fork. "C'mon, eat with me. This is fantastic! Almost totally worth the trip down from New York."

Unable to help himself, he laughed before taking a

bite—damn, it was really good. Better than the jambalaya he'd had for lunch, and that was saying something.

"Okay, so you did all this stuff and now you're thinking about where to move and finding a job. Anything else? Are you suddenly going to change careers and be a cruise director or…or go to med school to become a doctor?"

The glare she gave him told Carter she wasn't amused.

"The job thing is still up in the air. I really enjoyed working on the cookbook project for your mother, but it's not something I can make a career out of."

"Sure you can. You can work for a publisher doing that sort of thing all the time," he said, spearing his fork into the salmon for another bite. "You have a great eye for detail. I think you'd do a hell of a job."

She didn't look convinced. "It's an option, but not something I feel passionate about." She sighed. "I'm good with details. I'm good at taking a project and analyzing it and keeping it on task, but then I want to be done and move on. For some reason, lately I feel like I need to be challenged constantly. I don't want to just sit at a desk performing the same tasks day after day, but then I don't know what it is I want to do."

"You don't have to decide right away, do you?"

"Not this instant, but I've been out of work for two months, Carter. I have decent savings, but it's not going to last forever." She ate more of her meal and looked so happy and relaxed, like she didn't have a care in the world.

If it were him, Carter knew he wouldn't be able to relax at all. If he were dealing with half the things Emery was, he'd be a nervous wreck until every issue was resolved. And as he studied her, something came to mind.

He had a job for her.

Okay, it wasn't something he normally hired out, but in this instance, he thought the position would be perfect for her and it would keep her by his side for at least the next several months while she tried to work things out.

The only problem was he didn't want to insult her or make her feel like he didn't believe in her.

So maybe right now wasn't the time to bring it up.

Maybe he should wait until later, or at least tomorrow.

Or maybe—wait. Didn't she mention having something she wanted to talk to him about? He was just about to remind her, but when he looked at her and saw how much she was enjoying her meal and how truly relaxed she was, he figured it could wait.

Besides, she'd promised to let him have his way with her after she finished eating.

The sooner he let her eat, the sooner they'd get to have their fun.

Chapter 10

IT WAS AFTER TEN AND CARTER WAS LICKING CHOCO-
late sauce off Emery's nipple. Looking down at his handsome face, she could see the pure male satisfaction written
all over it. He'd taken her to places she hadn't thought her
body would ever go, and right now she just felt like a quiv-
ering mass of goo as she tried to calm her heartbeat down.

He inched his way up her body and placed a soft kiss on
her lips. "Mmm…delicious."

All Emery could do was hum softly before collapsing
against his pillows. Earlier, when he had mentioned having
plans for her, she'd had no idea he could be so creative. He'd
managed to combine her love of sweets with her love of
him, and it made for one hell of a combination.

Weakly, she reached up and raked a hand through his
dark hair. "You're mighty tasty yourself."

Carter relaxed next to her and tucked her in close to his
side, placing another kiss on her forehead. "I'm really glad
you're here."

"Mmm…me too." Exhaustion threatened to overwhelm
her and all she wanted to do was sleep. Last night at home
in her own bed hadn't been nearly as satisfying as she'd
expected and her mind had been going in a million different directions, making it impossible to get a decent night's
sleep. But now that she was here…

"Em?"

"Hmm?"

"Can I ask you something?"

"Anything."

"What would you think about…working with me?"

Slowly, she lifted her head and stared at him as if he'd lost his mind. "Excuse me?"

His expression never wavered. He met her gaze head-on. "You heard me. Come work for me."

Clearly, she was more exhausted than she'd thought, because there was no way she was hearing him correctly. "Um…Carter?"

"Hmm?"

"I think we both know I am a walking disaster in the kitchen and I'm a bit of a klutz when carrying heavy trays of food. I appreciate that you want to help me, but I don't think putting me to work in a restaurant is the way to do it."

Laughing softly, he gently guided her head back down to his shoulder. "That wasn't what I was talking about. Although the images in my head now are pretty damn funny."

Emery pinched his side and laughed when he cried out. "Making fun of me is definitely the way to kill the afterglow of some seriously spectacular sex."

"Spectacular, huh?" he teased, and she pinched him again for his smugness. "Ow! Cut that out!"

"Then stop being…you know, you!"

"Can't help it. This is who I am and you love it. Admit it."

And that's when she knew it was the perfect time. Lifting her head again, Emery met his gaze in the dimly lit room and said the words she'd been too afraid to say for some time now. "I do, you know." She swallowed hard. "I love you, Carter." Then she held her breath and waited for him to laugh at her, thank her, or simply pretend he hadn't heard her.

One strong hand came up and cupped her cheek. "I love you too, Em," he said with something that sounded a lot like relief. "I've been wanting to say it, but…"

"But…?"

His smile was that lopsided one she adored. "But as usual, you beat me to it." With his hand now anchored in her hair, he guided her lips back to his and kissed her so sweetly, so tenderly, she all but melted against him. When she lifted her head, he was still smiling. "You're everything to me. I should have told you sooner, but…I was scared. Everything that's happened between us has been so unusual and nothing at all like I thought anything should be. The last thing I wanted to do was add any pressure on you by telling you how I felt and then having you think you had to say it back to me. I kept waiting for the perfect time and—"

"This was the perfect time," she said softly, resting her forehead against his. "I was afraid to say it back in Montauk because my life was such a mess. And—let's be serious—it still is. But none of that matters, because the only constant in my life is you and I need you to know how I feel, because…well, you're stuck with me now."

He arched one dark brow at her. "Is that right?"

Nodding, she said, "Yup. You took me in and now you're stuck with me. I'm selling my house and I quit my job and—you know, for all the conversations we've had, I have no idea what a typical day in the life of Carter Montgomery is like. Or a typical month! How often do you travel? How long do you stay in one place? I mean, these are the things I'm going to need to know so we can at least see each other once in a while."

Maneuvering them so they were facing one another,

sharing a pillow, he explained to her what he meant by working with him.

"Something came to me on that last night in Montauk," he began, "a new idea for the restaurant."

She looked at him curiously and remembered that he'd never really explained to her what he was writing down in his notebook that night. "You mean like the design?"

"No, the menu." He chuckled. "You're not going to believe this, but you inspired the new menu and what I want to do with it."

"I…I don't understand."

"Do you want to know what the best part of our time in Montauk was?"

Emery blushed thinking of some of the amazing things she and Carter had done together while they were there. He lightly pinched her and she flinched. "Hey! What was that for?"

"Such a dirty mind you have," he teased lightly. "I'm being serious and your mind instantly went to the gutter. For shame."

Rolling her eyes because she knew he was teasing, she forced herself to be serious. "Okay, fine. Tell me what the best part of our time in Montauk was."

"It was the creativity you inspired in me—in my cooking," he amended. "It really got me thinking and now I want to incorporate comfort foods into the restaurant—maybe even make that the entire theme of the place. There are enough high-end restaurants out there already. Wouldn't it be nice to have something different? Something that's not a diner, but it's not a hundred dollars a plate, either."

The idea definitely had merit, she thought. How many times had she wanted to go someplace nice to eat and found she was disappointed because the food was overpriced and the portions small? And on top of that, most of the selections weren't what she was looking for. What Carter was suggesting was really intriguing.

"So what price point were you thinking of? Who is your target clientele? What will the interior look like?"

He laughed again and hugged her close. "These are all the things I'm trying to work out and want your help with. I want to set up a test kitchen with you and maybe get some of the locals involved to see what we can do."

The more she thought about it, the more excited she became. "It's so close to the holidays, Carter. I know you have an opening date in mind, but with all this new information, you may have to change that. Are you prepared to? Can you?"

"I'm going to have to, because I refuse to open the place until it's perfect. There's going to be a bit of trial and error involved that I haven't had to do before, but if we play around with ideas over the holidays, then kick off the New Year and hit the ground running, we just might be able to have a soft opening in the early spring."

"I guess we could. Where would we start? Where would we set up?"

"We go back to Montauk. We sit down and talk food and menus and options, and then we start cooking and testing. Once we have the menu set, we talk about décor, and then I start looking for staff to work for us."

"Us?" she squeaked. "You mean you, right? I mean…it's your place and you're the boss and—"

His finger rested on her lips to silence her. "Us, Em. We are going to create this together. If it wasn't for you and your

crazy eating habits and you forcing me to leave my pretentious comfort zone, I would never have thought of this."

Holy crap was that a lot of pressure on her.

Which was what she said to him. "Carter, just because
I'm a weirdo who likes to eat that kind of food doesn't mean
you're going to find customers who are willing to come out
and eat it. It's too much pressure on me. If this doesn't work
out and the restaurant tanks, I'd never be able to forgive
myself! Please tell me you have a Plan B!"

"There's always a Plan B," he said reassuringly. "That's
why we do a test kitchen and market research. We may
end up with this being just part of the overall menu." He
shrugged as if it weren't a big deal. "But it could also be a
phenomenal success and we start a trend and this new
model becomes the one I make into a chain. Can you imagine having dozens of restaurants with your menu?"

She was going to be sick.

"Carter, you've been mocking my food choices for over a
month and all of a sudden you're talking like it's the greatest
thing you've ever heard. Are you sure you're feeling all right?"

"Never been better. Trust me." Pulling her in close, he
kissed her again. Slowly. Thoroughly. When he pulled back
a few minutes later, he gave her a lazy smile. "Think about
it, okay? You don't have to decide right now. Tomorrow I'll
take you out sightseeing and we'll spend the rest of the week
here, and then—if you're up for it—we'll go check out my
other two locations so you can get a feel for my business.
And by the time we're done, it will be time to head out to
Megan and Alex's for Thanksgiving. What do you say?"

Right now she couldn't do more than yawn and fight to
keep her eyes open. "Sounds good," she whispered.

"I love you, Em."

"Love you too." And then she was asleep.

The next time she opened her eyes, the room was bright, the sun was shining, and she was sprawled out in Carter's bed alone. Slowly, she rolled over and sat up. Feeling a little disoriented, she looked around and saw the clock read eight fifteen.

Carter was already up and working in the kitchen. Emery could hear him moving around and could smell coffee brewing.

Bless him, she thought.

Yawning broadly, she stretched and was about to kick off the blankets when Carter appeared in the doorway. "Good morning."

She smiled and ran a hand over her hair in an attempt to smooth it a bit. "Good morning. What time did you get up?"

Pushing off the door frame, he walked into the room and sat on the bed beside her. "About an hour ago." He kissed her softly. "Did you sleep okay?"

Nodding, she replied, "I did."

"Hungry?"

"Always."

He smiled and kissed her again before standing to pull his robe from his closet, handing it to her. "Breakfast is almost ready. I hadn't gone shopping since I got back and did a quick run this morning so we would have something to eat. I know you favor waffles, so I whipped up a couple of Belgian ones and they're warming right now. And your coffee is waiting."

"You spoil me, Carter."

Gently, he pulled her from the bed and his gaze raked over her naked body. Before she could say anything else, he helped her into the robe. "Breakfast," he said gruffly. "I'm going to go plate everything." And then he was gone.

Part of Emery loved how he seemed tempted to forget about the food and start the day right back in the bed, but part of her loved how he took his food and her appetite even more seriously.

Securing the robe around her, Emery padded out to the kitchen just as Carter was putting their plates on the breakfast bar. She hopped up on a stool and reached for the mug of steaming-hot coffee waiting for her. The first sip was glorious. Not only could the man cook like a dream, but he made a fine cup of coffee too.

Truly the total package.

Last night there had seemed to be so much to talk about and they had barely scratched the surface. Although the most important things were said.

She loved Carter.

And he loved her.

All the rest would fall into place, right?

Today she was looking forward to having Carter show her around the city, enjoying all the magnificent food she'd heard about. Of course, she would do her best not to compare it to his cooking, but she had a feeling he was going to ask at some point. No doubt his ego could take a little comparison, but she was learning when to be playful with him and when to tread lightly. This was his career, after all.

It was humbling.

It was terrifying.

It was…awesome.

That one simple request from him meant more to

Emery than anything she'd ever been asked before in her entire life. It showed that he trusted her—no matter how much he teased. And because of that, because he trusted her, she wouldn't let him down.

Sitting beside her, Carter gave her a sexy grin. "Dig in, beautiful."

And she did.

Their time in New Orleans flew by and before she knew it, they were on a plane to Orlando to check out Carter's newest restaurant. They spent the weekend and a few days afterward playing tourists, hitting up the theme parks and enjoying more amazing food. All the walking they did during the day made her feel better about eating so much at night.

They stayed in Florida through the middle of the week before flying out to LA to do it all again. She enjoyed it, but soon realized she was an East Coast girl at heart and sitting around spotting celebrities wasn't really her thing. After only three days, they flew out to Vegas.

"You know," she said when they'd boarded the plane, "this is the one location you don't talk about. Why?"

He shrugged and accepted his beverage from the flight attendant.

"Come on," she urged. "There's a story there. I can tell."

He took a sip of his drink and shifted to face her. "LA and NOLA were more than I ever thought I'd achieve. I was riding the high of their success and was approached to do a spot in Vegas on the Strip." He took another sip. "I have a ton of investors and this one just sort of...I don't know, I don't have a connection to it."

"Why?"

Sighing loudly, he placed his drink down on his tray table. "I used to love traveling to New Orleans and trying all the food. To me it was like the ultimate eating destination. LA wasn't quite like that, but I got caught up in the atmosphere and the people. When I think of Vegas, it's not the food I'm thinking about. It's the shows, hotels, and gambling."

That comment stayed with her for a minute. "Okay, maybe I'm overthinking this, but if that's how you feel, then...why Montauk? What is it about that location that has you wanting to open a place there? Where's the connection?"

"You're not overthinking it at all," he assured her. "Montauk is...it's my happy place. Whenever I want to get away, it's where I go—just...never during the summer months," he added with a small laugh. "I love the town, I love the architecture, I love the privacy and the way I feel when I'm there. That's why the idea of comfort food hit me so hard. Montauk is my comfort, so it only makes sense for the restaurant to share that vibe."

"Interesting."

"I've tried not to push, but..."

She knew exactly where he was going. They hadn't talked any more about her working for him—even though she clearly wasn't putting much effort into looking for work anywhere else.

"There's so much to think about, Carter. I know you're excited about this and I love how you've put your trust in me."

"But...?"

"But we've spent so much of our lives competing with

one another and not trusting each other and...I don't know. I guess I don't want you doing this out of some sort of misplaced feelings or something."

"That makes zero sense," he said flatly.

Now it was her turn to sigh loudly. "Okay, hear me out."

"Fine."

"Right now we're in this really great place—this aspect of our relationship is new and wonderful and everyone is happy and in love."

"All good things."

"I know, I know," she said, organizing her thoughts. "But why are you just starting to trust me now? We've known each other for most of our lives. Sex didn't change me or the way I think or do things, so...why are you so willing to trust me now?"

Carter's expression went from pleasant to neutral to fierce in a matter of seconds, but he stayed silent.

"Don't get me wrong, I appreciate it. I do. But the timing seems a little odd, that's all. If we hadn't started sleeping together and hung out in Montauk exactly as we had—minus the sex—would you be willing to do this?"

"Yes," he said adamantly, fiercely. "Yes, I would. I'm not about to screw around with my business because you're good in bed, Emery."

The way he said it sounded crude and she was both offended and ashamed of herself for bringing it up. But if they were going to do this—if they were committed to this relationship—they were going to have to talk to one another about things that were uncomfortable. They'd never shied away from it before and she wasn't willing to change that now.

"I would hope not," she snipped, "but then again, I don't know much about your thought process and how you plan these things. I thought talking about it would help."

"And has it?"

Honestly, it was like he was trying to be difficult. "At the moment? No. No, it hasn't." Letting out a long breath, Emery glared at him before taking a sip of her drink. "What is it you want me to say, Carter?"

"I want you to say you've thought about my offer and you're going to work with me!" he said with a little more heat than she expected. The gentleman across the aisle leaned forward and looked at them, and Carter quickly lowered his voice. "I didn't think you were going to require so much time to think this over. You've always been decisive."

"So that should tell you I'm seriously considering it."

"Or...it could be you don't want to accept it and you're trying to find a way to break it to me."

It took her a moment to get her emotions under control. "Look, my life is at a crossroads right now. I'm afraid to make the wrong decision. I need to know you're offering me a job for the right reasons. And okay, maybe I was afraid to talk to you about it because I didn't want you snapping at me." She paused and glared at him to get her point across. "And honestly, I'm still not convinced it's the right thing to do. For either of us."

"How come?"

"At some point we're going to have to deal with not being together all day, every day! Right now it's fun and we're both able to do it without worrying about other commitments, but the bottom line is we're going to get on each other's nerves fast if we don't start having some time apart. I would hate for us to reach this place in our relationship—a place where we're happy and in love—and have it all go to shit because we're going crazy for lack of personal space!"

Then, in typical Carter fashion, he laughed. A full-throttle, hearty laugh.

Damn the man.

"This is funny to you?"

He was still chuckling even as he shook his head. After a moment, he took one of her hands and caressed it. "Emery, I get what you're saying. And yeah, there will be times when we get on each other's nerves, but that's a given. It'll happen whether we're working together or just hanging out together. I don't think that part of our relationship is ever going to end, and you know what? I don't want it to! Fighting with you is freaking awesome." Then he waggled his eyebrows at her. "And making up with you is even better."

Pulling her hand away, she swatted at him with annoyance. "Can't you be serious even for a minute here?"

"I've been serious for weeks now!" he cried, immediately cringing at his tone again. "If you're looking for some sort of guarantee, I can't give it to you! If you want me to promise that everything will be sunshine, rainbows, and unicorns, I can't give you that either! All I can give you is the truth. I want to work with you on this project. It's not going to last forever and we may very well find that it makes us both crazy. And if it does, we'll agree to let it go without letting it rip us apart. That I can guarantee you. Okay?"

He was being completely logical and making total sense, and for the life of her, she had no idea why she wasn't jumping at the idea.

Because you have been making terrible life choices for years...

If it wouldn't make her look like a complete crazy person, Emery would have shouted at her inner voice to shut up.

And speaking of choices, what was in this for Carter? What was up with Carter in general? Yeah, he had some self-imposed pressure where his business was concerned, but now that his father was gone, she would have thought that would be over. So why was he still beating himself up when he'd more than proved he was an excellent business-man and restaurateur?

"Can I ask you something?"

He smirked and finished his drink. "Seems to me that's all you've been doing."

Emery fought the urge to roll her eyes.

It was almost painful.

"What are you hoping to achieve with the Montauk place? I mean, you've talked about the food, the vibe, blah, blah, blah. But why are you doing this? Why are you open-ing another place when you're clearly on the fence about the whole thing?"

"I wouldn't say I'm on the fence."

"And I wouldn't say you were a man with a clear vision, either," she countered.

He studied her hard and for a moment, she thought he was going to get loud again. Instead, he seemed to relax a little as he straightened in his seat. "Old habits die hard."

"Um...what?"

Turning his head toward her, he explained. "I've told you the constant battle I had with my father over my career. Stuff like that doesn't just go away."

"Yeah, but…"

"My other places? It was one business model we kept copying and modifying for each location based on demographics and logistics. In the back of my mind, I know my father didn't think there was much to it because they were replicas of each other—I wasn't putting in an effort. This time, I want the effort. I need the effort." He paused. "I need to prove him wrong. That it wasn't luck and it wasn't laziness, that I'm good at what I do."

"Carter…you can't think like that."

He shrugged and faced forward again. "Easier said than done."

"Yeah, but—"

"The day of the funeral, Christian stayed behind at the cemetery after we all went back to the house. At the time, I thought he was crazy. When I went back to pick him up, he told me he stood there and had a one-sided argument with Dad." He laughed softly. "Now I wish I had thought to do it. I still might."

Reaching out, she captured one of his hands in hers and held it.

"Maybe I'm wrong. Maybe I should just be happy with what I have and what I've done and leave it alone. But the seed was planted, Em. The doubt is there, whether he intended to put it there or not. Now I need to know—to prove—I'm better than that. Better than he believed me to be."

And that's what it all came down to, really. Everyone wanted their parents' approval. Emery knew it was like that for her. It was why she'd had to confront her mother. There'd been that hope that she could change her mother's mind and she'd get not only her mother's approval, but an apology. Carter was never going to get that. There was no way to get approval or apologies from a ghost. So why? Why keep trying?

"Did it help Christian?" she asked softly. "Did all the arguing make a difference?"

"Eventually. I've told you my father was roughest on him. Made the most demands. There were times my brother was crippled by my father's words."

"And now?"

He smiled softly, looked back over at her again. "Now he has Sophie and all is right with his world."

Somehow she doubted it was quite that simple.

"And he no longer has any lingering issues because of your father?"

"Some. Like I said, old habits die hard. But he's getting better and he's living life on his own terms finally."

"Then so can you," she said simply. "You should be doing this because you love it—because your creativity is begging you to do it. If your only reason is to prove a point to someone who is no longer here, that's going to show, Carter. There will be a pall over the whole project that will never go away. You need to think about that."

Carter didn't get a chance to respond because one of their flight attendants was making an announcement.

"Ladies and gentlemen, we're making our final approach to McCarran International Airport and Las Vegas. Our crew will be coming up the aisle to collect all trash. Please place your seats in their upright position, along with your tray tables, and please secure your seatbelts. Thank you and welcome to Las Vegas!"

Vegas was okay.

Thanksgiving at Megan and Alex's was fun.

Returning to everyday life was harder than Carter imagined.

When he and Emery had left Portland, they had flown back to Albany with his mother. He had thought he was only going to spend a day or two before heading out to Montauk to check on progress with the building.

Then Emery had dropped a bombshell.

Several bombshells.

First, she turned down his offer for a job.

Turned. Him. Down.

After being majorly pissed off about it, he realized—begrudgingly—that she'd had a point. He was already putting enough pressure on himself over the restaurant for personal reasons, and she didn't want to be a part of that if things didn't work out. She didn't want to feel the guilt or that she was to blame if it didn't succeed.

However, she agreed to consult with him on his menu options or design choices as his girlfriend only.

With no other choice, Carter had agreed, but he wasn't happy about it. He was worried about her and her career options when bombshell number two hit.

She'd accepted a job from his Uncle William with Montgomerys.

Yeah, that one came completely out of left field.

Apparently when his uncle and Emery had spoken during the mock Christmas weekend, he had offered her a job working semiremotely for the company. When Emery finally told Carter about it, he had asked her why she had kept it a secret.

Her response? "You had a lot on your plate and so did I. I wanted to think about it without any input. Listening to other people is yet another reason why my life is a mess and not quite my own."

Once again, he got it, but it still stung a little that she hadn't shared it with him sooner.

But the final bombshell had come from both Emery and his mother.

The fundraiser they had created the cookbook for was having its gala that weekend and not only were Emery's parents going to be there, but so was her ex.

All this time, Carter figured he'd go to the gala, since his face was on the cookbook and all, but he hadn't given much thought to the guest list. Now it was all he could think about, and every one of those thoughts was negative.

He didn't want to see Emery's ex, and he didn't want her to see him, either! If it were up to him, he'd demand she not go and the two of them could simply head out to Montauk as soon as possible and not give the whole thing another thought.

And when he'd shared that logic with her, she'd been less than enthusiastic about it.

Actually, she'd thrown a shoe at him.

But only because he might have called her an idiot for considering going and being in the same room with all the people responsible for the shit-show that her life had become.

Yeah, not his finest moment.

Didn't mean it wasn't true, though. When he'd pushed

her on the subject, she said it was something she had to do—that they weren't going to force her to run or hide anymore. She had a prominent position with the charity thanks to his mother and therefore her attendance was mandatory.

As was his.

Dammit.

Now his main problem was how he could go and be cordial and sociable when all he wanted to do was hunt the three of them down and do some serious damage for all the ways they'd hurt her. Good manners demanded he have self-control and not make a scene, but that didn't mean he didn't want to. And really, he should be allowed to. Weren't these extenuating circumstances? Didn't anyone realize this was the sort of situation where normal rules didn't apply? And after all Emery had been through, shouldn't someone go to bat for her?

That last thought had been haunting him for days, and every time he mentioned it to her, the angrier she got with him—saying he needed to let her handle this her way.

But he couldn't. He absolutely couldn't.

They were staying at Emery's place for the time being, and she was currently on a conference call with Uncle William and Uncle Robert, talking about her new position. No doubt she'd be on the phone for a while, so Carter decided to take a ride over to his mother's. Emery may not agree with his line of thinking, but he was positive his mother would.

An hour later, he was proven wrong.

"You cannot make a scene, Carter! Why would you think that's okay?"

Seriously? Sitting at the kitchen table with his mother in his childhood home, Carter couldn't believe she wasn't backing him up on this. "Mom, come on! You know better than anyone what Emery's been through! How could you let these people come?"

"The Monaghans are prominent members of the community," his mother explained reasonably. "It's not unusual for them to be on the guest list. As for Derek Whitmore..." She shook her head and sighed. "I have no idea how that one got by."

"So stop it!" he cried. "You're on the committee for this thing—like one of the chair people, right? Why can't you simply say he's not allowed to attend? He's a disgrace! He's going to steal attention away from the cause!"

And that's when he knew he had her. How it was possible no one else had thought of this was beyond him, but right now he was thankful for it. Sitting back a little smugly, he smiled at his mother.

She didn't smile back.

"Believe me, I don't like this any more than you do, but it will also cause a bit of a scandal if the media gets wind of us refusing Derek entry into the gala. I'm sorry, Carter, but my hands are tied."

"What?" he shouted, coming to his feet. "I think you'll have more of a scandal if you let him in so he can...can prey on the people there! Seriously, why is this guy getting so much leniency from everyone?"

"It's not leniency," she reasoned. "He went and did his stint in rehab—"

"He left early."

"And he's trying to make amends. I'm sure he knows by now that Emery is going to be there. We've mentioned her in all the press releases about the event—"

"Great. So because you wanted to give her credit, now she has to deal with this unfortunate situation. Thanks, Mom." Eliza stood and smacked him on the arm. "Ow! What was that for?"

"For being a smartass," she snapped. "Contrary to popular belief, I didn't do this to Emery. She and I have talked about this at great length and the only one carrying on about it is you! Have you talked to Emery about this?"

"Of course I have!"

"And?"

By the look on her face, she already knew the answer. "Okay, fine. She says she's fine with it and she's not going to let it ruin her night." He let out a long breath and tugged at his hair as he began to pace. "But I don't understand how she could be! Did she tell you about her conversation with her mother when she came home? It was awful! Why would she want to be in the same room with her after that?"

"Maybe she needs to be, Carter. Maybe this is all part of reclaiming her life."

Yeah, that was exactly what Emery had said, but...he still couldn't bear the thought of her being hurt or embarrassed publicly.

Even though the behavior he was threatening would potentially do the same thing.

And that's when he knew what he had to do.

With a weary sigh, he faced his mother. "Then I can't be there."

"What?" she cried, taking a step toward him. "You have to be!"

But he shook his head, resignation wrapped around him. "If I go, I know I'm going to end up either making a scene or upsetting Emery in some way. No doubt you'll end up on edge because of me, too. And I can't do that. If I'm not allowed to protect her, then—then I shouldn't go."

"You're making assumptions," Eliza said with a bit of a huff. "For all you know, there won't be any reason to make a scene and Emery won't need protecting because everyone will behave themselves, have you thought of that?"

He shook his head. "I was there when she watched that press conference and I was there when she told me about the last conversation with her mother and I was there for all the time in between. You can have all the faith in the world that things are going to go smoothly, but I don't believe that will be the case."

"Carter, you're being an unreasonable brat!"

With a mirthless laugh, he turned and sat back down. "No. No, I'm not. I'm simply a man whose hands are tied. Emery doesn't want me making a scene, you don't want me making a scene, and I know myself well enough to know that's exactly what I'm going to end up doing. So I'm throwing in the towel and making things easier on both of you."

"You know that's not what we want! You need to be there. You're the reason we have such a fantastic product for our fundraiser! How am I supposed to explain your absence?" she cried.

But he wasn't affected by her tone or the tears welling in her eyes. He had to be strong for himself here. So many other people had let Emery down, and Carter could remember how many big events his father had ruined for his mother because of his behavior. There was no way in hell he wanted to repeat that pattern for either of them.

His solution wasn't ideal, but it was the best he could offer.

Even if the devastation on his mother's face said otherwise.

"It's for the best," he said, his voice gruff. "I need to head out to Montauk and see what kind of progress has been made. You can tell people I had some sort of emergency on the site and couldn't get back in time." He scrubbed a weary hand over his face and sighed. "It wouldn't be a total lie."

"I shouldn't have to tell *any* lie," she said quietly, taking her seat at the table beside him.

"Mom…"

They sat like that, staring at one another for several long moments.

"I'm not going to change your mind on this, am I." It wasn't really a question.

Shaking his head, Carter forced himself to stand and went to look out at the yard through the sliding glass doors. "Like I said, Mom, this is best for everyone. This way you and Emery can enjoy the night without me ruining it."

He expected some sort of push-back—another attempt at making him change his mind—but instead, his mother came and stood beside him, staring out at the property with him for a few minutes.

"Sometimes I used to wish your father would have stayed home," she said quietly. "Everywhere we went that wasn't something he had a part in, he would be difficult. Sometimes he would make me late, sometimes he would be rude to people, and other times he just critiqued every little thing for the entire night. It was exhausting."

"That's what I'm trying to avoid, Mom. I swear. I remember when Dad behaved like that. The last thing I want to do is be like him."

Beside him, her shoulders sagged and she let out a soft sigh. "I'm so sorry, Carter."

"For what?" he asked, his tone equally soft.

"I didn't do more to stop him or try hard enough to change him." She shook her head but didn't look at him. "I kept thinking he'd change, and in so many ways he did. Just…not enough to give his children anything but bad memories of him."

Carter knew he should argue that, but he couldn't. He wasn't a liar. Joseph Montgomery had had a lot of strong opinions and he'd felt his way was the only way in every situation. Still, Carter hated to see his mother beating herself up over it.

"It wasn't your fault, Mom. Dad was who he was and that's all there is to it."

"I hate hearing the way you and Christian and Megan talk about him. I know there were some good times— like the memories we shared during our mock Christmas weekend—but most of the times when you kids talk about your father, it's negative."

Raking a hand through his hair, Carter couldn't help but sigh again. "Yeah, I know. We should probably lighten up on that, but—"

"But he did a lot of damage with his words," she finished for him. "Your brother and sister wanted his approval. You did too, but he struggled with it the most because you went against what he wanted for you." Then she did look at him. "Here's something you don't know."

Curiosity had him facing her. "What?"

"He was really only mad for a little while," she said, a small smile playing at her lips. "Don't get me wrong, he always wished you would work with him just like all your cousins did with your uncles, but he had incredible respect for you and what you built."

"Mom," he said a little sharply, "you don't have to say that. I promise to stop laying into him so much and being disrespectful, but please don't make up stories. It's not right."

Her eyes went wide right before she got defensive—crossing her arms over her chest. "Now, you listen here—have I ever been one to lie?"

"Sorry," he mumbled.

"Anyway," she began again, giving him a harsh glare, "after you opened your first restaurant, it was almost impossible to go out to dinner with your father again and enjoy it."

"Why?"

"Oh my goodness, all he would do is compare! 'Carter's steak was better,' 'Carter's salad dressing was better,' 'Carter's place wasn't nearly as noisy,' or my personal favorite, 'Carter trained his bartenders right. They know how to make a damn good drink.' One night, he got up and demanded to talk to the chef at DuTorre's here in town. He walked back into the kitchen and told the man he should call you and learn how to prepare a proper rack of lamb! I'm telling you, on and on and on it went to the point where a lot of our friends stopped going out to dinner with us!" She laughed and—if he wasn't mistaken—wiped a tear away from her eye. "Ask Uncle Robert some time about the vacation we took with him and Aunt Janice and how much he hated eating out with us."

"But that's crazy, Mom. Dad always criticized, always—"

"Carter, your father criticized everything and everyone!

I don't think he knew how to have a regular conversation! It was like he was always trying to prove how much he knew or how he was smarter than everyone. I swear, what your father was—besides a pain in the ass—was insecure." She let out a long breath and reached to cup his cheek. "He hated that you chose a different path, even though he respected you for it and was blown away by what you created."

"Then why didn't he…just once—" Emotion clogged his throat and he couldn't finish the question, but his mother knew what he was asking.

"I wish I knew," she said quietly, sadly. "It would have made things so much easier for all of us after he was gone if we'd just understood why."

He nodded.

"I'm not saying you don't have a reason to be angry, but sometimes you don't know the whole story, and some-times…sometimes you have to forgive and move on. You've done something amazing with your life and you should be proud of yourself. Don't let anyone take that away from you. Any. One."

There were no words he could speak right then, he was so overwhelmed with emotion. He could almost hear his father's voice saying the things his mother just said to him, and no matter how hard he wished or hoped or prayed, he would never hear them for himself. It was both depressing and…freeing.

Maybe his father had never said the words Carter wanted to hear, but this conversation healed a lot of wounds. More than he'd thought possible.

"Thanks, Mom." Leaning in, he hugged her and placed a gentle kiss on the top of her head.

After a few moments, she asked, "So you're still going to Montauk?"

Pulling back, Carter looked down at her and nodded. "I am. Although…" He paused. "I have a much better attitude about it now. You helped me a lot today."

Her look of surprise was a little sweet and a little funny. "Me? How?"

With another quick kiss, he stepped back. "You just gave me the final piece to this whole new restaurant plan." Glancing over his shoulder, he checked the clock on the wall. "I need to get going. I'll talk to you when I get back."

"But—Carter, wait!"

"Sell lots of cookbooks!" he called out as he made his way to the front door. "I ordered a hundred of them for each of the restaurants and the money will go directly to the charity! Good luck!"

And as he climbed into his rental car and sped away, he really did feel like things had finally fallen into place.

Emery was typing up the last of her notes when she heard Carter come back. She had no idea where he'd gone, but by the loud slam of the door, she guessed it wasn't a pleasure trip. Hitting SAVE, she closed her laptop and walked out into the living room just as he was going into her bedroom.

"Hey," she said casually, following him into the room. "Everything okay?"

Her next clue that something was up was the way he went right into her walk-in closet and came out with his suitcase.

"Um, what's going on?"

"I'm heading out to Montauk."

"Why?" Stepping closer to the bed, she watched as he began haphazardly throwing his clothes into the case. "Did something happen at the restaurant?"

"Not really," he said vaguely, not stopping to look at her. "I'm just anxious to get out there and see what progress has been made."

Something was up. Carter wasn't normally evasive and he wasn't particularly spontaneous, so if he was leaving, there was a reason.

Carefully, she sat down on the corner of the bed and when he turned to grab another pile of clothes, she shut the suitcase.

His brow was furrowed when he spun around and looked at her. "Why'd you do that?"

"Because I want to know what your deal is. Why are you leaving? We have the fundraiser this weekend. Are you planning to come back for it?"

"No." He opened the case and resumed packing.

"Excuse me?" she said with all the pent-up aggravation she had. "What do you mean? We had plans, Carter! You're my damn date! So unless the restaurant burned to the ground, you need to be back here Saturday night."

He stopped and focused on her, just as annoyed as she was. "No, I don't, Em. I've got work to do. I've been playing tourist for weeks now and I need to put some serious time in out East to get caught up on things. With you turning down the job, I'm going to need someone I can rely on to help me out."

"Is that what this is about?" she cried. "You're paying me back because I didn't accept the job? What the hell, Carter!"

Emery reached out and grabbed his arm, which he promptly yanked away. "What do you want from me, Em?" he shouted. "I have things I need to take care of and I'm sorry it doesn't work with your timetable, but it can't be helped!"

"Bullshit! You're doing this to be spiteful and I want to know why." His expression was beyond angry. Rather than shrink back, she poked and prodded some more. "You owe me an explanation, dammit!"

That's when he took a step toward her. "Let me ask you something," he said, his voice low and rough, practically a growl. "If I asked you not to go to the fundraiser—if I asked you to come with me to Montauk tonight, would you come?"

It was the last thing she expected him to say and it stunned her into silence before she could collect her thoughts. "No," she said simply, feeling confused. "I know this shouldn't be a big deal to me. I mean, I wasn't part of the committee from the beginning, but I put in a lot of work in the short time I had on the project and I'd like to be there to see everyone's reactions. I'm no different from anyone else, Carter. I enjoy getting praised for my work."

Emery braced herself for a snarky comeback or at the very least more yelling. Instead, Carter's shoulders sagged as he said, "And you deserve to be praised. You'll have to tell me all about it afterwards." This time when he turned to finish packing, she didn't stop him.

She studied him. He seemed agitated but resigned. "Talk to me, Carter. Please."

He closed the case and zipped it shut, then set it by the bedroom door. He didn't come over to her, didn't sit down on the bed—he simply leaned against the door frame. "You sure about that?"

"About what?"

"Wanting to know what's on my mind?"

Right now? She wasn't so sure. He was acting…different. Wordlessly, she nodded and waited.

"I'm leaving because I can't go to this gala and watch everything you've worked so hard for these last two months all go to hell," he stated, his voice a little harsh.

"What do you—"

"You'll go in there feeling completely confident but as soon as your folks show up, you're going to cave, Emery. I know it. You may fight it for a bit, but they're going to wear you down. And what's worse is they're bringing Derek to help them."

"Carter…"

"And you and my mother both expect me to stand by and watch it all happen and not do or say a damn thing. I can't do it, Emery. I can't! I won't!" His voice grew louder with each word. "I've asked you not to go, I've told you how I felt, and you know what? It doesn't seem to matter! I can't understand why you want to do this. Is the praise you're going for worth it? Are a few smiles and pats on the back worth having to face that douchebag you almost married— the guy who publicly humiliated you? Can you sit there and tell me it's all going to be okay?"

Her heart was racing harder and harder with each of his statements. Honestly, she was worried about how it was all going to go, but not enough that she was willing to hide—to miss out on something she'd worked hard for. Which was what she told him.

Pushing away from the door frame, he walked across the room. "You don't get it, do you? With people like them, it's all you can do, Em. You aren't going to win! It won't matter that you're surrounded by a hundred people, they'll use that to their advantage because they know you won't want to make a scene. And that's exactly what will have to happen to get through to them—someone has to make a damn scene! Someone needs to stand there and tell them—to their face— that you're not playing this game with them anymore!"

"And I'm going to!" she cried, jumping to her feet. "I'm asking you to trust me, Carter! I'm asking you to let me handle this my way. Not everyone has to be a bully to get their point across, and that's exactly what you're trying to do. You...*you* want to bully the bullies! Where does it end?"

"It should have ended already! You don't need to prove anything. They'll ruin the night for you, and you know what? I'm not going to feel sorry for you because I warned you—I know exactly how it's all going to go."

"Believe it or not, you don't know everything," she said with a calmness she didn't feel. "You don't want to go because I won't allow you to make a scene, then fine. Don't go. I guess it's okay for you to go and be a bully and ruin my night, but not anyone else. How twisted is that?" Pacing the room, she couldn't bring herself to look at him. "You want to know the worst part of all this?"

He didn't try to respond.

"The worst part is no matter what, my night is ruined. There's no way I can enjoy myself now." Then she did look at him. "And the one who did that—the one responsible—is you."

And still Carter didn't say a word.

"So take your things, go to Montauk. I don't care." With a huff, Emery started to leave the room, but she stopped next to him. "For weeks you've been going on about how much you trust me—about how much you believe in me— but I guess that only applies when it's convenient to you. If you meant it, we wouldn't be having this discussion and you wouldn't be running because you can't bear the thought of me proving to you that I am, in fact, okay. Well, screw you, Carter Montgomery. Screw. You."

Without a backward glance, Emery stormed from the room, scooped up her keys and purse on the way, and went right out the front door.

Carter was going to leave. She knew that.

She just didn't want to be there to see it.

Chapter 11

EVERYTHING WAS WRONG.

Every. Thing.

Carter had been in Montauk for three days and not one thing had gone right.

The house he wanted to rent wasn't available, his hotel room was right by the elevator and was loud, the bed was lumpy, and dammit, he hated sleeping alone now. On top of that, the weather hadn't been cooperating and construction was at a standstill.

"Why the hell am I here?" he muttered, walking over to the hotel room window and looking out at another gray day. The rain was just heavy enough to mean no one could work outside and there was absolutely nothing for him to do.

Almost every hour since he'd left Emery's, he questioned his decision. She had a point—a completely valid point. No one else had screwed up, just him. Although he'd still bet good money that her folks were going to swoop in and do their worst. And then Derek would be there—the icing on the cake.

Food metaphors normally amused him, but not so much right now. Right now, Carter wasn't amused with anything and had no idea how to fix it. He could pack up and drive all the way back to Albany, but to what end? He still wanted to go in there and go all caveman on anyone who upset Emery.

Hard to go caveman on yourself, dude.

Yeah, yeah, yeah. He knew that and yet still had no clue how to fix things. His mother wasn't talking to him, no doubt his siblings knew what was going on and they wouldn't talk to him if he called, so who did that leave?

Emery.

Carter knew she was the only person he should talk to, but until he could do it without making things worse, he wouldn't.

Turning away from the window, he looked around the room and sighed. If things had gone as planned, he'd be in a house with a kitchen and could work through his anger and disappointment by cooking. So many ideas for new recipes were going through his mind and he was itching to try them out. Once he had them perfected, he'd try them out on his family at Christmas.

Of course, there was a good chance his mother was disappointed enough in him that she'd rather not have him home for the holidays. The season was already difficult enough for her since his father had died. No need to add to it.

Muttering a curse, he grabbed his coat and keys and left the room. Where he was going, Carter had no idea, but anything was better than sitting there by himself. He strode through the hotel lobby and out to his car and was speeding onto the main road minutes later. If it hadn't been raining, he'd be heading out for a walk on the beach, but since that wasn't an option, he simply drove into town to find something to do there.

It was just after eleven and he hadn't had breakfast or lunch yet. "Maybe eating will help," he murmured. Though he preferred his own cooking when he was in a mood, this would have to do. He slowed down as he drove through the heart of town and tried to figure out where he wanted to go and what he wanted to eat. At the corner was the fast food place Emery had gone to on the day that changed everything for them. Smiling, he contemplated going there, but decided against it. He wanted to sit down and be served and just...think.

There was an Irish pub and an upscale Italian restaurant on the left-hand side of the street, but neither piqued his interest. To his right there was a raw seafood bar, a burger place, and a deli.

"Pass," he said with a huff, wishing he had a clue what he was in the mood for.

Then he spotted it.

The place.

A slow smile spread across Carter's face as he drove to the end of the block and turned into the almost-empty parking lot. The building was in desperate need of repair, but he remembered eating here many a time since he'd started vacationing in Montauk years ago. It was a pub type of place—dark wood interior, booths lining the perimeter of the dining area, and a handful of tables covered in red-and-white checkered tablecloths filling in the rest of the space. The food was simple and had everything from burgers to whatever the local fishermen happened to catch that day.

Yeah, this was the place.

Stepping inside, his smile grew.

It was decorated for Christmas already with festive lights and garland draped along the exposed beams. There was a giant tree in the entryway, and along the bar were stockings with the names of all the employees. At least, that's what he figured they were. Stepping farther into the room, he spotted the hostess and she called out for him to pick a table. The place was fairly quiet with only a handful of diners seated, and Carter chose a booth against the back wall overlooking the ocean. Appealing as the view was, he couldn't seem to take his eyes off the interior. The whole place could use a good scrubbing and a fresh coat of paint, but this was the kind of place where people came to simply relax and have a good meal without breaking the bank.

The kind of place he wanted to create.

Maybe Montauk wasn't the right location for him. Did he really want to compete with places like this that were practically an institution in the town?

"Hey! What can I get you to drink?"

Carter looked up and smiled at the waitress—Karen—and ordered a Coke. With a smile and a nod, she was gone, and he was seriously contemplating scrapping this entire project because it suddenly didn't feel right.

Honestly, it hadn't felt right in a while—no matter what he kept trying to tell himself. It was probably why he hadn't been able to come to any decisions on just about every aspect of it—the menu, the décor, none of it. If he forced himself to take a step back, Carter could finally see he had been forcing the whole thing all along.

But why?

Karen was back, putting his glass down on the table. "You picked a great day to come in," she said. She was older, maybe late forties, early fifties, and looked tired though she was brightly cheerful. "Dad just made up an amazing batch of crab cakes. They're the special today, and you can get them plated or on a brioche roll with a side order of fries and slaw. I can get that going for you, or do you need some time to look at the menu?"

The menu hadn't changed much in the last ten years, if Carter remembered correctly, opting to have the special. Once Karen was gone again, he leaned back in the booth and sighed. If he didn't open his new restaurant here, then what? What was he supposed to do? Construction was underway—he supposed he could simply let it get to a certain point and then put it up for sale. But again, then what? What was he supposed to do with his time? He was already spreading himself thin by traveling back and forth between his other places. He'd been looking forward to settling in to someplace new for a while.

Here.

His head lolled back and his eyes closed as the gravity of his situation hit.

His business plan was shot.

His relationship with his mother was shot.

And his relationship with Emery was shot.

Right now, he wished someone would shoot *him* and put him out of his misery.

That wish was sort of granted by the appearance of his food. Karen set the plate down and studied him. "You doing okay?"

"Not particularly," he murmured, turning his attention to his lunch. It was so simple and there wasn't a fancy presentation, but it still looked and smelled delicious. Carter glanced at her and gave her a small smile. "Thanks. This looks great."

He figured it was the universal code for "go away," but she didn't move.

"You look familiar," she said. "You've been here before, right? But you're not a local."

Nodding, he picked up a fry and ate it. It was so damn good and his immediate thought was how much Emery would love them too.

Before he could respond, her eyes widened. "Wait a minute—you're that guy! You're the one building the new place over on Soundview, right?"

Realizing now that maybe the locals weren't going to be quite so impressed with the competition, Carter simply gave a curt nod and reached for his fork.

"Hang on," Karen said before turning and heading back toward the kitchen.

For all he knew, some angry mob was going to come out and start yelling at him, so he quickly wolfed down a couple of bites of crab cake before anyone told him to leave. And damn if they weren't the best he'd ever eaten. There was something to be said about getting your seafood right off the dock and making things fresh. Down in New Orleans he did, but none of his other places had the option. It made him long to be part of the community here even more—if for no other reason than to cook!

Out of the corner of his eye, Carter spotted Karen and an older gentleman walking his way. The resemblance between the two was strong—no doubt this was her father.

And this was their business.

Shit.

They came up to his table, and Karen made quick introductions. "I probably should have waited until you finished your lunch, but I wanted you to meet my father—Joe Mallin." She smiled. "And you are?"

Carter quickly wiped his hands and mouth. "Carter Montgomery." Standing, he shook Joe's hand and then Karen's. "Please. Join me."

Joe slid into the booth opposite him, but Karen stayed standing. "I'll keep an eye on the kitchen."

After taking his seat again, Carter had to fight to sit still. He had no idea how this conversation was going to go or if it would be a friendly one.

Thankfully, Joe started speaking first. "I've been watching the progress on your place." He paused. "Seems to be going a little slow."

Carter agreed. "Between permits and weather, it's been an uphill battle."

"We've all been wondering what you were going to do with the place. Everyone in town's been talking about it, but other than your name being attached to the project, no one knows what sort of place you're planning."

Unable to help himself, Carter let out a low laugh. "Neither do I," he said honestly and in that moment he knew he'd won the old man over.

"Surely you have something in mind. You chose this location for a reason and from everything I know about you, I would think you're going to open up a restaurant like your others."

He shrugged. "I was hoping to do something different this time around, but…" He let his words die off and took another bite of his lunch. "This is fantastic, by the way. Best crab cakes I've ever eaten."

Joe beamed with pride. "That's a real compliment coming from you. This place? I've been here for close to forty years. Started out as a little crab shack and then extended a bit. My wife and I did it because we loved to cook and we loved to fish. I don't fish anymore, not like I used to, but this place we built from the ground up. Neither of us had any formal training and our food is simple."

"But delicious," Carter added pleasantly. And since he figured the best way to speak was honestly, he said, "This is the kind of place I envisioned for myself this time around. Casual atmosphere, comfort foods, a place where everyone was welcome and could find something on the menu they'd enjoy."

Joe's face fell a little. "It's always done well for me. I'm sure your place will do even better, because you'll have your name and a big budget behind it."

Carter knew what he was saying and it bothered him. "Believe it or not, I'm having second thoughts."

"Really?"

He nodded. "Like I said, I can't seem to commit to anything, and…I don't know. I had my reasons for wanting to do something different this time around but nothing's sitting right with me. I keep looking for a sign—some sort of *aha* moment where it all becomes clear—but so far it hasn't." He took another bite of his lunch and then a sip of his soda. "So what about you, Joe? How did you know this was the right place for you?"

The older man chuckled. "It was my wife's idea," he said with a sad smile. "It was her dream and I made it come true for her. She's sick now and can't come in anymore and I hate leaving her alone all day." He sighed. "I always thought we'd retire together and leave the place to the kids, but…Karen doesn't want it and my son's a doctor down in Palm Beach." He shuddered. "Believe me, he definitely doesn't want the place."

"So why not sell it?"

He shrugged. "This place has been a part of my life for so long." He took a deep breath. "I hate the thought of it belonging to someone else. Someone who's going to come in and change everything and wipe away all my years of hard work."

Right now, Carter's heart was racing with excitement as idea after idea after idea came to mind. "What if someone came in and sort of…refurbished a little? You know, gave the place just a small facelift?"

Joe laughed. "I think the place needs a little more than that. But still, it would be nice if things didn't change too much."

"And what if someone came in and kept some of your recipes—some of your traditional meals—and then… added to the menu?"

Another laugh. "If you know someone willing to do that, you let me know! I can't tell you how many offers I've had over the years where they wanted to throw money at me and then change everything they claimed to love about this place. Or worse, knock it down to the ground and rebuild completely." He shrugged again. "I can't do it. Maybe that makes me crazy, but…"

Carter sat there for a long moment thinking, eating another fry. "Can I ask you something?"

"Sure."

"What did your family think about you doing this? You know, opening this place? And I don't mean your wife, I mean—"

"Yeah, yeah, yeah, my family. Like, my folks, right?"

"Yes."

"My old man thought I was crazy," Joe said with a grin. "He was a fisherman and that's all he ever wanted to be.

Cooking was for women, he used to say." He laughed as if lost in a memory. "When Elizabeth and I said we were doing this, my father just about had a fit—yelled and carried on about how no son of his was going to wear an apron! Oh my goodness...I haven't thought about that in years!"

Carter laughed with him. "Did he ever get over it?"

"Hell yeah! The first time he came in to eat, he was one hundred percent on board. For the first ten years we were in business, he was my main fisherman." He grew serious. "He died out on his boat. I remember that day like it was yesterday."

"I'm sorry."

"Thanks. We were in a good place, me and him. Sure, he'd still tease me about being a cook, but he died doing what he loved and he knew I loved what I was doing too. And that's all that mattered to him." Then he studied Carter. "How does your family feel about what you do?"

"Honestly? They approve—well, my father didn't, but...at least I thought he didn't."

Joe nodded. "Dads are always the toughest critics. Trust me, I know." He smiled. "We're also the worst at sharing our feelings. At least that's what my wife and kids tell me."

And then Carter couldn't help it; he laughed. Then he felt like crying.

But more than anything, he finally knew what he wanted to do. It was all there in his head with such clarity that he knew it was the right thing to do.

"So, Joe, I think I'd like to talk a little more about this with you and make you an offer."

Joe's eyes went wide. "Are you serious? But...what about your place? The one you're building?"

"I have no idea at the moment," Carter replied with a

nervous laugh. "All I know is it never felt right, but this? This conversation with you and the possibilities? That feels right."

With a look that was a mixture of relief and delight, Joe reached out his hand to Carter. "I look forward to talking with you more, Carter Montgomery."

Carter shook his hand. "Thank you, Joe Mallin."

"Actually, it's Joseph. But everyone calls me Joe."

Carter's hand froze midshake. What were the odds that he'd be doing business with a man who shared his father's name?

There's your sign.

And just like that, Carter knew he was making the right choice.

Emery opted to skip the little black dress and wear something festive and Christmassy by choosing a little red dress. Staring at her reflection and turning this way and that, she made sure it looked okay, wishing Carter was there to see her.

So he could eat his heart out.

Okay, that wasn't completely true. She missed him, dang it! For almost four days she'd been at war with herself about whether she should just be the bigger person and take the first step. Unfortunately, old habits died hard and she couldn't do it. He was wrong! So very wrong, and every time she thought about how little faith he seemed to have in her, she got angry all over again.

Still, she really wished he was here.

"Yeah, so I can prove him wrong," she murmured and

realized this wasn't getting her anywhere. Tonight after the party, she was calling him. It didn't matter how late it was or what happened, she was making the damn call.

And she was going to tell him how she was the more mature of the two of them.

Sooo…rubber? Meet glue.

Leaning in closer, she checked her makeup and then stepped back to take in her whole self again. Hair? Check. Makeup? Check. Dress and shoes? Check and check. Glancing over at the clock, she saw it was time to go. Eliza would be here any minute to pick her up and she didn't want to keep her waiting.

When Eliza had reached out to ask about driving together, Emery had pretty much broken down about her argument with Carter. Maybe it wasn't right to talk about such things with his mother, but right now she didn't have a whole lot of friends around to cry on their shoulders.

"Should probably start getting back into the swing of things on that end too," she said, grabbing her coat and purse off her bed and walking out into the living room.

And sighing.

Looking around, Emery hated everything she saw. Hated her furniture, hated the space, and most of all, she hated being here alone. Granted, that last one wasn't by choice, but she still hated it. Every place she looked, she saw Carter. How he had managed to make such an impression on her home in such a short time she had no idea. Right now, she'd kill to have it all wiped clean—the furniture, the pictures, the windows, the walls…all of it, if it meant she had some peace of mind.

If she didn't see him everywhere.

Or hear him.

On some level, Carter was right. There was a definite possibility of her parents and Derek ruining the night for her. She knew it. Actually, she was fairly confident they were going to. What had angered her the most about the entire situation was how he'd kept harping about it. It wasn't like he was bringing anything new to the table, for crying out loud. And if he knew her as well as he claimed, then he should have known all his snarky comments and worst-case scenarios were making her more tense and uncomfortable.

In a perfect world, she would love to let Carter loose on the bunch of them. The thought of him putting her parents in their place and then maybe beating the crap out of Derek was like a secret fantasy! But Emery was a realist and she knew that letting Carter defend her—no matter how satisfying—wasn't going to solve her problems. She didn't need him to save her because she was capable of saving herself.

That's why tonight was so important—not only because she finally felt strong enough to face her biggest fears, but because she wanted the man she loved by her side to be there to hold her tight and celebrate with her when she did.

When was she going to learn that some dreams just didn't come true and happily ever afters only existed in romance novels and fairy tales?

"And if there's one thing for certain about my life, it's no fairy tale." The doorbell rang and for a second her heart skipped a beat because she thought it might be Carter. Pulling the door open, she smiled at his mother and tried not to let her disappointment show.

"Oh, Emery, you look absolutely lovely! Red is a good color on you!"

"Thanks, Eliza. I wanted to be festive." Slipping her coat on, she grabbed her phone, keys, and purse, and walked out the door.

The drive took less than fifteen minutes and during that time, they talked only about the party and all the work they'd put in. Emery was relieved. The last thing she wanted was to have an awkward conversation about Carter, but she sort of felt like it was the elephant in the room.

Or rather, the car.

When they arrived at the country club, the whole place was heavily decorated for Christmas, and Emery couldn't help but smile. The twinkly lights, the garlands, the music playing...it was like walking into a wonderland, and all she could do was think of the wonderland she had created back in Montauk for Carter. The sigh escaped before she could stop it.

"Are you okay?" Eliza asked, concern written all over her face. "I love that you're here, Emery, but I know it's at a price. If you want to leave at any time, I don't want you to worry, okay?"

Tears stung her eyes because this was a woman who exemplified being a loving mother. Before she could stop herself, she hugged Eliza. "Thank you."

Eliza hugged her back with a soft laugh. "For what, sweetheart?"

"For just being you." Pulling back, Emery wiped her eyes. "It's too early for me to have my makeup ruined, right?" When she stepped away, Eliza put out a hand to stop her.

"I can't imagine how hard this is for you—to be here tonight and know you're going to face the people who hurt you." She gave her a sympathetic smile. "But I want you to know how proud I am of you for standing your ground and not letting them scare you off. You're far braver than I ever could be, and I'm a little in awe of you."

"Of me?"

Nodding, Eliza explained. "I'm sure Carter shared with you how my husband was…well, he was a bit of a bully. I rarely stood up to him and I used to get upset with the kids when they tried to. Maybe if I had—or if I had let them— things would be different now. Not that it would have saved Joseph's life, but maybe Carter, Megan, and Christian would have better memories of him." She paused. "I know this is going to be hard for you. If it comes to what we all think it will, then I know it won't be easy to confront them—but maybe this confrontation will pave the way to a better relationship. At least with your parents."

A trembly smile played at Emery's lips. "Thank you for saying that, Eliza. I'm not holding out much hope for a new relationship with my parents, but I need to know I stood up for myself and held my head high. No one is going to take that away from me. Never again."

"Good girl." Eliza looked around the room, pleased. Turning toward Emery again, she said, "This is going to be a good night. A great night!" she quickly amended. "And who knows? We may both be surprised before it's over."

Before either could say anything else, the event coordinator was rushing toward them to give them a tour of the room. Emery was thankful for the distraction and they had arrived early specifically for this. By the time they had seen everything and gone over the schedule for the evening, people were starting to arrive. As much as she hated herself for it, she kept one eye on the door at all times while stationed in the far corner of the room. Her logic was that she would have time to get her breathing under control by the time anyone arrived and made their way to her.

She only hoped it would work.

The room was filling quickly and she had a death grip on her glass of champagne. She smiled when she had to and made small talk with everyone she was introduced to. It was barely eight o'clock and she was mentally exhausted.

"You look beautiful, Emery."

She stiffened and then gasped as she turned and faced Carter. He looked magnificent in his dark suit and he smelled absolutely delicious.

The bastard.

"What—what are you doing here?" She looked around the room and wondered how she had missed his entrance. "When did you arrive?"

"I got here about noon and I've been working in the kitchen all day," he said smoothly, smiling at the server who brought him a glass of champagne. "Thanks."

"Wait—you got here...but how..." She let out a loud sigh. "Why didn't you tell me you were coming back?"

After he took a sip of his drink, he gave her a very serene smile.

So serene she wanted to smack it right off his face.

"I had things to take care of, and I knew you were busy too and I didn't want to disrupt your schedule," he said mildly. Just then another server approached them with a tray of appetizers. Carter grabbed two and thanked him before turning to Emery. "Here. Try this. You inspired it." He placed a small napkin in her hand and then put what looked like a small deep-fried ball on it.

"What is it?"

"Macaroni and cheese bites. Go ahead. They're delicious." He popped his into his mouth and hummed with approval. "I never thought those would be my thing, but they're a bit addictive."

But she didn't try it. Right now she was beyond confused and took a deep breath before she laid into him. "You know what?" she said loudly and then startled when he placed one finger over her lips.

"Uh-uh-uh. No making a scene," he teased. Next thing she knew she had a mouthful of macaroni and cheese that made her go a little weak in the knees. The grin on his face told her he knew it. "Good, right?"

She nodded.

Carter looked beyond her and waved someone over. "Now you have to try these." He snagged two sliders and handed one to her before thanking the server. "These are mini barbecue bacon sliders. Just the way you like them."

"Carter, I really don't understand—"

Burger. In. Mouth.

And dammit, it was delicious.

Self-consciously, Emery finished chewing and quickly wiped her mouth. When she saw him glancing around the room, she grabbed his face and forced him to look at her. "Stop. Putting. Food. In. My. Mouth. Got it?"

He nodded.

She released him and let out another long breath. "Seriously, Carter. What is this all about? You said you weren't going to be here, and last I checked, you certainly weren't going to be helping with the food."

He shrugged. "Last-minute decision. I made some calls,

brought in some of my top chefs, and prepared some of the dishes from the cookbook. It wasn't a big deal."

Emery wanted to growl with frustration. "Did your mother know about this?" Guiltily, he glanced away and that just fueled her rage. With a muttered curse, she wanted to stomp her food and storm away, but that was the old Emery. The new one was here to kick some ass and not feel ashamed of it.

"That was a really crappy thing to do," she began and secretly enjoyed the shocked look on his face. "How dare you show up here now after all the grief you gave me before you ran off. That's right. You. Ran. Off. But not before you made sure you freaked me out enough to have me doubting myself again. Well, let me tell you something, Carter Montgomery, it didn't work. I'm here tonight and I'm going to work this damn room and smile and make conversation with everyone. Every. One." She decided to do a quick scan of the room just in case she missed her parents' arrival.

She hadn't.

Turning her attention back to him, she glared. "Then you think you can just show up with your...your...delicious food, and that's supposed to make everything okay? Because it doesn't. If you think you're going to distract me with tiny burgers and melt-in-your-mouth macaroni and cheese, then you're sadly mistaken! There is no amount of food you could pull out that would distract me enough so you can go all caveman on my parents and Derek. So if you were hoping to do that and then stand there beating your chest in victory, you can forget it. Go back to the kitchen, because I've got some serious mingling to do!"

Her heart was racing and she felt a little sick to her

stomach, but she kept her head held high as she turned to walk away.

Carter's hand on her arm stopped her.

Unceremoniously, he spun her back around and hauled her in close. "For the record, I wasn't looking to distract you with food," he growled, his voice low. "Even though we both know I could. And I have no intention of going all caveman here or anywhere." His eyes scanned her face. "You were right. About everything. It was wrong of me to keep harping on the negative. It wasn't helping you, and more than anything, that's what I want to do." He paused again. "But you have no idea how hard this is for me, because…all I want is to take care of you. And maybe my behavior is a little outdated in these times, but I want to defend you. I want to fight your battles."

"Carter…"

He reached up and cupped her cheek. "I want to be your knight in shining armor, Em. I can't help that."

Everything in her melted at his words because…no one had ever wanted to be that for her. And the fact that this strong, confident, arrogant man wanted to be that for her simply meant more to her than she could ever have imagined.

While she knew she was going to fight tonight's battle on her own terms, having Carter there beside her helped more than anything else in the world.

"I love you, Emery Monaghan," he murmured, leaning in close. "You aggravate the shit out of me and you make me crazier than any human being alive, but at the end of the day, I want to be with you. I want to know all of your hopes and dreams. I want to comfort you when you're sad and celebrate all of your successes with you. Like tonight."

"Carter…"

But he wasn't done yet.

"I promise you I am here to support you," he vowed. "I'm here to hold your hand and give you strength if you need it." Then he laughed softly. "Although somehow I don't think you will, because you're the strongest woman I know. But I couldn't stay away, and I'm sorry I ruined things and I'm sorry I wasn't listening. Please tell me you forgive me so we can mingle and work the room together, and then later we can go home and I promise to make it all up to you." He rested his forehead against hers. "Please, Em."

Tears stung her eyes for the second time since she'd arrived. She cupped his face as she leaned in and kissed him. Carter maneuvered them to a quiet corner where he kissed her thoroughly until they were both breathless.

"Oh my," she said as she tried to catch her breath. "That was—"

"Just the beginning," he promised. He gave her a sexy smile that practically had her in a puddle at his feet as he pointed to the space above them.

Mistletoe.

"Is that the only reason you chose to kiss me?" she asked with a hint of sass.

"Seems to me you kissed me first. I was simply moving us out of the way of the guests." Then he pulled her in close. "But since we're here and that's up there…"

His lips claimed hers and all she could think of was how she wished they were back at her house, in her bed.

The kiss was full of promise and now Emery knew she'd be watching the clock tonight for a whole other reason.

When they finally broke apart, Carter took her hand and

said, "C'mon. Let's do this." A server was walking by with a tray of food she hadn't sampled yet, but when she went to reach for it, Carter stopped her. "Don't—I mean, you can try that later."

Emery looked at him curiously. "But...I want to try it now. What is it?" She studied the tray. "Stuffed mushrooms? I love those!"

"Just...trust me. Let's find the guy with the sliders again. I could go for another one, can't you?"

"Carter," she whined.

"Okay. Fine." He grabbed two of the mushrooms and thanked their server. "Here." He all but shoved the mushroom into her hands.

Suspiciously, she sniffed it and studied it. Then it hit her. "What's in it? What did you do to this innocent mushroom?"

"Try it."

"Oh no. You're not tricking me. Clearly there's something in here you know I don't like."

"Actually, I don't know if you don't like it. In all our time together, you've never eaten it."

"You're stalling, Carter."

"Fine!" he huffed. "The mushrooms are stuffed with sausage and...gouda. There. You happy now? I said it. There's gouda on the menu tonight."

He looked so adorable as he stood there trying to be defiant. It was impossible to be annoyed with him, and... she supposed now was as good a time as any to confess.

"As a matter of fact, I happen to enjoy gouda," she stated and took a bite of the mushroom. It was fantastic, but what did she expect? Everything Carter made was.

His dark brows drew together as he studied her. "But...

you…" A low growl came next. "You carried on about the gouda when we started on this project!"

She shrugged and popped the rest of the mushroom in her mouth. "I simply suggested there were other cheeses. I never said I didn't like it."

The blank expression changed to a big smile as he pulled her in close and hugged her. "Like I said, you make me crazier than any human being alive." He pulled back. "But I love you."

"Good. Because I'm not letting you go again."

"I'll let you in on a little secret," he whispered close to her ear. "You're stuck with me." He kissed her cheek and they turned toward the crowd.

"There you two are!" Eliza approached and hugged them both. "Carter, everything is delicious! Everyone is raving, and we've sold the first batch of books we put out. I have people restocking the display already!" Then she looked at Emery. "Please don't be upset with me for not telling you about this. I really wanted it to be a surprise."

"It was," she replied with a laugh. "It most definitely was." Then she looked at Carter. "But it was the best kind."

"Oh, this is wonderful! I swear, you don't have to get me anything for Christmas this year, Carter, because this is the best gift I could ever get," Eliza gushed.

"The food?" he asked.

Eliza shook her head. "Seeing the two of you together again. This makes me so happy!"

"But the food's good too, right?" he teased.

"Stop fishing for compliments," Emery chastised, playfully elbowing him in the ribs.

"Everything's fantastic, Carter. You're going to have

to promise to make those macaroni and cheese bites on Christmas Eve," his mother said before getting distracted and telling them both to have a good time, then heading over to join some friends.

"It's hard to believe Christmas is still three weeks away. It feels like it's happening right here, right now," Emery said, still looking around the room in awe. "This is like the ultimate winter wonderland, isn't it?"

With his arm around her waist, he tucked her in close to his side. "It's okay. I liked our winter wonderland out in Montauk better."

With a soft gasp, she turned and looked at him.

"What? What did I say?"

"That's exactly what I thought earlier when I got here."

Placing a gentle kiss on the tip of her nose, he said, "That's because we are one. And it's amazing."

Together they walked around the room, talking, eating, and socializing. Eliza stood up on the stage an hour later and made her speech thanking everyone for their hard work and for all the donations to The Hospice Foundation. Emery listened, smiled, clapped, and all the while scanned the room, wondering if somehow she had missed her parents. But they weren't there.

Odd.

Several members of the board joined Eliza on the stage and gave impassioned speeches about the importance of giving—especially at this time of the year—and as hard as she tried to pay attention, Emery's mind began to wander. When the last speaker was done and the room erupted in applause, she finally shook herself out of her reverie. Carter leaned in close.

"Are you all right?"

Nodding, she said, "Sure. I mean...yes. I'm fine. I'm good. I'm—"

"Em," he interrupted. "What's going on?"

Knowing she sounded crazy, her arms dropped to her side and she faced him. "Why didn't they come?" she cried. "I've had myself worked up now for weeks, and for what, huh? Why would they say they were coming if they weren't? I mean, maybe something came up or maybe they just wanted to mess with me. I shouldn't be surprised, but..."

Eliza walked over. "What a fantastic night! Oh, I feel like I am floating on a cloud!"

Forcing a smile, Emery praised Eliza for all she'd accomplished and for the successful event, but clearly the older woman wasn't fooled. "Will you both follow me?" she asked pleasantly. "I'd like to show you something."

They made their way through the crowd but it was slow going, because everyone wanted to stop and talk with them. When they finally made it to a small office, Eliza shut the door behind them and let out a long breath.

"My goodness. That was quite a feat, wasn't it?" she asked with a nervous laugh.

"What's going on, Mom?"

Moving around them, Eliza reached into her purse and pulled out her phone. "I just found out about this, and... dang it. I hate trying to search for things on my phone."

Carter stepped forward and took the phone from her hands. "What are you looking for?"

"I think I saved it in my searches. Just...you'll see."

He glanced at his mother and then Emery before returning his attention to the phone. Emery had no idea what he was looking for, but Eliza's face showed it wasn't good news.

Carter's gaze narrowed, but his expression remained neutral. He scanned the screen before handing the phone to Emery.

For her?

Cautiously, she took the phone and saw the headline and gasped. Eyes wide, she looked up at Eliza.

"Tabitha Skinner just showed it to me," Eliza said, her expression sad. "Her husband was the arresting officer."

"Congressman Derek Whitmore was arrested tonight and charged with sexual battery. Unlike the previous allegations, the victim called the police immediately after the attack. Police arrived to find witnesses who were willing to confirm what had happened," Emery read out loud and then stopped, feeling like her heart was going to beat right out of her chest.

Her parents were the witnesses.

The attack had happened at their home.

This time when the tears came, she let them fall. "All this time they defended him," she said, her voice shaking. "All this time they chose him over me. It didn't have to come to this. They let a predator into their home because they ignored all the signs and all the reports, and now this happens."

Carter took the phone from her hands and immediately wrapped her in his arms.

"All night I've been watching you looking at the door and searching the room for them," Eliza said quietly. "I thought you should know why... well, you know."

"Thanks, Mom," Carter said quietly and Eliza nodded and left them alone. His arms tightened around her and he placed a gentle kiss on her forehead. "I'm so sorry, Em. I really am."

And she knew he was. She also knew he was probably

fighting to keep his words and opinions to himself so he didn't upset her any more than she already was.

"You want to know something funny?"

He laughed softly. "Right now? Sure."

Pulling back, she looked up at him. "I'm not sad that they aren't here. And I'm not sad that I didn't get to confront them after I'd prepared myself for it. I'm angry because their actions caused someone else to get hurt. In my opinion, they're as much to blame as Derek."

His expression was full of compassion. "You're an amazing woman, Emery, you know that?"

"Me? Why?"

"Because you have the biggest heart. Even through your own pain and disappointment, you're concerned for someone else."

"She's a victim, Carter. And if she was in my parents' home, she trusted them." Moving out of his embrace, she took a couple of steps away. "I have no idea who she is and yet I'm angry for her! And I'm sick to my stomach over this—like, seriously sick! When is it going to end?"

"I have a feeling it ends now. Tonight. If your folks are willing witnesses, I'd say things may finally turn around. Like you, I'm sorry it had to come to this. I'm sorry you had to be hurt again. But more than anything, I'm sorry this ruined your night."

She gave a mirthless laugh. "I think we can both agree it was bound to happen. I just didn't expect it to happen like this." She groaned and then wiped away some stray tears. "I need to fix my makeup, and then we're going back out there to eat, dance, and socialize."

Carter took a step toward her. "Are you sure? Because

we can go. We can leave right now and just…I don't know, not be here."

But Emery shook her head. "No. This is me not running away. I'm sure people out there know what happened tonight and they may want to talk about it. And if they do, I'll let them. This situation has kept me running and hiding long enough. I'm not happy to deal with it here tonight like this, but…again, I'm not surprised that they managed to ruin my night without being here."

"Baby," he said softly, "they're not ruining it. You're brave and strong and…" His gaze raked over her. "You're incredibly sexy. Have I mentioned how much I love you in red?"

She blushed and Carter reached up and caressed her cheek.

"You're not letting them ruin anything. You're willing to walk back out there and show everyone what a class act you are. You're amazing."

He kissed her then—and it was deep and wet and had her wanting to wrap her legs around him and beg him to take her right there.

But there'd be time for that later.

She smiled at him. "Give me five minutes and then let's go eat."

He chuckled. "There's my girl."

Emery turned to leave the room, but then looked back at him. "Any other culinary surprises I should be on the lookout for? Any other sneaky uses of gouda?"

His hands slid into his trouser pockets. "There may be. But I promise to let you know before slipping any onto your plate."

"That's all I ask," she said with a wink, and then she was out the door.

"We should go get a tree today," Carter said. It was after midnight, the house was dark, and Emery was naked in his arms.

And all was right with his world.

"Nope," she said simply.

"What do you mean, nope? Why not?"

"I'm not putting one up this year."

Okay, now he was curious. "Why?"

She pushed up on one elbow and looked down at him. The only light in the room was from the moonlight, but he could see her perfectly. Her hair was tousled and the sheet dropped just enough that he could see her breasts; he had to hold his hands still and not reach out to touch her yet.

"Because I don't want to celebrate Christmas here. The house is on the market, we've had some offers, and I'd rather pack things up than deal with decorating and having to rush to take it all down. It's not worth it to me."

With a dramatic sigh, he did reach out and pulled her back down against him. "Then it's a good thing I have a plan," he said quietly.

"You do?"

Nodding, he explained. "Our house in Montauk is available again and I've booked it through the end of February, but if I don't find a place to buy, I may extend the lease." When she went to straighten up again, he held her firm. "So, I know tonight was all about the fundraiser and the work you and my mom did, but I had some stuff to share and didn't want to take away from your night."

"What are you talking about?"

"The restaurant. I'm going to want to live in Montauk

for at least the first year it's open. I'd rather invest in a house than keep renting. It just makes sense."

"Oh, right. I guess I never thought about that." She paused. "But…that's not really anything new, Carter. Has something else happened?"

He told her about meeting old Joe Mallin and about his pub. "I'm buying it."

This time she did straighten. "What? I mean…how? Why? You're building a place already, Carter!"

"I know, but… So much about the project hasn't felt right with me, and when I walked into Joe's place, it was like everything made sense. It all fell into place. Everything about it felt right—the atmosphere, the location, the menu. I'm going to make some changes but I'm over the whole idea of trying to reinvent the wheel. I want to just get back to the joy of cooking good meals for everyone to enjoy."

"Not just those who like gouda?"

Laughing, he hugged her close. "You have to get over that one. Although…you are going to love his fries."

"His fries? You're keeping his menu?"

"Not all of it, but at least half. He and I discussed it and he's going to stay on with me part-time as we transition, and he'll help me tweak the menu and figure out what to add."

"Hey, I thought that was my job?"

"You decided working for my uncle was a better deal," he teased and kissed her again. "But don't worry, I'm sure we'll let you try some of it when you're not too busy wowing the Montgomery corporation."

Now it was her turn to laugh. "Knock it off. You know this offer from your uncle was just to bridge the gap until

I find something else. I'll be freelancing and working remotely, so…wherever you go, I go."

"Nothing could make me happier," he said, and he meant it. Knowing things were heading in the right direction finally gave him a sense of peace he hadn't known in a long time.

If ever.

And for the first time in years, Carter had something to look forward to that wasn't about his business, it was about his life. He was looking forward to Christmas in a way he hadn't since he was a kid. The thought of spending it with Emery already had the wheels in his mind spinning with all the possibilities. He wanted to make it the best one she'd ever had.

Beside him, she yawned broadly. "I'm exhausted. It's been a long day and an even longer week." She placed a kiss on his chest. "I missed you."

"I missed you too," he said softly. "What have you got planned for tomorrow? Anything?"

"No. I had planned on taking the day as a mental health day. After getting myself so worked up over what might or might not happen at the fundraiser, I thought I would need it." Then she laughed softly.

"What's so funny?"

"Before I left here tonight, I vowed to call you and straighten things out."

"Oh yeah?"

"Mm-hmm."

"And what were you going to say?"

"I was going to tell you what a colossal jerk you are and how you better come back here and apologize. Pronto."

He chuckled, loving how she was trying to sound like she was tough. "Pronto?"

"Yup. Pronto."

Slowly, he maneuvered them until Emery was on her back and he was stretched out on top of her. "Hmm...very bossy of you, Em."

She nodded in agreement. "It helps get things done."

"And that's important to you, huh? Getting things done?"

Another nod. "Absolutely."

"I just have one more question," he murmured, lowering his head until his lips were a breath away from hers.

"Just one?" she whispered.

"Yes. Are you really hung up on the whole pronto thing? Because I prefer to take things...slow. I'm thorough like that." And then he began to move against her until she was panting and begging for more.

Yet another thing he loved about her.

"Carter?" she said breathlessly, as his hands and mouth traveled along her silky skin.

"Hmm?"

"You're killing me."

"But what a way to go, huh?" he said between kisses along her thigh.

She sighed his name again right before telling him how much she loved him.

Yeah...he'd never get enough of hearing her say that. Just like he'd never get tired of saying it back to her. And he did, over and over as he loved her.

And much later, when they were both nearly asleep, she said his name again.

"Yes?" he asked.

"If I don't remember to say it later, thank you for making this the best Christmas ever."

He frowned. Best Christmas ever? It was only the first week of December. "Em, sweetheart, we still have a few weeks until Christmas."

Slowly, she shook her head. "I already got the best Christmas present ever. You."

She may think he was the best Christmas present ever, but he had a few tricks up his sleeve to change her mind.

Well, maybe not change it, but he already had some plans in motion to guarantee Emery would remember this Christmas forever.

Epilogue

"YOU KNOW, I'M REALLY NOT TRYING TO SOUND SNARKY, but...just what is the deal with your family?"

Carter looked up from chopping vegetables and smiled at Emery—who was wearing the new cashmere robe he'd given her as an early Christmas present. "What do you mean?"

"I mean these Christmas family newsletters are a bit insane. No one should have this much good news to share!"

He couldn't argue with her. It was true. Things were especially good in the Montgomery family, it seemed, and Christmas was the perfect time to share that. Besides the abundance of Christmas cards he received this year at their new address in Montauk, each one had contained some form of family news. Luckily, his aunts managed to consolidate it all in newsletter form. No doubt his own mother had done the same.

"Okay, like this one from Uncle William and Aunt Monica."

"What about it?"

She held up a finger and read it out loud to him. When she was done, she looked at Carter. "I had no idea families were really like this."

He nodded and shifted the vegetables from cutting board to bowl before tackling the next batch. "Did you read the one from Aunt Janice?"

Emery shifted through the stack of envelopes and pulled

it out. "I only glanced at it, but I figured it was more of the same."

He chuckled. "No doubt. But read it out loud. I was distracted earlier and didn't get to read the whole thing."

Emery took a seat on one of the upholstered bar stools and read it to him. Putting the paper down, Emery sighed.

"What? What's the matter?" he asked.

"It's just a lot to take in. I've never experienced anything like this. Even with two sisters of my own, we don't celebrate like this, we don't share or gush over family news like yours does." She flipped through the stack of Christmas cards again. "I think your mother's came today too."

"Really? Why would she send one when she's coming here? That seems a little crazy."

"Relax. So she wasted the cost of a stamp. It's not a big deal." After a minute, she found it. "Got it!"

With a dramatic sigh, he cleaned up the food he was prepping and said, "Go ahead and read it. Let's hear about how fabulous my siblings are."

Amused, Emery reached for a carrot he had missed and munched on it before she read the final bit of Montgomery news.

When she was done, she slammed the paper down on the counter with a hint of outrage. "I had no idea she did that on purpose!" Emery cried. "She helped me out in hopes of setting us up?"

Smirking, Carter wiped down the countertop. "And you're surprised why? You've heard all about the crazy matchmaking that has gone on in this family."

"But...doesn't it bother you?"

"Hell no! Look how it all worked out. We're here

together in this fabulous house, deliriously in love, and planning our future. I say we buy her more Christmas gifts to thank her!"

To her credit, Emery wasn't upset for long and soon she was stacking the cards back up again. "I guess…since we're deliriously in love, I guess that makes it okay."

"Damn right."

She looked around the kitchen. "Anything I can help you with?"

"No. Everything's prepped for dinner tonight. But…" Spotting the envelope he was looking for, he reached for it and handed it to Emery. "This one came today for you." He knew the instant she figured out who it was from, and before she could say a word, he grinned. "Relax. They just wasted the cost of a stamp, right?"

The angry glare she shot at him told him she wasn't amused.

"Look, I know it's going to be a little awkward, but we talked about this. Inviting your parents here for Christmas was the right thing to do," he said. "There will be plenty of people here to make sure nothing gets out of hand, and need I remind you what you said to me about the whole thing?"

She huffed. "It's the season of charitable forgiveness."

Then she muttered a curse.

"That's my girl," he said with a grin. "Now come on, we've got work to do. Everyone's arriving tomorrow and I want us to have our own Christmas celebration tonight while it's just the two of us."

Walking around the kitchen island, he came to stand beside her, kissing her soundly. "Look at this place. I think we outdid ourselves, don't you?"

They were back in the house they had rented before, but this time all the decorations were theirs, the tree was one they'd picked out themselves from a tree lot, and all the ornaments were a combination of Emery's and new ones they had chosen together. And in his opinion, it was the best tree in the history of Christmas trees.

"We did," she agreed. "I never had a twelve-foot tree. I can't believe how much we had to buy to decorate it."

"Totally worth it. And this is just the beginning," he said. "Every year we're going to add to it."

She laughed. "We may need a bigger tree."

"And a bigger house."

Now she laughed harder, turning toward him. "Carter! I know you're teasing, but that's ridiculous!"

"Hey, you read all the Montgomery newsletters. Our family is forever expanding. We're definitely going to need a bigger place."

She groaned. "I know you're right and this place is just a rental, but…this has been the best house I've ever lived in. The memories we made here? They'll stay with me forever."

He kissed her softly and was about to take it a little bit deeper when the doorbell rang.

"Please tell me no one's surprising us by showing up early," she whined.

"They better not. I have plans for the two of us under that tree later," he said, heading toward the door.

"Again?" she cried.

At the door, Carter accepted the package with a big grin and walked back into the living room, where Emery's eyes went wide.

"Oh my goodness! What is it?" she asked.

Carter placed the box on the table, careful to keep it positioned in a way that wouldn't give anything away. It was a red box with a big white bow on it. "Your name is on the tag, so I guess it's for you."

She eyed him suspiciously. "Carter Montgomery, what did you do?"

"Me? How do you know it's from me?"

"Carter..."

"*Woof!*"

The box seemed to jump slightly and Emery let out a shriek.

"*Woof!*"

"Ohmygod, ohmygod, ohmygod!" she chanted excitedly as she opened the box. A small furry head popped up.

And snorted.

"Oh my gosh! It's a mini Maylene!" Emery cried, reaching for the puppy. "She's adorable, Carter! Oh, I'm in love already!" She cradled the puppy, which was wearing a big red bow instead of a collar. "What's her name?"

Crouching down beside her, he scratched the puppy's head. "Well, she is a he and we have to name him," he said, smiling at her. "I figured you'd want the honors." Then he turned serious. "I remembered the story you told me about wanting a dog for Christmas. We never talked about different breeds, but you seemed to love Maylene when we were all together last month. I figured maybe we'd start with a small dog for now and once we get settled into our forever home, we could add to our family."

She snuggled the puppy close and kissed his head. "Well, I'm not sure Stanley will want to share the attention with another dog. I mean…he's just a baby. He should get some time to himself with us, shouldn't he?"

"Stanley? Stanley the pug? That's what you're going with?"

"Too generic?" she questioned with a grin. "How about…Cheddar? Or…Gouda! Oh, Gouda the pug! How does that sound?"

"Like if he went to dog school, he'd get wedgies," Carter deadpanned. "C'mon. Be serious. This little guy needs a name befitting a Montgomery."

"A Montgomery, huh?"

Nodding, he petted the dog, who then tried to lick his way up Carter's entire arm.

"Okay, think. Think, think, think…" She giggled when the pug turned and started licking her chin and cheek and entire face. "Easy there, Schmoopie."

"Do not call him that," Carter said firmly, but he couldn't keep a straight face.

"Why not?"

"Because we're going to have to use his name in public and I'm not going to be caught calling my dog…Schmoopie. I have my limits."

"Fine," she said dramatically. "But then you need to give some input too."

"I just did. Don't call him Schmoopie."

"How about we name him something for Christmas? Since he's my Christmas present, we should give him a good Christmas name."

"I'm on board with that. But what?"

"Oh! Let's name him after one of Santa's reindeers! Please! Can we?"

"That sounds great, but which one?"

Emery immediately began to sing the lyrics of "Rudolph, the Red-Nosed Reindeer"—off key, of course. "You know Dasher and Dancer and Prancer and Vixen." She paused. "Definitely not Vixen."

Carter quickly agreed.

"Comet and Cupid and Donner and Blitzen." She paused again and looked at the dog. "He's definitely not a Rudolph."

He agreed again.

"How about Comet?"

"I can live with Comet." And clearly the dog agreed because he squirmed out of Emery's arms and began to run around the living room. "I think he likes it." Together they sat and watched the puppy explore his new surroundings, and after a few minutes, he came back and fell asleep on the floor at Emery's feet.

"He is so incredibly sweet, Carter. Thank you."

"You're very welcome."

"I still can't believe this is my life and this…this is the Christmas I always wanted."

He reached up and tucked his hand behind the nape of her neck. "That was my plan. I wanted to give you everything, Em. You deserve everything."

Resting her forehead against his, she said, "Well, you're not the only one with surprises up your sleeve."

Straightening, he looked at her curiously. "What does that mean?"

Jumping up from the sofa, Emery carefully stepped over Comet and went to the tree. She pulled out one of the wrapped boxes from the stack and handed it to Carter. "I know we said we'd open gifts on Christmas Eve, and then we said we'd open some tonight when it's just the two of us, but I really want you to open this one now."

"O-kay…" Out of the corner of his eye, he could see her biting her lip nervously as he opened the gift. It was a small box—like the size of a hardcover book. Taking the lid off, he moved the tissue paper aside and…

He stilled.

Gently, he lifted the picture frame out of the paper and simply stared.

Beside him, Emery cleared her throat. "The week after the fundraiser, I was over at your mom's house helping her go through the Christmas decorations. We were up in the attic and she found an old box of family photos. She seemed surprised to find it and said she hadn't seen it in years. So we brought it downstairs and went through it, and when I found this picture, I knew I wanted to have it framed for you."

It was a picture of Carter and his father—he was maybe five years old at the time, and he was wearing a Santa hat and a chef's apron and so was his father. They were laughing together while they were cooking.

"I…I had forgotten about this," he said, emotion clogging his throat. "Those meals I made? The ones from the book?"

She nodded.

"This was how some of them started. Dad and me goofing around in the kitchen." Tears stung his eyes. "He went through this phase where he seemed to enjoy cooking or helping in the kitchen. We were all little then, but then he just…he stopped." He looked at her and there weren't enough words to convey all he was feeling. "Thank you."

"I have one more gift I'd like you to open," she said. "It kind of goes with this."

Carter had no idea if his heart could take it, but he

nodded and tried to make light of it. "If we keep this up, there won't be anything for us to open later."

She motioned to all the gifts under the tree. "Somehow, I doubt that." Then she reached for a larger, slim box that was standing behind the tree. There wasn't a tag on it and he had wondered who it was for. Emery handed it to him.

Without a word, Carter took it from her. It was about three feet long and ten inches wide. What in the world…?

If he thought the picture was a surprise, it was nothing compared to this.

Joseph's Place.

It was a sign made out of teak and the words looked like they were burned into it. He stared at it until his eyes blurred.

"We also found this up in the attic," she said quietly. "Your mom said it used to hang down in the basement when your father had his version of a man cave down there years ago. I thought you might like it for the restaurant. It's a tribute to your dad, but also a nod to Joe Mallin." When he didn't say anything, she quickly added, "Of course, you can do whatever you want with it. It was just an idea, and I…I…"

Carter quickly closed the distance between them and kissed her. When they broke apart, his eyes scanned her face. "Never in my entire life have I ever gotten gifts that meant more to me. I already was in awe of how much I was looking forward to Christmas this year because of you, but what you gave me today was priceless. You gave me something I didn't think I had—happy memories of my father. You'll never know what this means to me. There aren't enough words." He kissed her again. "I love you, Em."

"I love you, too. Merry Christmas, Carter."

"Merry Christmas, Emery."

William & Monica Montgomery

We're always amazed at the abundance of blessings in our lives and this Christmas has us feeling doubly blessed. We're adding twins to the family! Yes, twins! Jason and Maggie are expecting in April and just shared the news with us. For those of you counting, that will make babies three and four for them! Jason is walking around with a perpetual smile on his face and Maggie has never looked lovelier. We can't wait to meet these sweet babies and I am already making plans to do some renovations on the house so we can have a new nursery here for sleepovers!

Lucas and Emma are busy keeping up with their three girls, and I have to admit, I simply adore watching my son being a dad to them! Emma's bakery is thriving—especially this time of year—and we are all benefitting from her sweet confections! My hips aren't benefitting, but that's what New Year's resolutions are for, right? On top of baking and business, both of them are busy with dance recitals for our three beautiful granddaughters. Having raised only boys, this has been a real treat for us. Their oldest daughter, Lily, has the lead in *The Nutcracker* and we're all so proud!

Not to be outdone, Mac and Gina's daughter Brianna is singing the lead in her school's holiday concert! Such talented grandchildren we have! And speaking of Mac and Gina, they just purchased a new vacation home in San Francisco near Gina's mother. The view there is spectacular and their son Harry has developed a real interest in the architecture of the city. We know he's only three, but Mac insists his interest is real and that we have a future architect in the family! We'll see...

As for William and I, we will be celebrating our anniversary this year in Europe. I've been begging him for years to take me on an eating tour of Italy and he's finally agreed! We're looking forward to a little time away, and with our anniversary being around Valentine's Day, I plan on making sure it's absolutely the most romantic trip ever!

Merry Christmas, Everyone!!

Robert & Janice Montgomery

Greetings from the Montgomerys! What an incredible year it's been, and we're bracing ourselves for quite a big spring. We're expecting three new babies! Three! Zach and Gabriella are expecting their second child in March and Summer and Ethan will be right behind them in May! You know those cousins are going to be best friends, just as Autumn and Willow are. Maybe we'll get some boys this time for our West Coast babies. But if you can believe it, Summer is most concerned with how her sassy little pug Maylene is going to adjust to having a new baby in the house! I'm sure she'll be fine...

Back here on the East Coast, there also seems to be some baby fever. Casey and Ryder just had sweet little Emily back in

September and we are looking forward to celebrating her first Christmas with her and her two siblings. Matthew and Jax weren't too thrilled with getting a new sister, but we think they'll adjust just fine.

And then there's James and Selena. After years of thinking little Jamie would be an only child, it seems like their prayers have been answered! Their new addition will be here this summer and we all couldn't be more pleased. This Christmas is going to be extra special because we all have so much to be thankful for. Every day Robert and I look at one another in amazement at the family we created and how much we've grown.

Merry Christmas &
Love to ALL!!

Eliza Montgomery

Where has the year gone? Last year at this time, I felt like I would never be happy again, and I've never been happier to be wrong. Losing Joseph was so hard on all of us, but I know he'd be thrilled to see how we've persevered and flourished.

And now how we're growing!

I'm going to finally be a grandmother! Oh my goodness! I have a long way to go before I'm caught up with my sisters-in-law, but I think I'm off to a good start! At Thanksgiving, Megan and Alex announced they were expecting their first child. I was beyond excited and had already begun making plans to spend a large portion of the next year on the West Coast. It's not every day a woman finds out she's going to be a grandmother for the first time, right? And before I could come down from my euphoria, Christian and Sophie just gave me an early Christmas present with a picture frame that said "Nana" and had a sonogram picture of their little one in it. I'm a little ashamed to admit how hard I cried when I got it. Two babies within two months of one another! I am going to be one busy woman in the New Year.

I only wish Joseph was here with me.

And then there's my Carter. He surprised us all by scrapping his original plans for a new restaurant out in Montauk and instead purchasing an existing one and putting his stamp on it. They're not planning on getting to work on it until after the New Year, but I know it's going to be amazing! This could definitely be the start of something new for his business and we're all very excited about it.

But as exciting as that is, the biggest announcement was his engagement to the lovely Emery Monaghan. For those of you who might not know, Carter and Emery have known one another since the fifth grade and were bitter rivals all through school. To know they found one another again—thanks to some of my own match making skills I learned from my brother-in-law William and his wife Monica—has made my year complete. And who knows, maybe I'll have more baby news to share next year!

I know my fingers are crossed...

Merry Christmas to All and
Blessings for the New Year!!

About the Author

Samantha Chase is a *New York Times* and *USA Today* bestseller of contemporary romance. She released her debut novel in 2011 and currently has more than forty titles under her belt! When she's not working on a new story, she spends her time reading romances, playing way too many games of Scrabble or Solitaire on Facebook, wearing a tiara while playing with her sassy pug, Maylene…oh, and spending time with her husband of twenty-five years and their two sons in North Carolina.

Also by Samantha Chase